I0544622

UNEXPECTED TROUBLE

THE UNEXPECTED SERIES, BOOK 3

STACY EATON

Copyright © 2020 by Stacy Eaton

All rights reserved.

No part of this book may be reproduced in any form or by any electronic or mechanical means, including information storage and retrieval systems, without written permission from the author, except for the use of brief quotations in a book review.

✸ Created with Vellum

CHAPTER ONE

GREGORY

"*W*hy can't we just buy another damn coffeemaker?" I growled as I stared at the barren space on the counter in the small kitchenette of our office. "I'll even pay for the damn thing."

Trevor chuckled as Alex responded with a smirk. "You haven't been here long enough to realize how things go."

"Have you not figured out that Jake likes things a specific way, Blaire? He'd rather wait three extra weeks to get the coffeemaker that he wants than to replace it with something else."

"It's fucking coffee," I groaned. "You add grounds and water, and it brews. What the fuck does Screamer need a special machine for?"

A hand slapped me on the shoulder, and I turned to find Jake behind me, a brow hiked. "I bet you are one of those guys who use tap water in your machine too and doesn't care what kind of beans are in the machine, right?"

"That's exactly the type of guy that I am. It's fucking coffee, Screamer."

"Yeah, and that's why I'm not letting you buy the machine.

God knows we drink enough of it around here, and if we are going to do that, the least we can do is have a good brew."

"When did you become such a coffee snob?" I asked. "Last I knew, you'd drink all the swill you could get, and you didn't care where it came from."

"Yeah, well, some of us have grown up and acquired taste."

"Acquired?" I laughed. "Next, you'll be telling me that you go to wine tastings now too."

He scrunched up his face. "I'm not quite that much of a dork."

We all laughed. "When is this new machine supposed to be here?"

"I don't know; the one I want is on backorder, so until then, you can schlep it down to the coffee shop on the corner and pick us up some for the meeting at nine." Jake started to walk away.

"Me?"

Jake paused and glanced back. "Yes, you got a problem with that, Blaire?"

"Can't—"

A woman's voice called from down the hall, "Don't even suggest it, Gregory Blaire. Go get your own damn coffee! I'm not the coffee girl."

I rolled my eyes as everyone laughed again, and I called out my response a little louder so I would know she heard me. "I was not going to suggest that, Alice."

Trevor leaned forward and whispered, "Yeah, you were."

I shrugged as I began to walk down the hallway. "Fine, I'll go. What does everyone want?"

"Ask Alice, she knows," Alex said as he punched me in the arm and stepped around me.

"How does she know?"

Trevor grinned as he moved to my side. "Because she keeps track of those things for us."

2

"Yeah, right," I muttered as Trevor and Alex walked away. She probably went to pick up coffee for them regularly. Why was I being sent out on this errand?

I paused by her desk, and she didn't even glance up as she reached into a drawer and pulled out a three-by-five card that was laminated—laminated!—and handed it to me. Printed on the card in neat handwriting was a coffee order for everyone in the office. Well, everyone but me. I frowned. "How come my name is not on here?"

She lifted her warm brown eyes to mine. "Because you haven't been in the office since the coffeemaker bit it." She was right; I had been in training classes and traveling the last two weeks.

"What did happen to the machine?"

She glanced over her shoulder, leaned forward, and spoke softly. "Jake got pissed about something and took it out on Mr. Coffee. Picked the thing up and smashed it on the ground."

"Did the machine do something?"

She shook her head and leaned back. "Nope, he was just in one of his moods. Make sure you pick up three more cups, black with sugar and creamer on the side for the clients." She turned her head to the side. "And you better hurry. It gets busy around this time, and the clients will be here soon."

"I don't see your name on here. Did you want something?"

"No, but thanks. I already have mine." She lifted her brown paper cup.

I stared at the cup. "Isn't that from where I'm going?"

"Yes," she said sweetly.

"Why didn't you pick this up when you were there?"

She lifted her eyes to mine, and even though I knew she wanted to take my head off for that comment, that did not stop me from noticing again how beautiful she was. Her dark hair pulled back from her oval face, warm brown eyes almost the color of whiskey, and a breathtaking smile. Well, breathtaking

3

when she was smiling. She wasn't doing that now, though. "Because I'm not the coffee girl."

"Alright, sorry for asking." I was about to step away when I saw the newspaper sitting beside Alice, and a small picture captured my attention.

I collected the paper and turned it around to read the heading. *Is he the man for you? Ten ways to know if he is.* The name under the article was Maggie Valor, and I stared at her photo. Damn, she looked amazing.

What was Maggie doing back in town? The last I knew she had moved to Atlanta. "Hey, Alice." I held the paper up as she gave me her attention. "How long has this woman had a column in the paper?"

She grinned. "Why? Do you need some advice on romance?"

"Hardly, Alice, of course, you'd know that if you'd let me take you out."

"And I might have let you take me out if you knew anything about romance," she quipped back, and I laughed.

"Touché, but seriously, do you know how long she's been writing this column?"

"Um, I think it's been a couple of months. The last romance guru kicked the bucket."

"Nice way to say she died."

Alice rolled her eyes. "No, she literally kicked the bucket and said she was giving up on romance. Said that all the advice she had ever given was bullshit and laughed at all the people who asked for her advice."

"You're kidding?"

"Nope, she slipped the article into the paper one night when the editor was busy, and when they saw it the next day, they tried to get her to print an apology, but that's when she kicked the bucket and said love was dead. Of course, she was fired, and when Maggie Valor started, she had a lot to deal with after the fallout."

"Is she any good?"

Alice barked out a laugh. "She writes a romance column, of course it's good. She's full of wit and sarcasm, and just enough advice to seem like she's trying to help you. I love her. Why the interest?"

"I knew her way back when," I stated as I set the paper down. "Been a long time, but I knew her in high school."

"What are you still doing here?" Jake barked as he came around the corner.

"Oh, he's getting romance advice," Alice said quickly and held up the paper, pointing at the column.

"Get the fuck out of here, Blaire! The clients are going to be here in fifteen minutes."

"I'm going," I told him and walked toward the door as Alice rolled her eyes. I would have joined her, but Jake might have seen my reflection in the glass.

The sidewalks were busy with people hustling to wherever they were going. Alice was right; it was going to be hectic at the coffee shop if the number of cups passing by me was any indication. As I went on my way, I stayed closer to the buildings, rather than the curb, and watched every single car I walked past.

I'd seen too many car bombs in my tours overseas, and having vehicles parked along the sidewalks still made me nervous—one of the gifts from my enlistment in the Marines. It's a shame I didn't have a return address, or I'd send it the fuck back.

I stepped into the coffee shop and sighed. It was packed, and there were about ten people in line in front of me, with another six or seven waiting on the other side for their orders. Around the small interior, there were nine tables, all in use, and four chairs off to the side at a bar table area, all occupied too. A few people had computers open and appeared to be working; others messed with their phones, and a couple of people were actually talking to one another.

Conversation was a lost art—sadly. I enjoyed talking to people, and just about anywhere I went, I tried to strike up a conversation. It made me more comfortable, especially if I was in a crowd. I glanced around again as I shuffled forward a few more steps.

There was a constant level of noise in the place, the door opening and closing, the chatter of people, the clicking of keys, the whooshing of steam on the espresso machine, and the dinging of the cash register. If you didn't bunch the sounds together in a group, it could have been overwhelming.

Someone bumped me from behind, and I glanced over my shoulder to see a woman with her phone glued to her ear, her blond hair blocking her features and a huge-assed shoulder bag over her arm. That's what hit me, not her, her damn bag. I shuffled a few inches to the side to avoid it.

We moved up another foot as the next person was helped, and then someone leaving cut between the woman in front of me and me, making me step back to avoid getting stepped on. I frowned at the guy as he passed by, not even saying excuse me—fucking millennials. They thought they owned the world. I shook my head and got poked by the woman's bag again.

I ignored it and wiped my brow, which was starting to bead with sweat. It wasn't just the heat in the room; it was the noise, the people, the feeling of being herded toward something.

A sharp jab nailed me in my back near a bruise from a recent training incident, and I spun around. "Would you mind watching your bag, please?" I said roughly. Even though I was pissed, I was trying to keep my cool.

The woman's face snapped to mine, and we both jerked back slightly. "Mags?"

"Greg?" she said at the same time. "Heather, I need to call you back." She hung up without even waiting for a reply. "Gregory Blaire, what are you doing here?"

"Getting coffee with the rest of the damn city. I could be

asking you the same thing. Last I heard you were going to Atlanta."

"I did go to Atlanta, and the last I heard, you had gone back overseas for another deployment."

"Yep, I did. I just finished twenty. I'm out now."

She let her gaze drift over my face and down to my chest. "You look good, Gregory."

While she had been checking me out, I'd been doing the same, and she looked better than good. She looked fucking edible. "Thanks, you too, Maggie."

"Do you mind moving up?" the pregnant woman behind Maggie said abruptly with a bit of a bite to it. Someone needed a caffeine fix. Didn't she know that wasn't good for her baby?

"Sorry, ma'am. I'd be happy to." I gave her my best smile, and she relaxed a little—even smiled back. I turned my attention back to Maggie after I had shifted closer to the register. "How long you been back in town?"

"A few years, what about you?"

I grinned down at her, noting that she had a few lines around her blue eyes now, but they didn't detract from her beauty. In fact, it was quite the opposite. "About sixteen months."

I glanced at the counter and saw I was up next, so I dug into my side pocket to retrieve the laminated coffee order card. I stared at it for a moment; who fucking laminates something like this?

Maggie took the card out of my hand and laughed. "Are you serious? Your office needs a laminated list of how everyone takes their coffee?" She skimmed the list and laughed again as she lifted her pretty, smoky-blue eyes to mine. "Are you the coffee boy? Is that the best job you could get?"

I removed the card from her hand. "No, I'm not the coffee boy. I haven't spent much time in the office, so I got sent on the errand."

The barrister called out, "Next!" and I shifted to the register.

I looked down at the card, ready to start reading it off when I thought better of it and thrust it toward him. "One of each of these, then four blacks with cream and sugar on the side to go."

The guy rolled his eyes but took the card and began to punch buttons faster than I could have read them. I had no fucking clue what half-caf-soy with an extra skinny shot meant. What happened to regular coffee with cream and sugar?

"Is that it?" the clerk said, and Maggie pushed in beside me. "Add another large black with extra room for cream, please."

I raised a brow toward her. "Sure, by all means, add your order to mine."

She grinned and leaned forward slightly, lowering her voice, and seductively said, "With all that, I didn't think you'd notice one more. Besides, I think you owe me at least a cup of coffee."

Damn—she kept smiling up at me, and I had this crazy-ass idea to lean forward and kiss those lips. Fuck if the idea didn't get something moving below the belt too.

I was opening my mouth to tell her just what I had noticed when the front door opened, and someone screamed. Two men with masks burst into the place, both holding handguns. I grabbed Maggie's arm and pulled her behind me before I took hold of the pregnant woman's arm, too, and yanked her around me also. They were no sooner behind me when a gunshot went off into the ceiling, and my demeanor went from sexual to lethal in the time that it took for the firearms slide to move backwards and then snap back in place.

CHAPTER TWO

MAGGIE

"No, I told you that I was going to break the segment down into more than one column—I specifically told you it would be ten days. I did say there were ten ways to know if he loves you."

"You should have just put all ten points into one column," my editor complained.

"Jeff, it would have been too long. There is no way I can put all ten reasons you should be with a man in less than five hundred words."

"You could have if you had tried, Maggie."

"No, I couldn't, Jeff." I stopped on a dime as a man barreled past me, almost plowing into me as he crossed the sidewalk.

"Move." The man glared at me, his hazel eyes devoid of emotion to the point that I shivered and looked away, noting the black SUV parked at the curb, still running.

Man, didn't they know that was a crime? It was illegal to leave your vehicle running with no one in it. The two men had disappeared into the store, so I slipped closer to the vehicle and peeked inside, checking the back seat to see it was empty, too.

"What are you going to do now?" Jeff asked, snapping me back to the conversation as I glanced over my shoulder and didn't see anyone in the jewelry store. They must have gone toward the back.

"I'm going to finish the series. Look, just give it a day. I promise you that more people will tune in tomorrow, and more will keep reading the column over the next ten days. They aren't going to want to miss even one of the reasons that I give."

As I spoke, I went around to the other side of the SUV and tried the door handle. Unlocked, of course. I made sure there wasn't a car coming, then opened the door, reached in for the keys, and turned the SUV off. I stared at the keys for a moment, chewing my bottom lip, tempted to throw them into the street, but I decided to toss them into the rear storage area behind the second row. With that done, I pushed the door closed, checked the traffic, and then ran across the street as my phone began to beep in my ear.

I glanced at the screen. "Jeff, I will be in the office in a few minutes. I have to take another call." I hung up on him before he even uttered a sound. "Hey, Heather, are we still on for tonight?" I asked as I cut through pedestrian traffic on the sidewalk to get to the coffee shop door.

"Yep, I'm totally game. I have been dying to try out one of those speed dating things for months."

"It will be great for my next series," I told her.

"How is the current one going?" she asked as I stepped into the coffee shop and tried not to sigh at the long line in front of me. The only benefit to the line was getting the chance to check out the sweet buns in front of me, and I wasn't talking about the ones in the glass display case. I glanced from the man's feet, up his long legs covered in black slacks, to his thick waist and wide back, pausing at the neatly trimmed brown hair on the back of his head.

The guy had to be a cop, or something, with the way he was dressed and the way he stood. I'd dated a cop a few times, and it hadn't gone over very well. He was too damn macho for me and thought I should be doing cushy things in an office, not trying to dig through the news for a story with grit. I sure as hell didn't want to be a romance advice columnist for the rest of my life. Hell no! No wonder Babs had kicked the bucket!

"Jeff is still pissed that I broke it down into segments, but he needs to get over it. If I'm going to help this column grow to be something serious, then he needs to give me some space."

"Good luck with that."

From the corner of my eye, I saw the man spin around on me. "Would you mind watching your bag, please?"

I turned to snap an apology, and my jaw dropped as I stared into the deep blue eyes of my first love. Holy crap!

"Greg? Heather, I need to call you back." I hit end call without a second thought. "Gregory Blaire, what are you doing here?"

Oh man, the sight of him had shivers tearing all the way down to my toes, then reverberated right back up to my scalp. He looked incredible, and his voice was just as sexy as it had been back when we were teens. The memory of him whispering in my ear the first time we had sex—my first time ever—that he would love me until the day I died, flashed into my mind. Not that I would mention that, nope. I wasn't going to point out to him that he had lied. That he had broken my heart when he enlisted in the Marines two weeks later and that when he found out he was leaving for overseas a year after that, he'd broken up with me. I'd cried for a month, and then I'd finished high school, gone off to college, and went about my life.

It was hard to believe that I hadn't seen this man in nineteen years, and I was ready to drag him into the tiny restroom in the back and do dirty things to him. He might be impressed that I had learned a few things over the years. I was no longer that shy teen.

Nope, now I was a woman who took romance by the balls—I could say that, right? Of course, I could. I was a contemporary woman in charge of her life and in control of her sexual needs. We shuffled toward the cashier, chatting about inconsequential things, and I was dying to ask if he was single or dating or married, or maybe he was gay now. Who knew!

We reached the cashier, and he handed over the card with the coffee orders on it and then added a few more. I didn't think he'd mind throwing one more on there; I mean he did owe me at least that for breaking my tender teenaged heart—right?

I leaned toward him, waiting for him to say something as I inhaled his subtle aftershave. Oh, Lord, it made me want to rub my face all over his neck and chin so that I'd have something to enjoy for the next few hours. With a scent like that, I could write some rip-roaring romance articles.

Greg's gaze drifted to my mouth; would kissing him be as incredible as it had been in the past? Did he remember how incredible our kisses had been? I sure did. I had measured every kiss I had ever gotten from other men to his, and I had learned that he had ruined me for most men. Uh, there was my time with Ben, but that was so long ago it didn't count anymore.

I was about to open my mouth and ask him what he was doing tonight when things got a little crazy behind me, and before I could figure out what was going on, I was standing behind Greg. People were screaming, and a gunshot made me flinch like every other person in the room. Well, everyone but Greg, that is. He seemed to grow taller, rather than make himself smaller, and I cozied up to his back beside the pregnant woman who had been right behind us.

"Everyone get down on the floor!" a man shouted, and I peered around Greg to see a man in a green army fatigue jacket wearing a black ski mask that covered all of his face, except his eyes. Was that the guy that had cut me off on the sidewalk a few minutes ago? It had to be. Whoops! Did he know that I was the one that had removed their car keys? Did they see me get into their car and think that I still had them? Had they come over here to get them back? Holy crap! Had they come here for me?

"Get down!" the second man wearing a black jacket and matching mask shouted, his voice sounding slightly shaky, and he looked around frantically.

Green jacket guy turned the lock on the coffee shop door and pointed a gun at someone. "Close the shades on the front window." The woman had been going to her knees, and she jerked back up, shaking as she sobbed and moved to the window to do as he asked.

I helped the pregnant woman to the ground. "How far along are you?"

"Eight months," she whispered.

I helped the woman shift so that her back was resting against the counter behind us. Greg squatted down and pulled his cell-phone out of his pocket. Without even looking at it, he started fiddling with it.

"Get their phones," green jacket guy snapped at black jacket man, and he nodded before he started coming around and collecting the phones. Greg's screen went dark right before the guy reached him, and he hesitated as he stared up at the guy.

"Give me your phone!" the guy said, and Greg's chin went up higher like he was challenging him. Was he crazy? Black jacket guy seemed confused that Greg wasn't doing as he asked and frowned. "I said, give me your phone."

Green jacket guy appeared at his side, his gun pointed at Greg's head, and my stomach turned upside down. "Give him your phone, now!"

Greg held the phone out, and the man snatched it. "Don't be

a fucking hero here, you got it? I'll put a bullet in you before you could even see it coming."

Greg didn't say a word, and outside sirens approached the area. Black jacket man peeked around one of the window shades that were in place now. "The cops are here! What are we gonna do, Len?"

"Shut up, you fucking idiot!" green jacket man snapped. "Of course the cops are here! We just robbed a jewelry store. Did you think they would just let us go?"

"Let's just go out the back door. Can't we do that?"

"No, they will have cops everywhere," he said. "We are staying here where we have hostages."

"You aren't going to kill them, are you?" Black jacket man looked around, his eyes wide.

"I'm not going to kill them as long as they don't do something stupid."

Greg glanced back at me, lifted a brow at me as if to ask if I were alright, and I nodded slightly to him. He glanced at the pregnant woman's face, her belly, and then sighed as he turned back to the two men.

The woman was rubbing her stomach, and I squeezed her arm. "Are you doing okay?"

The woman nodded as Len turned toward me. "Shut up!" He came toward us with long strides, and Greg tensed. "There is no talking; you got that, lady!"

"I was just checking on her," I said, and Greg put his hand behind his back on my ankle. Was he trying to tell me to shut up too?

The guy pointed the gun at me, and I cringed, every muscle in my body tensing in fear. The guy glanced at the woman beside me, frowned at her swollen stomach, and then growled at me, "Shut up, woman!"

I swallowed the retort I wanted to lash out at him. Holy crap, I'd never had a gun pointed at me before, and I wasn't sure if I wanted to have a panic attack or go all sorts of female hysterical on him.

More sirens filled the air, and you could hear people yelling outside. Greg shifted slowly backward, and I scooted to the side so he could slide in between the pregnant woman and me. I saw him looking at the mother-to-be, and then he took hold of her hand and squeezed for a moment.

He sat with his leg straight out in front of him, his hands flat on his thighs. I leaned slightly toward him as the two men talked in a whisper at the side of the room. Everyone was quiet, nervously looking around at each other as if searching for someone who would end this situation. Strangely, most of the people kept bringing their attention back to Greg. Did they all think he was a cop like I had once thought?

He had that look about him, but I guess after twenty years in the military, he would have that look. Greg was watching them through his lashes, and I wished that I had a window into his brain. I would love to see what he was thinking right now, what he was planning. What had he done on his phone before they had taken it? I was dying to ask but knew that now was not the time.

The guy in the black jacket kept looking at me, and it was making me nervous. Suddenly, his mouth dropped. "I know who you are!" Greg tensed beside me as I shifted as far back against the counter as I could.

Oh, my god! He knew that I'd seen them without masks! They knew I was the one that had removed their car keys. Would they kill me now? I was ready to jump to my feet and apologize for taking the keys out. If I had just left it alone, they would be long gone. This was all my fault! If anyone died, it was going to be my fault! I was ready to hyperventilate.

The black jacket guy stared down at me from a few feet away, his blue eyes bright behind the black mask. "You're that lady that writes about romance! My girlfriend loves you; what's your name? Something Valor, right?"

I wanted to melt into the floor. He knew me from the paper, not the sidewalk. Holy smokes. Len, his very angry cohort, came to stand next to him. He opened his mouth to talk, but just then a loudspeaker called out from the street, and he dismissed me.

CHAPTER THREE

GREGORY

*B*efore shit could get too out of control, I pulled my cellphone out and sent a message to the last person I'd spoken too. Luckily, that was Trevor. In my training, I'd learned how to send messages without looking at the keyboard too much. The one I sent Trevor was: *in deep, 911, java, listen.*

Hopefully, he would figure it out quickly that there was trouble at the coffee shop. I was pretty sure that by now, Trevor and Alex were already on the street watching what was going down and letting the cops listen to the open line I had given them.

I had no trouble figuring out who the boss was on this job. The guy in black was probably Len's lackey, possibly a relative he didn't think highly of. What had gone wrong with their plan? If they had robbed the jewelry store, why hadn't they taken off? What had stopped them? Was there a cop on the street when they came out?

It didn't make sense to leave a robbery and move into a hostage situation. Sometimes they went hand in hand, but you sure as shit didn't do a robbery and then change locations to take hostages if you could get away. It didn't make sense.

Len was frustrated and trigger-happy. He'd already let loose one in the building. I did not doubt that if something happened in here, he'd pop off another shot. I just hoped that it didn't hurt anyone when he did.

When Len had pointed the gun at my head, I'd almost laughed and said go ahead. I mean, it would be fucking ironic to make it through six tours overseas in war zones to die in a coffee shop picking up half a dozen foo-foo coffees. This wasn't the first time I'd had a gun pointed at my head—probably wouldn't be the last either—so I just rolled with it.

What I didn't want to roll with was the asswipe aiming his loaded weapon at Maggie. Oh, fuck, no! That almost put me over the top. I wanted to get in his evil-looking grill and knock the shit out of him. I didn't, though. I kept my cool until the lackey came toward her again, his voice tinged with excitement that I wasn't sure was good or bad.

I felt her fear blast from her body as she tried to back away from him, and I wished I could have blocked her somehow. Even though she had her chin up and she was staring him down, I knew she was afraid. I knew Mags well. I might not have seen her in years, but that expression was one that I remembered all too well.

I had been nineteen and about to leave for overseas. I cared a lot for Maggie, and yeah, I loved her. I was two years older than her, and we'd been together since she was a freshman in high school. Even though I cared about her, I just couldn't ask her to put her life on hold for me. I knew I wasn't ready for a serious commitment like marriage, and neither was she.

I had been getting ready to head into a war zone and fight for freedom. Maggie was going to finish high school, go to football games, dances, hang out with friends, and take advantage of the freedom that we fought for.

The day I'd come to say goodbye, she had looked up at me

with that same look. There was fear in her eyes for my safety, and anger for what I was doing. That was an image that had never faded in my memory.

There had also been something else in her eyes that day—love and pain—and I knew I hurt her. I hurt myself, too, but I knew it was the right thing to do. One day she would under-stand—or so I hoped. How long had it taken her to realize why I had broken it off?

The guy in the black jacket kept looking at Maggie, and she was squirming under his scrutiny. He approached her, and his words were a punch to the gut. "I know who you are!"

Ah, shit! Maggie pushed herself back as far as she could.

"You're that lady that writes about romance! My girlfriend loves you; what's your name? Something Valor, right?" What was he going to do? Use her status as a reporter to help him get something?

An amplified voice rang out through the café. "This is Sergeant Wilkins; we'd like to speak to the man in charge. We are going to call into the shop, so please answer the phone."

Len and his accomplice looked at one another, and then the phone behind the counter started to ring. They both turned to stare at it, and man two turned to Len. "You gonna get it?"

"No," he growled.

"Why not? We can demand a getaway car and leave."

Len laughed at him. "You are so stupid. They aren't going to let us go. They'd just as soon kill us."

The guy looked surprised and then disappointed. "We can give ourselves up."

"We are not going to give ourselves up, numbnuts," Len hissed at him.

"Maybe you won't, but you can't tell me what I'm going to do." He planted his feet firmly as he squared off to Len. "I'd rather go to jail than be stuck six feet under."

"You keep that shit up, and that's the only place you're going to end up," he snapped back at him. "Now, stop your yapping so I can think." He turned and pointed the gun at one of the employees who was on the floor near the back. "Go pick that phone up and hang it back up."

The kid blanched but got off the floor and went behind the counter. The phone stopped ringing, and it was so quiet in the room that you could hear the phone being hung back up. Len waved his gun toward the kid to sit back down.

I observed them from the corner of my eye, waiting patiently for a moment that I could step in and take control of Len's weapon. I had a feeling that if I could subdue him, I could talk the other guy into giving himself up. I hoped that the cops were listening so that they were aware that we had one subject who was willing to turn himself in.

The phone started ringing again. "You!" He shouted at the kid again just after he got seated. "Stand by that phone, and every time it rings, you hang it up! Got it?" The kid rushed back to the phone, and a moment later, it stopped ringing.

I glanced around the café; a variety of people were scattered along the floor. An elderly man glared at the two men as he shifted on the ground, looking uncomfortable. A frazzled-looking woman was in the corner, her legs curled under her as she kept glancing at her watch. A couple held hands on the far wall, both wore wedding rings, but not matching. Were they merely lending support to the other or having an affair? Several businessmen were seated near the back, looking annoyed or bored. Some held coffee cups as if they had just received their orders.

What I wouldn't do for a freaking cup of coffee right now; at least I hadn't paid for all that coffee yet. After this, I was buying a damn coffeemaker, and I'd put it at my desk if I had to. Jake could kiss my ass.

The pregnant woman next to me winced and sucked in a breath. "You okay?" I asked softly.

Numbnuts was watching us; she nodded at me nervously.

"Hey, guys." Len spun around as I spoke, pointing his gun toward me. "Whoa, no reason to point that gun at me. I just want to suggest that you have a little heart here and let this pregnant woman have a chair, along with the elderly gentleman over there. Neither of them are threats to you, but being kind to them might go a long way in your defense."

"No," he hissed back.

"Can I at least use the restroom?" the woman surprised me by asking. "My baby is kicking my bladder."

Len stared at her and her large abdomen. "Fine."

She looked immediately thankful but then struggled to get to her feet. I went to get to my feet and felt the muzzle of the gun at my forehead.

"I'm just going to help her get off the ground," I said.

"Sit your ass down; Chuck can help her up."

And just like that, Numbnuts had a first name. I sank back to the ground, and Chuck held out a hand to the woman. I took her other hand and helped the best that I could being seated on the ground. She waddled herself to the bathroom and disappeared behind the door.

I sat there, trying to figure out the best way to play this. How long would it be before Len spoke with authorities?

Chuck was pacing and turned on Len. "How are we gonna get out of this?"

"I'm thinking," he said as the bathroom door opened and the woman emerged, looking slightly distressed.

She shuffled back to my side, and I helped her get down to the ground. "Are you alright?"

She shook her head and threw a look in their direction. "No, I'm bleeding, and I'm having some small contractions."

Damn. "How far along are you?"

"Eight months," she said.

Len turned his attention toward us. "No talking."

"Look, you have to let this lady leave," I said. "She's going into labor right now."

Len's expression didn't change a bit, but Chuck grinned beside him. "Really? That's cool."

The guy was obviously short a few screws, and Len glared at him. "She's not going anywhere."

"Then can you at least see if there are any medical employees in here to help her out?"

"I'm a nurse," a woman on the far side of the room under a table called out.

"Fine," Len finally relented, and the nurse slowly got to her feet. She was wearing light-purple scrubs and kept her head down as she approached us, going to her knees beside the woman.

"Hi, I'm Carol." I listened to her ask a few questions about the pregnancy and quickly learned that this was a high-risk pregnancy. When a contraction began to hit her, I took her hand and let her squeeze hard.

Chuck seemed enthralled with what was going on. Len, on the other hand, looked pissed off at the world as he leaned against the wall and scrutinized all of us.

I glanced at Maggie; she was watching the pregnant woman but glanced my way and tried to smile.

"Do you want to sit next to her?" I asked, and she nodded. I started to move and saw the booted feet coming toward me.

"Stay right where you are!" he hissed at me as he put the muzzle to my head. "I don't trust you one bit. You're up to something."

"No, sir, I'm not. I was just trading places with the lady so she could help them. I'm not looking for trouble." This guy was itching to get into it with someone. I already had a few pieces of shrapnel in my body, but I didn't think a bullet in the brain would be good for the collection.

"You just sit. Don't talk, don't move. If you make one more move or say one more word, I'm going to put a bullet right between your eyes."

I lifted my face, the muzzle of the gun dragging over my scalp, down my forehead until it was lined up right between my eyes. "Understood, sir."

He hissed, "Crazy motherfucker." He dropped the gun from my head and stepped quickly back from me. Had he not moved so fast, I might have shown him just how crazy I was. Maybe he wasn't as dumb as I thought he was.

Chuck had been watching us, and Maggie settled herself back against the counter, peering up at him. "You are that lady, right? The one that writes about love and stuff in the paper?"

"Yes," she said softly and then lifted her chin. "You know I do more than just write advice columns; I write real news too. I could write an article about you two, tell your side of the story."

"Could you?" Chuck asked excitedly.

Len raised his arm and shot into the ceiling again. Everyone jumped, a few screamed, and Maggie slipped closer to me. "Shut up! Just shut the fuck up, all of you!"

He smacked Chuck on the back of the head. "She ain't gonna write a story on us, you dork. She's lying to you."

"No, she's not. I know she's in the paper." Chuck looked around. "Hey, anyone have today's paper?"

The frazzled woman raised her hand and then pointed at the table where she'd been sitting. Chuck made a beeline for it and then started flipping pages.

"Section two, page two," Maggie said, and Len rolled his head toward her, his eyes spitting venom.

Chuck found the page and handed it to Len. "See, it's her. You can tell by the picture."

"Well, look at that, we have a reporter in our midst," Len said

23

as he looked back at Maggie. The way he stared at her made the hair rise on the back of my neck. "Nice to have you with us, Maggie Valor; maybe you might be of use to us."

"Oh, shit," she murmured under her breath.

CHAPTER FOUR

MAGGIE

I'd been really thankful that the police had shown up when they had, and the two guys had forgotten about me—at least for the moment. The last thing I wanted was to have their attention. Instead, I preferred to remain unnoticed so that I could note everything that they did. I had every intention of hitting my editor up and asking for front-page space. How could he deny me that? This story would most definitely be front-page news, and who better to report it than someone present at the scene.

So I watched, and I prayed that Len wouldn't do anything stupid, like put a bullet into Greg's head. Was he crazy—Greg, not Len. We all knew the bad guy was crazy. Greg had lifted his face directly to the guy, rested his forehead right against the gun, and smiled. Okay, so maybe he didn't outright smile, but I swear there was a little hint of a grin on his face. I remember that Greg had always been outgoing and daring when he was a teenager, but had he gone nuts after his years in the service? He had to have because no sane person would have done what he did.

I felt for the pregnant woman, and I'm glad that they let her at least use the restroom, although, with the way she was moving, I was beginning to wonder if the stress of this situation might send her into labor right here in the coffee shop. Now that was a story to tell the kid when he got older.

Yep, I was hankering for a shot of espresso and ended up getting held hostage instead. You were born right there on the dirty floor of Cocoa's Coffee Café with twenty or so people there to witness your entry into this world. It wasn't nerve-racking in the least that two men were waving guns around and the kind man that had tried to help me had gotten shot for doing so. I named you Greg after him.

I cringed when Chuck asked me again, "You are that lady, right? The one that writes about love and stuff in the paper?"

"Yes," I replied meekly. Maybe if I told them I was also a serious journalist, they would make sure I lived to tell their story. "You know, I do more than just write advice columns; I write real news too. I could write an article about you two, tell your side of the story."

His blue eyes sparkled. "Could you?"

I screamed when Len fired another shot into the ceiling and cowered behind Greg. "Shut up! Just shut the fuck up, all of you!"

I was hoping that was the end of it, but no, Chuck just had to push and prove it was me. When they located a paper, I volunteered the location and earned a glare for my trouble. Why did I even bother?

Chuck pointed at the picture, tapping his finger on it. "See, it's her. You can tell by the picture."

"Well, look at that, we have a reporter in our midst." Len turned to me, and I would have had to be blind to miss the scary joy in his gaze. "Nice to have you with us, Maggie Valor; maybe you might be of use to us."

"Oh, shit," I mumbled and didn't miss the stiffening of Greg's back beside me.

Len glanced around the room. "I have an idea. Everyone, take your wallets out."

No one moved, and then he shouted the command and waved the gun around. Most of the people began to rummage around in their pockets or purses, including me. Greg didn't move.

One woman began to cry. "I don't have a wallet. I just brought enough cash with me to get my coffee. I work in an office building across the street." Len grunted at her.

"Everyone take out your licenses. I want to see them." He turned to Chuck. "Collect them from everyone, and if they don't have one, I want to know."

His eyes cut around the room, and I leaned toward Greg and whispered, "Get your ID out."

"No," he replied, not looking at me.

"Greg—" I started to plead with him and garnered Len's attention again.

"What's so important that you need to talk to him about, Ms. Valor?"

I shook my head instead of answering, and he approached us, glaring at Greg. "Where is your license?"

"I don't have one."

"Bullshit. A guy like you doesn't go around without identification on him."

"You can check me, but I don't have a wallet."

"Then how were you going to pay for your coffee?"

"With my phone."

He frowned. "Mr. Fancy Pants, using his technology to pay for things. Look at that." He glanced at me. "Is this your boyfriend, Ms. Valor?"

I shook my head at the same time that Greg spoke. "I don't even know the woman."

I frowned at the side of Greg's head. Why would he say that?

Granted, we hadn't seen each other in almost twenty years, but to say he doesn't know me? What the hell?

Len looked at the pregnant woman. "Did you hear these two talking in line?"

The woman looked immediately scared, and Greg spoke up again. "I admit that I was talking to her. I was hitting on her, trying to gauge if she'd be worth asking out. She's pretty enough."

My brow furrowed. Pretty enough? Was he serious?

"She's not your girlfriend?" he asked him again.

"Nope, not really my type, seems a bit prudish, if you know what I mean."

My jaw dropped. Prudish? Was he serious? Oh, man, when we got out of here, I was going to show him just how prudish I was.

Len grinned and looked me over from head to toe. I felt violated by his leer, and I looked away, noticing that Greg had his hands fisted. Len turned to the pregnant woman. "Is he telling the truth?"

She nodded quickly. "Yeah, he was flirting with her."

"Turn around and get on your knees." He grunted toward Greg, waving the gun toward him.

Greg didn't look at me as he spun around on the brown tile floor and then got to his knees slowly. Len called Chuck over. "Check him, see what he has in those pockets."

Greg laced his fingers behind his head, stared straight ahead and let Chuck pat his waist down, and then his side pockets. "What's that?"

"A note pad and a pen," Greg responded. "And before you check the other side, I have a pocketknife."

"Take the items out of your pockets carefully and hand them to Ms. Valor," Len commanded.

Greg slowly took one hand off his head and pulled a small leather-bound notebook from his pocket and then a pen and held them out to me. I took them. He shifted his hand to his other side and dug around in a pocket for a moment. He held his hand out toward me, and I gave him my palm. The contents dropped into mine, and I stared at the half roll of breath mints, a Chapstick, a black pocketknife, and a condom. My eyes snapped to his. He didn't carry a wallet, but he brought along a freaking condom? I glanced at the wrapper and saw it was a super magnum. I almost started laughing because I knew damn well that he wasn't a super magnum size. Not that he was small, but he wasn't *that* big.

Greg winked at me, and there was just a touch of humor on his features before they went blank again. Chuck checked his other side to make sure nothing else was there.

"That's all he has on him."

"Give me that stuff," Len said, and I held my hands up for him to take it. He removed the knife, glanced at the notebook before putting it back into my hand, and walked away. Greg seemed relieved when I put my hands down, and for a second, he closed his eyes.

Len and Chuck went to a table, and Chuck laid out all the ID's. Len glanced over them before he took his phone out and started snapping pictures of them. Why was he doing that?

The phone rang again, and Len turned to the employee and waved his gun at him. The ringing stopped, and then the phone clicked as he put it back down.

"There were four that didn't have a license on them," Chuck said.

"Fine, get them, we are going to move them."

"Move them?"

"Yeah, we're going to move them."

A muscle in Greg's jaw ticked against his cheek a couple of times, and a few lines crossed his brow momentarily before his face calmed back to nothingness. What was going through his mind?

Chuck pulled the gun out of his waistband where he'd stored it while getting ID's and went to gather the woman and two men who were on the other side of the café. "Get up," he told them. "Leave your stuff there."

They got to their feet, and he told them to move toward the back of the business.

"Sit them there, and go find something from the back to tie them up with."

Chuck nodded and disappeared into the back for a moment as the three people he'd collected sat around a small table. I glanced at Greg; he was still on his knees, hands still laced behind his head. Why was he still sitting like that? Why didn't he turn back around?

The bullhorn from outside filled the room again. "This is Sergeant Wilkins again. We really would like to settle this peacefully, but we can't do that if you don't speak with us. We need to know if everyone is alright in there. We heard that last gunshot. Please answer the phone so that we can discuss options and make sure everyone is alright."

The phone began to ring, and Len glanced at the employee. The phone stopped ringing and clicked as Chuck returned. "I found duct tape," he announced, and I swear I heard Greg scoff.

"Fine, bind their wrists, feet, and mouths, and put them in the bathroom," Len stated.

"You want me to take him too?" he asked Len as he pointed at Greg.

"Yeah, but get those three done first. He might give you trouble."

As Chuck disappeared into the bathroom with one person at a time, Len walked around the room and looked carefully at all the people, especially the men. Finally, he stood in front of one of the employees and nodded.

Chuck finished with the three people and came back to get Greg. As he got to his feet, he stared at me hard, and then he was turned and marched to the bathroom. I sure hope no one else needed to use the bathroom. From where I was seated, I could see the people gagged and bound on the floor. Gross.

Chuck returned a moment later, and the phone rang again. This time Len walked toward the phone. The phone rang three times, and then he picked it up.

He didn't say anything at first, and I wondered what they were saying. "No one is injured," he stated gruffly. "Yes, I'm telling you the truth. Here." He must have grabbed the employee. "Tell them that everyone is okay."

The employee's voice cracked as he spoke. "No one's injured."

"The gunfire was warning shots," Len stated as shuffling was heard behind me.

He grew quiet again, and a few of us traded looks. Two people were staring at him and then the door, probably wondering if they could make it there and unlock it before they were noticed or shot.

"Give us five minutes, and we'll give ourselves up," Len stated gruffly and then hung up the phone abruptly. I glanced at the pregnant woman and the nurse in surprise. They were going to give themselves up? I hadn't expected that. Did he realize there was no way out of this? If he did, why did he put those four people in the bathroom?

Len called Chuck behind the counter, and the two of them whispered for a few moments. Chuck came back around the counter, and so did the employee that had been answering the phone. Len went to another employee, a slightly older man who I knew from my visits was the manager and told him to get up.

He pointed the gun at him and told him to walk into the back. What the hell was he doing? Was he going to hurt the guy?

Chuck paced around the room and came to stand in front of me. "After we give ourselves up, will you come to see me in jail and write my story?"

"Um, sure. I can do that."

He looked excited for a second, but that disappeared quickly as he stared at the front door and realized that he was about to be arrested.

The phone rang a minute later, and Chuck went around to answer it. "Yeah, give us one minute, and we'll give ourselves up." He hung up the phone without waiting for a reply.

I heard footsteps behind the counter as if Len and the employee had come back, but they didn't come to this side of the counter.

My hands were clammy as I wondered if this was going to be as easy as it seemed. Would they give themselves up and just let us go?

"This is Sergeant Wilkins again; your time is up; let the hostages go."

Chuck glanced around the room and swallowed. "Okay, get up and go toward the front door slowly."

Holy crap, were they just going to let us walk out of here? A few people got to their feet quickly, and I got to my knees, intent on helping the pregnant woman up, but one of the employees rushed to her side and helped her off the floor. She kept her arm around him as he ushered her to the door.

We all walked out, our arms up around our heads. Well, except for the nurse, the pregnant woman, and the employee who was helping her.

I glanced behind me as I reached the door. Chuck stood in the center of the room, looking nervous, and Len was standing at the back of the room. I hadn't expected him to let us go this way. I raised my hands over my head and slipped out the door.

CHAPTER FIVE

GREGORY

*T*hese guys were both idiots. Sure, stick me in the bathroom and put duct tape around my wrists and ankles. Like that was going to stop me. My wrists were bound behind my back, and the tape was off in less than ten seconds. It took another fifteen seconds to get it off my ankles and mouth. It took me longer to get the others out, but within two minutes, we were all free. I spoke quietly to each of them, moving to the side of the door in case they came in to check on us. If they did, I'd take them out then, but in the meantime, we didn't need to be uncomfortable.

A few minutes after we were locked in there, I heard the police loudspeaker, and then Chuck told the group of hostages to get up and leave. Chairs scratched the floor, and muted footsteps could barely be heard from the main room. Why put us in here if they were going to let the hostages go?

If they were letting them leave, then surprising Len and Chuck by opening the door would be a bad idea, especially since I didn't have a firearm with me. I heard the police announce that cops were coming in, and I told the three people with me to get on their knees, face the wall, and put their hands behind their heads.

"Why are we doing this?" one of the men asked.

"So when they yank open the door and have a gun on you, you don't freak out and move. You move—they shoot. Just sit still and wait for the police to find us. They will direct you when and how to move from there."

I heard the police giving commands to the two men in the main room, and I dropped to my knees. It wouldn't take long for someone to check the bathroom, and I was right—only twenty seconds by my count.

"Which one of you is Blaire?"

"Me," I said as I unlaced my fingers and waved my hand.

"Who are these people with you?" he asked.

"All innocent victims," I said as I looked at the tactical dressed man over my shoulder. He told me to get to my feet, and then I helped the woman get to hers. The cops in the main room told one of the guys to stand still.

When we stepped into the main room, Chuck was seated in a chair. His hands were cuffed behind his back, and his mask was on the table next to him. He watched the cop pull the cover off of Len's face and gasped.

"That's not Len!" Chuck exclaimed.

My face snapped to the other man, and I saw tape over his mouth. His green eyes were wide and frightened. The cop yanked the tape from his mouth, and the man sputtered, "I'm not him! He made me trade clothes with him. He told me he knows where I live, and he'd kill my family if I didn't do it. He walked out of here with the woman who was pregnant."

I turned to the cop beside me. "That's not Len, he's telling you the truth. His voice is not gravelly enough, and his eyes are the wrong color."

I started rushing toward the door as one of the cops got on his radio. As I breached the door, there was a bit of commotion off to the side, and a few police officers began to run that way. I scanned the crowd, saw Trevor, Alex, and Jake near one of the police SUVs, and then I saw Maggie off to the side talking to two cops.

I made a beeline toward Maggie. I wanted to check on her before I gave my statement to the police. I was a few steps away from her when she turned from the cops and launched herself into my arms the moment that she saw me.

"Oh, my god! You're alright!" I held her tightly for a moment, glad to see she was unharmed.

"Yeah, I'm fine. How are you?" I leaned back to check her and cupped her cheek.

"I'm a little rattled, but I'm okay and glad it is over without anyone harmed."

I pulled her back to me and kissed her brow as I tucked her against my chest.

"Yo, Blaire!" I heard my name shouted, and I shifted my body and Maggie's so I could see Trevor as he approached with Alex. "Dude, where's my coffee?"

I started laughing. "Sorry, my order got interrupted."

"Glad you're alright," Trevor said as he checked Maggie out. "Only you would go to retrieve coffee and find yourself a woman."

"Funny." I chuckled as I tucked Maggie into my side. "Maggie is an old friend. We go back to high school."

Maggie spoke up from my side, "Yeah, back when I was a prude."

I glanced down at her, lifting her chin. "I said that to get him off the scent. If he had known that we had any connection, he would have used it. Speaking of which—" I glanced around. "He got away."

"What?"

"He got away. He traded clothes with an employee and slipped out with everyone else."

"Oh, my god! He helped the pregnant woman out!"

"Do you see him around here?" I asked her.

She started looking around. "No, he was here a couple of minutes ago, but I don't see him now."

"Did you get a look at his face, Maggie?" Trevor asked her.

"No, not when we were leaving," she answered.

"Not when you were leaving?" Alex echoed back. "Did you see him earlier?"

"Yeah, actually, I did."

"What?" I barked. "When?"

"Before they came into the coffee shop. I saw them go into the jewelry store. One of the men, Len, almost knocked me down and then glared at me."

"Shit," I muttered as I swiped a hand along my jaw and searched the area again.

"Why? I can give the police a description now."

"Yeah, you can," Alex replied to her.

"If he remembers that he saw you before the café, he will know that you can ID him."

"So," she said with a shrug.

"Mags, he knows where you live."

Her brow furrowed. "How?"

"He took photographs of all the licenses. He knows where everyone lives."

She looked like someone had just tossed a bucket of cold water into her face. "That's why he did that?"

"Yes, and that's why I didn't give him my ID."

She frowned at me. "But you didn't have one on you anyway."

"Yeah, I did. It was tucked into the back of the notebook, along with my retired military ID."

"Oh," she said as she glanced around nervously.

"You think he will come after her, or anyone?" Trevor asked.

I shrugged. "I don't know. It depends on what Chuck has to

say. I have a feeling that Chuck will give up his accomplice to get a better deal. I'm sure that he is smarting now that Len got away and he was apprehended. It was obvious by the look on Chuck's face in there that he didn't know Len was going to leave him behind."

"Good, I hope he tells the police everything," Maggie said.

Alex spoke up. "The police sergeant wants to speak to you. He was impressed with your message and how you put the call through."

"What call?" Maggie asked.

"I called Trevor when things first went down. Everything they did in there was aired out here to them. The police knew what was happening because the line was open."

Her lips parted in surprise. "That's what you did? What made you think to do that?"

"Training, darling." I winked at her. "And for the record, I do not think you are a prude."

"Oh, that's a good thing because I had been stewing over how I could prove to you that I wasn't."

I leaned down and whispered into her ear, "You could still try to prove it."

She laughed and slapped my chest as we began to walk toward the police vehicle with the most activity around it. Alex and Trevor walked in front of us.

"What I'd like to know is how you could possibly think that you are a magnum?" Maggie said with a grin.

Trevor burst out a laugh in front of us as he turned and walked backward. "Is he still carrying that around with him?"

"Yes, he is. I assume that's a joke."

Trevor, Alex, and I all laughed as I replied, "Yes, it is."

"Are you going to explain it to me?"

All three of us sobered and said, "No!" at once, startling her.

"Where did Screamer go?" I asked, changing the subject on purpose.

Alex shifted to the side of us to answer. "He said that since you were alive, he was going back to the office and told you to hurry the hell up. He's not paying you to dilly-dally around anymore."

"Screw him." I snorted a laugh.

"Who is Screamer?" Maggie asked.

"My boss."

"And his name is Screamer? Do I want to know why?"

Trevor chuckled. "We all did a tour together overseas. Jake got the nickname Screamer because when he went into battle, he had a wild war cry, and when he gets pissed, he screams at the top of his lungs."

Her eyes were wide as I peered down at her. "Sounds like a wonderful guy."

"He has his moments," I told her wryly as we paused next to the police vehicle.

Trevor introduced me to Sgt. Wilkins, and I explained more of what I knew. Maggie helped me explain a few of the things for the time I was in the bathroom.

"Well, we thought we had all the hostages detained, but he must have slipped out somehow."

"Maggie saw him before the jewelry heist."

"You did?" The sergeant turned to face her more fully, his gaze slipping down her body quickly, and I found myself a little irritated with that. Not that I had a right to be, or that I would say anything, but still— "What did you see?"

"On my way to the coffee shop, he cut me off on the sidewalk. I was on the phone with my boss. Oh crap! I need to call my editor. When do we get our phones back?"

"Not for a little while. What about when you saw the guy?" The sergeant attempted to get her train of thought back on track.

"Nothing really, he almost walked right into me and then glared at me as he passed."

"That's all that happened?"

"Yes," she said, and her eyes cut off to the side. What was she not saying?

The sergeant studied her for a moment. "Okay, well, we'll need you to work with a sketch artist to get a good composite of him."

"What about Chuck? Can't he just tell you who the guy is?" I asked him.

"Chuck isn't talking right now. He said he wants a lawyer."

"Okay, but won't he eventually talk when he decides that he wants to make a deal?"

"Not sure the DA's office will offer a deal. The guy got away with over three hundred thousand dollars' worth of diamonds and kidnapped nineteen people."

"What?" Maggie exclaimed. "But where were the diamonds? He wasn't carrying anything with him."

"Mag, the package would have fit in his pocket. It wouldn't be that big."

"Oh, yeah, I guess it would. They are expensive little suckers."

"Damn, don't I know that," Trevor grunted, and I knew he was thinking about the engagement ring he had bought for Davina. He bitched about it being more than four months' worth of mortgage payments.

"We will need you to come down to the station and give your statement, ma'am, and work with our sketch artist."

"Okay, I need to call my boss first. He probably wants to fire me right now for not showing up at work."

"Here." Alex handed her his cellphone. "You can use mine, and I'm Alex Miller, by the way. This funny-looking guy is Trevor Vaughn."

"Thank you. Maggie Valor." She took the phone, shaking both of their hands before she stepped a few feet away and dialed. "Hey, Barb, it's Maggie, can I talk to Jeff, please?"

"Not bad," Trevor said in a hushed voice from beside me.

"No, she's not," I replied as I let my gaze drift down her light-pink blouse and navy-blue slacks.

"You really knew her in high school?"

"I not only knew her, but I dated her for three years until I deployed on my first tour."

"How could you leave *that* for a war zone? Are you stupid?"

I glared at him. "Yeah, like you were ready to settle down when you were nineteen."

"Ah, true."

The two of us watched her as she started talking. "Oh, I'm sure he's pissed, but I couldn't help it. Just put him on the phone, please."

She rocked back and forth for a moment as she waited for him to answer and stared at the sidewalk. I knew when he got on the line because she yanked the phone away from her ear, and we could all hear him screaming like a banshee. Maybe he was related to Jake. Alex, Trevor, and I all shared looks and laughed to ourselves.

"Will you just shut up, Jeff!" she hissed into the phone. "I couldn't help it! I'm not sure if you've heard, but there was a jewelry heist and then a hostage situation down at Cocoa's. I was one of the hostages, and they took our phones."

She was quiet for a second. "Yes, I'm fine. Yes, I was in there, and I want the story." Her face turned red as she pursed her lips. "No, I'm not telling anyone a damn thing. This is my story! I was in there, and I want to tell the details."

"Um, Mags—" I touched her arm, but she waved me away. I shared a look with the cop and then went to stand directly in front of her. "Mags, you can't do the story."

"Why?" she asked, totally ignoring the barking on the phone. "I was there; I can tell this story. You might not think I'm a good reporter because I write a romance column, but I am!"

"I don't doubt that, but you can't. At least not right now. You are a witness to a host of felony charges. You can't talk about it with anyone. Not until it goes to trial. If you do, you could jeopardize the case."

"What? That's not fair! Wait!" She put her hand up to stop me. "Jeff, I'm alive, and I have to go down to the police station. I'll call you when I'm finished." She hung up the phone and handed it back to Alex. "Are you telling me that I can't talk about this case to *anyone?*"

"No, you shouldn't, not even me."

She frowned. "But you were there. Why can't I talk to you about it?"

"Because talking about the details that you have in your mind to someone else who has their own version can taint the eyewitness account—influence it."

Her brows dropped low over her pretty smoky-blue eyes. "Well, damn, that sucks! I was going to use this as my big break."

"Sorry, Mags. After the trial is over, you can share your story, but not until then."

CHAPTER SIX

MAGGIE

That was stupid! If I didn't tell my story now, then someone else would tell it, and by the time I was allowed to talk about it, it would be old news, and no one would care. I growled to myself, and Greg put his hand to my lower back. His thumb rubbed gently over my spine and caused tingling in my toes and a few other places.

"Come on; they want us down at the station."

"Do we have to ride in the police car?"

"No, I can take you down."

"Actually," Trevor said, "I have to go down too because you were nice enough to call on my phone, and they want me to write a statement. I can drive you guys down."

"Thanks, Trev," Greg said.

"Alright, I won't say no to a ride," I replied as Greg put his hand to my lower back again to escort me through the crowd, but once we were out the other side, he dropped it and stepped away from me. His eyes scanned the area, just as Trevor did, also.

Were they looking for Len? Or were they just wired to be always looking for some unknown enemy? I had read a few articles about military veterans, and some of the interviews talked about how they could never really relax. That they felt that at any moment a new threat would appear, even when they were walking through their hometown where nothing disastrous had ever occurred; what would that be like to be fearful of the unknown all the time? To expect something to happen around every obstacle?

I couldn't imagine it—I honestly couldn't. We walked around a corner and down an alley. Both Trevor and Greg stood close to me, flanking both sides as if they were sentries. Every few seconds, one of them would look over their shoulder.

A nervous laugh slipped from my mouth. "What's so funny?" Greg asked as he glanced my way.

"You two are. Do you guys have any idea how serious you look? I mean, you are both walking beside me like you are private security guards, and I'm some important person to protect while you check behind us every few steps to make sure the boogeyman isn't back there. It's creeping me out a bit."

"Good to know we're doing our jobs." Trevor chuckled.

"What do you mean, doing your job?" I asked him.

"We work for a security company, although most of our work is for clients overseas. We do protect a few people and locations in the states," Trevor shared.

I glanced at Greg. "You're really out of the military now?"

"Yep, private security and training. I did twenty and got out."

"And you live here?"

He gave me a cocky smile. "Yes, I live here, where I assume you do too."

Why did that give me a little thrill? "Yes, I do."

We took the stairs up four flights, even though there was an elevator, and Trevor led us to a newer shiny pickup truck. Greg opened the rear passenger door, and I paused. Somehow, I had not expected there to be a child's seat in the back.

"You have something against car seats?" Greg asked as I stood there, staring at it for another second.

I shook my head. "No."

Greg leaned toward me. "Are you going to get in?"

I turned my face toward him; our noses almost brushed, and we locked gazes. Did Greg have children? Did he have a wife? Had he ever been married? Did he ever think about me over the years? A hundred other questions zipped through my mind in an instant, and I just kept staring at him.

If Greg and I were back in the same town, could we try again? Was it too late? Had our relationship hit its high point when we were only sixteen and eighteen? What would he be like in bed now?

"Mags?" His voice was husky. "You alright?"

Trevor started the truck, and the sound yanked me out of my head. I jerked back from Greg. "Yeah, fine. I was thinking about something."

"Were you still wondering how to prove to me that you weren't a prude?"

"Ha! You wish!" I said as I brushed past him and climbed into the truck. I peered at the car seat again as Trevor pulled out.

"I have a son, Devon. He's four months now."

"Are you married?"

"Not yet, engaged." Trevor grinned right before he turned around.

"Aren't you doing things a bit out of order?" I joked. He grinned at me in the rearview mirror.

"Davina is not his birth mom. Carol was, but she died during childbirth, and no Carol and I were not really a couple. I didn't even know she was pregnant until after Devon was born. Then Davina, who was Carol's best friend, dropped Devon in my lap."

Greg laughed. "I'm sorry; the whole thing was funny. You taking care of a baby by yourself was hysterical."

"That was not funny. Thank god for Alex and Lexi." He

glared at Greg for a whole half a second before he laughed and looked in the mirror at me again. "Anyway, Davina and I hit it off and got engaged, and once we get married, she's doing to adopt Devon as her legal son."

"Aw, that's sweet. I'm sorry about his mom; even if you weren't in a relationship with her, that had to be hard."

"It was, but I'm lucky to have both Davina and Devon in my life. It's why I stopped traveling overseas."

I studied the back of Greg's head. "Do you travel overseas?"

He peered over his shoulder. "Yes."

"But you don't go to dangerous places anymore, do you? I mean, you're not in the military anymore, so you are safe, right?"

Greg shifted to see me better. "No, I go to dangerous places, too. We train civilians to go into hostile areas, give them critical thinking skills and a little tactical and medical training, and then we help them get from place A to place B for their job."

So, he wasn't in the military anymore, but he was still doing military type stuff. I wasn't sure what I thought about that. The truth of the matter was, I didn't have the right to have any opinion on it as it was his life and not mine. It wasn't like we were a couple. We'd only run into each other again a few hours ago after nineteen years.

Not to say that I wouldn't mind getting to know him better. Although, when he had walked away from me all those years ago, he had said it was because his career was too important to him. Had that changed? Or was his career still as critical to him as it was before? Why the hell I even wondering this?

"Are you married?" I blurted the question before I could even try to stop myself.

Trevor laughed loudly, and Greg grinned. "No, you?"

"No. Have you ever been married?" I rephrased the question. "No, you?"

I squirmed for a moment and looked out the passenger side window briefly. "Yes, for a couple of years."

"Do you have kids?" he queried.

"No, you?"

"Nope, none that I know about."

Trevor laughed again. "Who knows, some woman might show up at the office and hand him a child."

I frowned, and Greg turned back around to face forward. "That's how Trevor learned of his son. Davina showed up at work and dropped the baby off."

"Whoops," I said as I winced. "You really had no idea?"

"None. Carol and I had a nice weekend together, and then I left for another overseas job. When I came home, I found out I was a father."

"Well, okay then," I said from the back seat. "I'm glad it worked out for you."

Trevor glanced in the mirror. "Thanks." He tossed a look toward Greg and grinned. "Maybe it will work out for you two."

Was that a two, as in Greg and me, or a too as in just me?

Greg gave him a funny look, and I chortled from the back. "If you mean Greg and me, there is not a chance in hell of that happening."

Greg's forehead lined as he turned my way. "Why do you say that? Wouldn't you like to get to know me again?"

"Sorry, Charlie, but you already broke my heart once. It might have been nineteen years ago, but I can remember it as if it were yesterday."

"Wait! I want to hear this story," Trevor urged from the front seat.

"No, you don't," Greg stated firmly.

"You want to hear how he broke my tender teenage heart, Trevor?"

"Yes!" Trevor said with a grin as Greg gave an emphatic no.

"I'll tell you since you are nice enough to give me a ride to the police station. Greg and I started dating when I was a freshman in high school. He was a total jock, one of the most popular guys in school, because he was not only good at sports but a nice guy and took his classes seriously. Then he graduated and became this hotshot young Marine, and when he heard he was going overseas, Greg decided that he didn't want me to wait for him. Said he wasn't sure he would ever come back and didn't think it was fair of me to wait. Wasn't that sweet of him?" I said sarcastically. "And just after that, he told me that I should find someone else and move on with my life. He kissed my forehead, handed me back a box of my stuff, and walked away."

"You bastard!" Trevor tossed toward Greg, who shook his head and stared out the windshield.

"He had the nerve to tell me that he would always love me, but he just couldn't be the man I wanted or needed him to be."

Trevor cackled behind the steering wheel and then smirked at Greg. "So, do you still love her?"

"What?" Greg's head snapped toward Trevor, and then he peered back at me momentarily. I cocked a brow, suddenly wondering that myself.

Trevor responded, "You told her you would always love her, do you? Or did you lie to her?"

"You're a dick," He muttered to him.

"No, wait." I put my hand on Greg's shoulder. "That's a good question, Gregory Blaire. Did you lie to me all those years ago?"

He shifted so he could turn his head all the way around to see me. "I cared a lot about you, Maggie, but that was nineteen years ago. I don't know you, and you don't know me, so I can't tell you that I love you."

I pursed my lips. "So, basically, you lied."

He sputtered, "Those were stupid words from a stupid kid."

"Who ran away and joined the stupid military."

"Whoa, don't go bashing the military," he stated huskily.

"Sorry, that wasn't what I meant. I have a lot of respect for our men and women who serve. I just meant that you ran away."

"I was not running, Maggie. I was following my heart."

"I thought I was your heart."

He sighed, and Trevor snickered and said softly, "I don't think you're going to win this one. I'm on Maggie's side. You broke her heart, and you lied to her."

"Shut up," Greg growled toward him.

"I got your back, Maggie. You stick with me, and I'll help you get even."

I laughed as we pulled into the parking lot of the police station, and then sighed. "Do I really have to tell them what he looked like?"

"Yes," Greg said as he took off his seat belt and spoke over his shoulder toward me. "The more detail you can give them, the better it is for the case."

"I still don't see why they need this when Chuck will probably tell them who Len is."

Greg exited the vehicle and then opened my door for me and gave me his hand to climb down from the seat. The minute I was out, he let go of me and stepped away. I guess he really didn't have any feelings for me after all these years. That kind of sucked, because after only a few hours of being in his presence, I was totally crushing on him again.

Oh, Maggie, Maggie, Maggie, you need to just let this go and be happy that you got to see him again after so many years. If you thought he hurt you as a teenager, he could probably destroy you as an adult.

CHAPTER SEVEN

GREGORY

That whole conversation in the car irritated me. Maybe I didn't love Maggie, but that didn't mean that I didn't have fond memories of our time together. But come on, it was almost twenty years ago. I'd been in half a dozen relationships since then. I'd seen a hundred different war zones, seen a lot of death, screwed a lot of women, and kept moving forward. It was always better to move forward and not look back.

At first, when I'd gone overseas, I'd thought a lot about her. I'd carried her photo in my pocket with me for the first few months, and then I'd stuck it in one of my notebooks that I always took with me. Over the years, that damn photo had moved from one notebook to the next. Damn, if it wasn't in the one that was now burning a hole in my pocket.

Why had I kept her photo all these years? Maybe it had just become a habit, or I'd come to think of it as a good luck charm. Or perhaps it had become a symbol of what I gave up to fight for our country's freedom. I wasn't sure, and I didn't know that I wanted to dwell that much on it now.

When we reached the door, I took hold of her arm, pulling

her to a stop. "Hey, Trevor, go on in; I want to have a word with Maggie."

"Alright," he said as he stepped around us with a knowing smirk. Not sure what he thought he knew.

I let go of Maggie's arm as she studied me. "I'm sorry about what I said in the truck."

Her once curious look turned into one of annoyance with one blink. "Forget about it, Greg. Yes, you hurt me a long time ago, but that was *a long time ago*. I'm a big girl now, and I know those were silly adolescent words. Trust me, I'm fine, okay?"

"You're sure? You're not upset with me?"

"Hardly," she retorted and stepped away. She said she understood, and maybe Maggie did, but I still had the feeling that she wasn't happy with me.

I followed her into the police station, and we were led back to a conference room to have a seat. Wanted posters and updates to general orders were posted all over one of the walls, announcements on another wall, statistics on the opposite side. They must do roll calls in here, I thought to myself and noted that Trevor was also skimming over the walls and stopped at the wanted poster.

A few minutes later, a detective came in and took Maggie away to interview her. Trevor was handed a statement form to fill out since his involvement was limited to the cellphone, and I was escorted to another room to give my interview.

Giving a statement was very similar to a debrief after a critical mission. You told them the facts: the good, the bad, and the ugly. No emotion, no opinion, no unnecessary details. I was done in less than twenty minutes and found Trevor kicked back in the same chair, a cup of coffee to his lips. At least he'd gotten some. I still needed to get my own fix. There were several other victims now seated in the room with him, along with a couple of people I didn't know.

"You done?" he asked when I approached him.

"Yeah, Maggie come back yet?"

He laughed. "No, and I don't think she'll be done for a while. Alex is bringing your truck over so you can get Maggie home when she is finished. I need to get back to the office; I forgot how long it was going to take for her to do a sketch and give a statement."

"Ah, that's true." I winced. Maybe I should leave her a message to call me after it was done, and I could come back. Who knew how long it was going to take her to get this done.

"Hey." He slapped me on the back. "Stay here; don't worry about work. I'll fill you in on anything you need to know later. Make sure Maggie gets home safely and that she's okay."

"All right, I appreciate it."

He started to walk away and stopped, coming back and leaning toward me to speak softly. "And find a way to make it up to her. I think you owe it to her after walking away from her all those years ago."

"Give me a break," I muttered as I shook my head.

He grabbed my shoulder. "Blaire, she seems like a great woman, and I see interest in your eyes, and in hers. Take a few moments to check it out."

"The last thing I need right now is a needy woman in my life, Vaughn."

He leaned back and laughed. "Needy? That woman is anything but needy. She's hysterical and could probably keep you on your toes. I get it; neither of us ever wanted to be in a serious relationship, but look at me now. I'm a dad and soon to be a husband, and I couldn't be happier."

"That's great for you Trev, it really is, but I have never been interested in settling down, not then—not now."

"Okay, but you don't know what you're missing," he said as he started to walk backward. "Give me a shout after you get Maggie home, and I'll fill you in on the day."

I mock saluted him, and he did an about-face and was gone.

I searched around the room and poked my head out into the hall. A cop was standing farther down the hallway, and I approached him. "Is there someplace I can get a cup of coffee?"

He laughed. "You still want some after that debacle?"

"More than ever," I replied. He pointed me in the direction, and I found a new pot just about finished brewing. I leaned back against the wall, skimming my eyes over the bulletin board above the water cooler as I waited. More rules and regulations covered the cork surface, but these focused on cleaning up after yourself. You would think that these adults wouldn't need those continual reminders. I guess I was lucky for the training I'd received twenty years ago. My drill sergeant had nailed into me that I was responsible for myself, and no one was going to clean up after me. I could not tell you how often I had heard him screaming in my ear, "What did you do this morning, boot, get up and inject yourself with some stupidity?" I learned in quick action that if I didn't do it for myself, I would just make everyone else look bad, especially myself. I had taken that to heart.

The coffee machine finally stopped dripping, and I sighed as I reached for it. I poured the dark brew into the waiting Styrofoam cup that I had ready with a little powdered creamer in it. I stirred it with the wooden coffee stirrer and then lifted it to my nose, inhaling the scent and sighing internally—finally.

I knew better than to take a drink yet and risk scalding my tongue, mouth, or throat. I finally had my fix in my hand; I could give it another moment or two before I enjoyed it. I heard Maggie's voice around the corner and peeked out of the little kitchenette area to see her walking toward me. No sooner did she reach me before she snatched the coffee cup from my hand.

"God bless you, soldier. I was dying for this!" She winked and disappeared around another corner with the detective she'd been trailing.

"Well, shit," I muttered and spun around to make myself

another cup. I was tempted to hide in the bathroom so I could drink this cup in peace, and if one more person approached me, I might have. Luckily, I managed to get that first sip in, and I wanted to scream in joy. I meandered slowly back to the conference room, checking things out as I went.

I paused when I saw Maggie on the other side of the room, bent over a desk, looking at something. Her slacks tight over her buttocks, and something kicked below my belt. Damn—

I tore my eyes from the sight, cleared my throat, and then noticed another cop staring at her from his desk. I should have gone back to the conference room, should have minded my own business, but I didn't. I strolled right over to Maggie like I owned the fucking place—or in the least—worked there. Instead of just stopping beside her, I placed my hand on her lower back as I nailed the cop with a look that I was pretty sure was a dare.

I wasn't sure what I was daring him to do, but in my gut, I felt like I had the right to protect her, and that was what I was doing. Now, what I needed to figure out is if someone else should be protecting her from me.

Her back tensed, and her head snapped to the side. When she saw me, she gave me a tight-lipped smile and turned her attention back to the computer in front of her.

I locked on to the computer image they were staring at as she spoke. "His nose needs to be a little wider in the bridge, and his eyebrows were a bit more chaotic."

"Chaotic?" I laughed.

"Yeah." She stood to face me. "They were kind of like all over the place." She wiggled her fingers over her eyes. "Not neatly groomed, and his pores were a little larger than normal, even for a man."

"You noticed his pores? How long did you stare at the guy?"

She shrugged. "About two, maybe three seconds."

"And you noticed how large his pores were?" I asked her doubtfully.

She crossed her arms over her chest and leaned forward into my face. "You might have forgotten this, Gregory Blaire, but I have a photographic memory. I am incredible at remembering details, especially from years ago. Little details—" she held her hand up, pinching her fingers together—"like how you are not a magnum."

I glared at her. "We already told you that was a joke."

"Uh-huh." She nodded and turned back to the computer. "Yeah, that's more like it. But the bag under his right eye was a little more pronounced."

As the detective adjusted the image, I realized that she was right. I hadn't seen the guy's face, because of his mask, but I had seen his eyes, and his right one did have a larger puffy area below it.

She was also right about her photographic memory and me forgetting about it. I hadn't thought of that in a long time, and now that I remembered it, I winced internally. She probably remembered a whole lot more than I did about our time together. It wasn't that I didn't want to remember; I had just replaced many of those memories with other things—some not so great either.

I remained quiet as she worked with the detective on the sketch to get it just right. While they worked, I studied her every move. She was a confident, in-charge woman, who was so damn gorgeous that I couldn't understand why she was single.

She had mentioned that she'd been married before, for a few years, I think she said. What kind of a douchebag would have let a woman like her go? I winced as that question rattled around in my mind. I was that kind of douchebag. I'd walked away from this one, and if I were going to admit it, it was because I was very selfish—or had been. Was I still selfish? Maybe.

Was it time to change that? Was Trevor right? Was it time to settle down and enjoy life, stop living for the thrill? I wasn't so sure, but I did know that right this moment, if someone ordered me *not* to see Maggie again, I would have bristled at that—maybe even have wanted to defy the order.

That brought me up short. I'd never in my life defied an order purposely; what was it about her that made me consider it now?

CHAPTER EIGHT

MAGGIE

he statement process was less painful than I had anticipated. Luckily, details were easy for me, and the fact that I'd kept my mouth shut—for the most part—during the incident had allowed me to retain more descriptive facts. Sometimes my ability to recall details so entirely was a pain in the ass. There were many things that I sure wished I couldn't remember or hadn't seen so up close and personal.

Mrs. Tompkins dead cat was one of them. I'd been nine, and I found her half-decayed cat in the woods behind the house. The image had burned into my mind, and I'd had nightmares for a year. To this day, I still couldn't be around a cat without shuddering.

I was able to zip through the interview rather quickly, and then they had a sketch artist come in and work with me. I enjoyed doing that part. I wasn't artistic in the slightest bit. I couldn't even draw a straight line with a ruler, but with my comprehensive details and the detective's computer program, we blew out the composite in short order.

We were heading to his desk when I spied Greg with a cup

of coffee, and my mouth began to water. I'd been jonesing for one since eight this morning. The brew was kind of gross and very bitter, but it was coffee and contained much-needed caffeine, so I practically sucked it down in seconds.

Detective Highmore and I were almost done with the final touches to the composite when I felt a hand on my lower back and was getting ready to swing around and punch someone for being so brazen with their contact—but found it was Greg. I wasn't sure that I should allow him to have such intimate contact either, but at least it was better than a stranger.

I wasn't surprised that Greg didn't remember my ability to recall details. Back in high school, I hadn't said much about it. People were always jealous because I could remember things so easily, and I usually just shrugged it off. No one in their teenage years wanted to be different than their friends. Nope, that could get you ostracized even faster than not dating the right guy or wearing the right clothes.

Of course, I'd dated the right guy—until he left me—wore the right clothes, had all the proper friends, and hid my abilities from everyone. Every once in a while, I even purposely screwed up on a test or an assignment so people wouldn't get suspicious.

Of course, once I went into journalism, I found that my knack for remembering details after only seeing or hearing them for a moment was a blessing and helped gain me high honors in my classes, and a job. Sadly, the position wasn't exactly what I wanted, but it had gotten me in the door.

I had learned that no matter where you worked, you had to start at the bottom and work your way up. While in Atlanta, I had done well for myself, and I was finally reporting serious news. I didn't get many articles on the front page, but I was at least in the front section and not buried in the back of the paper. I had even started to get more of a following when we finally went digital, and I was able to track my links and shares on my articles.

I had hoped another year or two, and I would have been in the running for the headlines. Only my mother got sick, and I decided to come home. What kind of daughter would I be if I didn't help her? A few of my friends in Atlanta had told me to put her in a nursing home and let them take care of her, but I couldn't do that. She had given everything of herself to me, been there for me every step of my life, so how could I not do the same for her when she needed me—especially with the fact that her faculties were diminishing.

Now, there were full days that she didn't know who I was. The first time I realized that she didn't know me was a karate kick to the solar plexus. I had quietly reminded her that I was her daughter, Maggie, and then I had kept on talking. When I had finally stepped away from her, I had sunk to the floor and sobbed into my hands. I was used to it now, but somedays it still hurt a lot.

"So, Ms. Valor, would you say that this is a correct representation of the man you saw in front of the jewelry store?"

"Yes, that is the man I saw."

"Alright." He grinned. "We will put this in front of Chuck and see what he says. Maybe knowing that we have a photograph of him, he might be more willing to give him up. He's got to know that we'll find him sooner or later."

"Until you do, should I be worried?"

The detective stood. "No, I don't think so. I'm sure he is trying to get out of the area. He's going to want to sell those diamonds as quickly as he can, and he won't be able to do that anywhere local."

"So, you don't think that I should be worried that he has my address? All of our addresses?"

"No, he's not going to do anything. If the guy is smart, and I have to think that he has a few brain cells in that skull with the way he disappeared, he's long gone from here. He probably hightailed it out of town within an hour of leaving the coffee shop." I glanced at Greg and wondered if he agreed. "I appreciate you both coming down. If you'll excuse me, I need to get this approved and out to patrol and then start my next interview. I'll call you if we hear anything, or once we have the guy in custody."

Greg and I both shook his hand, and then Greg led me from the area and to the hallway that led to the front. At the counter, he stepped away. "Did someone drop off keys for Gregory Blaire?"

"Yes, sir." He tossed them to him, and Greg thanked him as we left. We found his truck, and he helped me into the passenger side. I found myself glancing in the back to make sure there were no car seats back there. He must have noticed because he chuckled and shook his head but didn't say anything.

"What's your address?"

"Why?"

"Because I'm going to take you home."

"I don't want to go home. I need to go to work. My boss was already pissed at me this morning about my latest column; I'm sure he wants my head on a silver platter now since I haven't been to work yet, and it's—holy crap! It's almost two in the afternoon. No wonder I'm starving."

"Want to grab a bite to eat on the way to your office?"

"No, I keep snack bars in my desk drawer. That will have to do today. I have to get the next three articles written."

"Do you know what those are going to be about?"

"Yes, they will continue today's subject: ten ways to tell he is the one." He chuckled. "What are you laughing at?"

"Nothing, I never imagined you writing an advice column, especially about romance. I figured you'd be knee-deep in politics."

"Oh, I wish I were, but jobs in journalism are tough to come by around here. Maybe if I were still in Atlanta—"

He peered my way. "Did your divorce send you back this way?"

"My divorce? Um, no. I came back to take care of my mom."

That grabbed his attention; he had always liked my mom. He thought she was cool. Probably because she didn't give him grief about hanging out in my bedroom for hours at a time. She might have even known what we were doing, but she never said anything. She *had* been a cool mom.

"Is your mom okay?"

I sighed. "No, she has early-onset dementia. She was diagnosed seven years ago. I came home to take care of her then."

"Does she live with you?"

"Actually, I live with her in my childhood home. When I moved back, I knocked down the wall between my bedroom and my father's old office and made it all one big room; it even has a door to the bathroom. It's not perfect, but I'm close to her, and I can help her."

"What does she do during the day when you are working? Is she well enough to be home alone?"

"She goes to day care." I frowned. "I hate saying that; it makes it sound like she's a child, but in many ways she is. She forgets things, sometimes doesn't know who I am, and gets confused on simple tasks. She gets picked up every morning by their bus and brought home at night. If I have to work late, I have a couple of neighbors that I can call to come over and sit with her."

"Wow, I can only imagine how difficult that is."

"It has its moments. I'm lucky that Mom has been stable for the last few years, and the treatment that we have her on slowed the progression, until recently. Her doctors say that she is in the next phase, and things are going to move quickly again. I've been thinking that it might be time for a home, but I don't know. She still has good days, and I don't want to miss out on that time."

"Take advantage of that, Mags. That is one thing I regret, not having extra time with my parents in the end."

"Your parents have passed?"

"Yeah, Mom about six years ago, and Dad three. Mom had breast cancer; Dad stopped taking care of himself after she passed, and he ended up with diabetes. He refused to follow the treatment plan the doctors gave him, and it ended up killing him. To be honest, I think he just wanted to go so he could be with her."

"I'm sorry, Greg. I remember how close your parents were."

"Thanks. I got the notice of his death a week before I was set to come home on leave. Leave was pushed up, and I returned for his funeral instead."

"Where are you living now?"

He grinned my way. "At my old childhood home."

I laughed. "How funny that we both came back to our childhood homes. If you had asked me fifteen years ago if I ever saw myself doing that, I would have laughed at you. I was just getting married and had plans of grandeur and traveling the globe, reporting the news with my husband."

"He was a reporter?"

I pursed my lips. I didn't want to talk about my ex-husband, but I had brought it up. "Yes, he was, and we got divorced because we should never have gotten married in the first place. I knew it, he knew it, and his inability to stay faithful was just the added proof; eighteen months after we married, we joint filed."

His jaw went slack as he turned toward me. "You're shitting me? He cheated on you?"

"Yeah." I laughed. "Why do you seem surprised by that? People cheat all the time."

He compressed his lips tightly. "Because I can't believe someone would cheat on *you*. I mean, look at you."

I snorted in laughter. "Oh, come on, Greg. You make it sound like I'm something special. I'm just a woman, and he liked women. He liked *lots* of women, and he liked to do some damn kinky things with them, too."

His brows spiked high. "How do you know that?"

"Because I saw pictures and videos. He liked to keep a record of them."

He turned his head slowly toward me. "He made sex tapes of other women and kept them?"

"And a couple men, too."

He choked slightly, and his mouth opened and closed before he finally spit the words out. "Are you serious?"

I threw my head back and laughed. "No, I made that up. Yes, he liked women; yes, he made tapes. He never asked to tie me up or spank me or use crazy toys, but he did with other people. I think he might have married me to keep up a certain persona. When I found the tapes and confronted him, he almost passed out. I told him he would give me a nice amicable divorce, and I would not destroy him in our social circle."

He chuckled. "You are nicer than I am."

"Oh, that is for sure."

He was stopped at a traffic light and turned to me. "Why do you make that sound like I'm a terrible guy?"

"You are. I'm still not over you breaking my heart."

"Mags, that was nineteen years ago, almost twenty now. I never took you for a woman who held a grudge."

"I don't, but I guess seeing you again has brought back memories."

He flipped his blinker on and pulled into the parking lot at the paper. He parked his truck and then turned to me, reaching for my hand. "Maggie, I'm sorry for hurting you. I truly am. Believe it or not, it hurt me too, and I missed you like crazy when I went overseas, but I made the right decision. I've never been interested in getting married, having a family, staying home, and building that kind of life. I have always had one foot out the door, ready to go, ready to fight, ready to do what was needed."

"And now, Greg? Is that the kind of life that you still want?"

He swallowed and squeezed my hand. "That is who I am, Mags. It is who I always will be."

CHAPTER NINE

GREGORY

*S*hould I feel guilty for saying that to her? Maybe, but I couldn't feel guilty because it was the truth. If I couldn't be truthful to myself, who could I be honest with?

"I'm glad that you know what you want, Greg." Her words were laced with an edge of sadness that made my heart ache.

"And I'm sorry that you haven't found the right man." Perhaps I should have said that someday she would, but would that be another lie for her to throw back in my face? What if she didn't have a soulmate out there that she would one day find? What if she never fell in love again, or had someone love her back?

"I'm sure I'll see you around, Greg. It was good seeing you again." She leaned over the console and pressed a kiss to my cheek. I turned my face to hers, so close that our breath mingled, and I could see the flecks of lighter blue in her eyes that always made me smile.

I had the sudden urge to pull her over the console and rest her on my lap. Maybe toss her in the back seat and join her there. It wouldn't be the first time that we had sex in a truck. Her pretty blue eyes searched my face, pausing on my lips as her hand touched my cheek. Her fingers traced down the line of my jaw, and then she ran a finger over my bottom lip. Damn, if I didn't want to nip it with my teeth and suck it into my mouth.

"Bye, Greg."

"Bye, Maggie."

Her eyes held mine again as if she were daring me to lean forward, to kiss her just once. Nope, not going to happen. I was pretty sure if I kissed her once, I wouldn't be able to stop. I wasn't going to do that after what I'd just said to her. She wanted more, and I couldn't give her more.

I heard her soft sigh as she shifted away from me and climbed out of the truck, never looking back—kind of like what I did when I said goodbye to her nineteen years ago. I had broken up with her all those years ago to protect her, to allow her to find love, to have happiness, and to achieve all she ever dreamed out of life.

It pissed me off that she never accomplished those things. That she didn't have the family she had once talked about, didn't have a man who treasured her more than life itself. She deserved that. Hell, she was worthy of a lot more than that.

I watched her head into the building from over my shoulder. Once she disappeared inside, I pulled out and headed to my office. It had been nice to see her again, but I needed to get focused and forget about the past.

I hit a deli and grabbed a sandwich before I parked in the parking garage behind our office building and made my way up to the office.

Alice was on the phone when I stepped in and put her hand up to stop me from disappearing. As I studied her, I found myself comparing Maggie with Alice.

Total. Opposites.

Alice had dark-black hair, an olive complexion, and dark, mysterious eyes. Maggie was fair, blond, and had those damn beautiful smoky-blue irises that could be seductive as hell one moment and so damn sweet the next that you could get a cavity staring into them.

I growled to myself as I whispered, "I'll be right back." I went back to my desk, dropped my food bag, and then hit the head before I returned to the reception desk again.

"You have three messages, and Jake wants you to call him the moment you get back in the office."

"Where is he?"

"He had to run out to a job; that's why he wants you to call him."

"Alright, I'll give him a call."

I started to turn away, and she leaned forward, causing me to pause. "So tell me about her?"

"Who?"

"Maggie Valor. I thought you were joking when you said you knew her, but I saw you two on television hugging. You really do know her, don't you?"

"What news?"

"The local, you fool. The paper has a picture of you two on their website, with a link to the television station."

"I'll check it out," I told her as I started to leave again.

"Wait! Why didn't you tell me you two were a thing? I want you to hook me up with her. I have some questions."

"About what? Me?"

She rolled her eyes. "About her column, Blaire. Who cares about you?"

"Nice, Alice." I laughed as she stuck her tongue out at me playfully and then answered the now ringing phone.

Back at my desk, I started logging into my computer and then pulled out my hoagie, unrolling it from the paper wrapping as my stomach growled. I took a massive bite from the sandwich before I logged on to the internet and searched the paper.

Right there on the front page was an article about the incident and a photograph beside it with the heading, *"Local reporter taken hostage along with eighteen others."* I stared at the photo of us. I had an arm around her waist, and my hand cupped her cheek. I was leaning toward her like I was about to kiss her; behind us, a few cops watched. "Well, crap."

"Greg," Alice yelled back to me. "Take your phone off do not disturb; I have Jake on the line for you."

"Okay," I called around my mouthful and hit the button. A second later, the phone on my desk began to ring. "Hey, what's up?"

"Why didn't you call me? I told Alice to have you call me as soon as you got in."

"Jake, man, I've been in the office for less than five minutes, and I'm trying to eat my sandwich. I haven't had anything to eat all damn day."

He sighed. "Fine. You're going to need the fuel. You have exactly five to finish what you are eating, and then you need to grab your go-bag and meet me at the airport."

I was chewing as he spoke and asked my next question around another mouthful. "What's going on?"

"We need to get down to Washington and explain why we have to oversee that damn shipment. They think they can just send those relief medical supplies over there and no one will mess with it. They are stupid fucking bureaucrats that only think about saving a buck to line their own damn pockets."

"You can't go alone?"

"No, I can't. This is your job. I'm going because it's my company, but you're the one that has been overseeing this entire project, so finish stuffing your face and get your ass in gear. Alice has the details. I'll see you at the gate." He hung up before I could even give him a Roger.

I shoved another bite into my mouth and was about to close my laptop so I could put it in my bag, but I stopped and stared at the photo again. I clicked on the picture, saved it, then brought it up and sent it to the printer.

In between bites, I collected all my work off my desk and tucked it all into my briefcase. On the way back from the locker room where I stored my go-bag, I passed the printer, grabbed the photo, and slipped it into my briefcase.

One last bite and I wadded the paper and tossed it into the trash can as I gathered my two bags and headed toward the door. Alice pushed a folder toward me as I reached the reception desk, "Thanks. See ya when I see ya, Alice."

"Bye, Greg. Don't do anything that I wouldn't do." She gave me a finger wave as I laughed. I was pretty sure that Alice would do just about anything she wanted. It was one of the things that I liked about her. She was outgoing and didn't let you get away with shit.

Maggie wasn't letting me get away with shit either. I frowned as I thought that and hit the stairs. I needed to stop comparing Alice and Maggie. There wasn't a reason to, and I wouldn't be getting involved with either of them, so it was a moot point.

When I got through security at the airport, I found Jake pacing like he usually did while he spoke on the phone. Even in his office, he was restless when he talked. The man was so damn high-strung that after being in his presence for a few hours, you were exhausted. It was like he used all of his energy and then fed off you to get more. I sure hoped that this meeting went quickly, I was already exhausted, and we haven't even left yet.

After he hung up, he came to stand next to me as I surveyed the crowd. "Took you long enough."

"I'm here, relax already."

"What happened with that incident this morning?"

"Two subjects robbed the jewelry store on Market; for some reason instead of fleeing the area, they came into the coffee shop and decided to take hostages."

"I heard one got away."

"Yeah, but Maggie gave them a good description."

"Who is Maggie?"

"She was in there with me. I knew her in high school, dated her back then. Haven't seen her in nineteen years."

He chuckled slightly. "Small world."

"Yeah, it is."

A few minutes later, we were boarding the plane, and luckily Jake hated flying commercial. He was tall and couldn't stand the cramped seats. Because of that, we were going first class. It was one of the benefits of traveling with the boss.

We discussed things on our way down and devised a plan of attack, along with the essential points to make them aware of the security and loss risks. Our meeting was supposed to have been this evening, but it got moved to the morning. That's what Jake had been dealing with when I arrived at the airport. He was on the phone with Alice making sure we had hotel reservations and a car to pick us up.

The flight was quick, and our ride was waiting for us near the luggage pickup. Sixty-five minutes after we landed, we were walking into the lobby of our hotel, and Jake checked us in and gave me my key.

"We aren't sharing a room, are we?" I asked him as we approached the elevator.

"Oh, hell no. I haven't shared a room with anyone since my last deployment five years ago."

I was glad to hear that. The last thing I wanted was to deal with his hyper ass all night long.

"I have a few calls to make. I'll meet you in the lounge at seven, and we can grab dinner," he said as we got off the elevator.

"Sounds good to me."

Inside my room, I set my duffel down, tossed my computer back on the bed, and then kicked off my shoes. I got settled on the bed and dug into my computer bag, pulling out everything, including the photo I had printed before I left. I carefully folded the paper around the picture to give it sharp creases and slowly tore away the excess paper. When it was complete, I pulled the small notebook out of my pants pocket and dug around in the back pocket. Behind my license, a credit card and my retired military credentials was Maggie's junior year high school picture.

It was tattered and dog-eared, but in decent shape for all the miles it had on it. I held the two pictures side by side. Maggie had been so pretty in high school, and her beauty had done nothing but grow over the years. I stared at them for a long moment before I folded the printed picture in half and put them both back into my little notebook.

I didn't know why I did that, but for some reason, it felt right. Putting Maggie out of my mind, I focused on my work and spent an hour catching up on emails before I went to meet Jake for dinner.

Every once in a while, her image would come to mind, and I'd wave it away again. I didn't need a distraction. My job was too critical, and if I let myself be, I could totally be distracted by Maggie.

Part of me almost wished that I hadn't run into her again, but then there was that other part of me that told me that I would be a complete idiot not to take advantage of this second chance.

I was used to war in the world, but I hated being at war with myself.

CHAPTER TEN

MAGGIE

I was in my room, digging through a box I'd pulled from the attic when my mother wandered into my room. "What are you doing, sweetheart?"

"Oh, hi, Mom. How was your day?" I asked, happy to see she was lucid and smiling today. Over the last week, she had been a little more confused than usual, and fretful. As if she knew she was confused and not sure why. I hated this disease. Hated that it robbed her of her life and memories, and hated that it stole my strong-willed, active mother.

"It was a pleasant day. How was yours?"

For all of two seconds, I considered telling her about my day, but I didn't want to waste good moments with her by sharing horrible things. Instead, I grinned at her. "It was a great day. I ran into an old friend."

"You did? Did I know them?"

I dug around inside the box and grinned as I pulled out the photo album dedicated to one, Gregory Blaire. "Yep, you sure did."

She blinked at the album I held out for her to see. "Oh, I remember that. You were madly in love with him in high school. He was a nice boy, and then he went away someplace, and he broke your heart. Isn't that right?"

"Yes," I replied as I moved the box and took a seat on the bed, patting the space next to me to invite her to join me. "He joined the military and went to war."

She sat beside me, and I opened the album to the first page. I hadn't looked at this in at least sixteen years, and the sight of us together on the front page stole my breath away.

"My, he is handsome, what was his name?"

"Gregory Blaire."

My mother smiled at our photo. "Is this who you ran into today?"

"Yes, I ran into him while I was getting coffee today."

Her eyes sparkled. "Tell me everything. Was Greg happy to see you? Is he still as handsome as he was? Did he give you butterflies in your stomach? I seemed to recall that he used to give you butterflies."

I blinked back the tears that threatened to explode into my eyes. My mother could remember how Greg used to make me feel. To be able to share that with her again was a real gift.

"He did give me butterflies, and he is even more handsome now. He seemed taller, but not much, and his shoulders were wider. He has a beard now, not a heavy one, but one of those sexy scruffy ones."

My mother put her hand on my arm. "Oh, I remember when your father would let his beard grow in; it was so sexy." She lifted her eyes to mine. "Until it wasn't."

We both laughed at the memory of my father refusing to shave for six months and looking like a grizzly old man.

"So how is Greg? Was he visiting his parents? How are they?"

"No, Greg lives around here now. He retired from the military and came home to live here. He works in security or something, but I'm not too sure of the details. We didn't get much of a chance to talk."

She stared at me for a moment. "And his parents?"

"They passed, Mom. His mother had breast cancer many years ago, and his father passed a couple of years ago."

"Oh, I'm so sorry to hear that. I think I remember them being nice people." My mother had met them a couple of times when we were dating.

"They were nice people," I echoed.

"Are you going to see him again?" She frowned. "Did you break up with him, or did he break up with you? I don't recall the details."

"He was going overseas and not sure how long he would be gone. He didn't want me to wait for him or be tied down either."

"Is he married now?"

I shook my head as I turned the page. "No, he's never been married, and I don't think he ever will be either."

"Such a shame," my mother said as she looked over the page with me. For a few minutes, we laughed about a couple of the pictures, and then as if someone had flipped a switch, my mother changed as I went to a new page of the album.

"Look at me in this picture; I was so thin back then, and my hair was so blond." She pointed at one of the shots, but the image wasn't her, it was me. I was in my bathing suit, and Gregory was holding me in his arms, getting ready to toss me in the pool at my friend's house. I was clinging to his neck and laughing. I remember saying if I go in, you go too, and he had.

I swallowed the immediate lump that lodged in my throat. "Yes, it was." I knew better than to say that it wasn't her. We looked enough alike at that age that she was easily confused. If I tried to convince her that it was me and not her, it would only upset her.

For the next few minutes, we looked over the photos, and I treasured the memories that expanded in my mind with each photograph. When we were done, my mother made mention of the time and said that she needed to get dinner ready because Dad would be home soon.

As she rushed out of my bedroom door to head downstairs, I knew I needed to follow her. She would either get to the kitchen and forget what she had wanted to do, or she'd start cooking and leave the pans on the stove.

I sighed as I stared at the last page of the album. It was a picture of Gregory and me the day he graduated from boot camp. His parents had brought me with them to see it, and I'd never been so proud of him. I also hadn't thought that he could ever get more handsome, but he had. Man—had he!

As I set the album down and went to find my mother and prevent a disaster, I wondered what Greg would have done if I had kissed him goodbye. I had been very tempted to do so, and the only thing that stopped me was knowing that one kiss with that man and I would be opening myself back up to heartbreak. He had told me straight out that he would never be available for anything more, and I had to accept that.

I helped my mother get dinner ready and somehow managed to get Greg out of my mind as we ate and cleaned up. After dinner, Mom and I went out to the front porch like we did many nights. While she sat on the porch swing, I weeded the flower garden while she talked about memories that she had. Of course, those memories she thought were brand new and would jump from year to year in a matter of minutes. Sometimes it was rather enlightening; other times, it was depressing. Tonight, it kept reminding me how short life could be and as I finally got my mom settled for the night, I curled up in bed with the photo album and took another trip down memory lane.

~

J was at work the next day when I received a phone call from Detective Highmore on my office line.

"Ms. Valor, we know who the other man is now."

"You do? Do you have him in custody?"

"No, we don't have him in custody yet, but we now have a good lead."

"Okay, that's good to hear. I appreciate you letting me know. What is his name?"

"Jefferson Lenard Bunker. Um, I tried to call Mr. Blaire but got his voicemail. Will you be talking to him today?"

"Uh, I don't think so."

"Oh, I got the impression that you two were a couple. Alright, I will try to get ahold of Mr. Blaire later then. I will let you know if we hear anything else."

"Alright, thank you, Detective."

"You're welcome; also, you can come by later today and get your phone."

"Great, thank you. I'll be by soon to get it."

Now, wasn't it funny that he had thought Greg and I were a couple, and Len had even suggested that we had known each other too? Why did people automatically believe that we were together?

My desk phone rang, and I set that line of questioning aside to answer it.

"Who was the hottie in the picture with you yesterday?" my friend Heather said as soon as I answered.

"You saw that, huh?"

"Um, yeah! Was he like your personal savior or something?"

"No, an old friend."

"Friend? Is that why you didn't make it to the speed dating last night?"

I slapped my palm to my forehead. "Holy crap! I'm so sorry, Heather. I completely forgot about it! After yesterday's drama and spending a few hours at the police station, it slipped my mind."

"Yeah, I figured as much. I tried to text you like a dozen times. Then I thought you'd already had your speed dating while you were on lockdown in Cocoa's."

"No, definitely not." I chuckled. "It was a long day, and it slipped my mind, and as for my cellphone, the police still have it. I can get it back later today."

"Well, you didn't miss too much. I mean, there were a couple of interesting people there, but no one that grabbed my heart-strings and tugged."

"Glad I didn't miss much. When do they do it again?"

"They have it there every Monday night, so if you want to try and not get kidnapped next Monday, I will give it another try with you."

"That sounds like a plan, but remind me tomorrow after I get my phone back to put it on my calendar. I'm lost without my phone right now." We both laughed, and I told her I'd talk to her later.

Jeff called me into his office as soon as I was off the phone, and I was dreading getting into it with him again. When I had arrived this morning, the first thing I had done was to check my stats for my column. This series of articles was already higher than any of my last publications in the previous month, and we are only on day two of ten. I didn't have a chance to read all the comments yet, but people seemed to be enjoying the sincere advice that was sprinkled with a little bit of sarcasm. I just hoped my boss appreciated it too.

"Hey, Jeff, you wanted to see me?"

"Yeah, close the door."

I closed it and took a seat in front of his desk as he shuffled papers around and then leaned back and stared at me for three full seconds. "So, I talked to Hobart."

He paused, and I waited. Talking to his boss, Hobart, I

assumed was a daily thing; why was he making such a big deal out of it? When he didn't continue, I spoke. "And what was that conversation about?"

"You."

Again, I waited—and nothing. "What about me?"

"I asked Hobart if he would consider giving you some front-page space for your story from yesterday."

As the words came out of his mouth, my hopes started to soar. A moment later, those hopes took a nosedive like a parachutist without a parachute.

Greg had told me that I shouldn't talk about it, and the police had also reiterated that fact during the interview.

"That's great, Jeff. When I'm allowed to speak about it, I'll be happy to share every detail."

"What do you mean, when you are allowed to speak about it?"

"I can't talk about it right now, Jeff. It is an active investigation, and I can't discuss what I saw until after the men are prosecuted."

"Yes, you can. You have the freedom of speech behind you."

"And if I spoke, it could affect the outcome of the trial."

"If you don't talk, it could affect your job."

I startled back. "What are you talking about, Jeff? You'd fire me for not doing the article?"

"No, I wouldn't fire you, but any hope you had of getting out of romance advice would be cut short."

"That's not fair, Jeff! You know that I'm a damn good reporter. If they have room on the news floor, you know I should be there. I'm too damn good to be writing a stupid romance column."

"Then maybe you should have stayed in Atlanta since you were such an up-and-coming big-shot reporter."

"And you know that I came home to be near my mother so I could care for her."

"That was a sacrifice that you were willing to make, Maggie. I didn't make it for you. You have to decide how important your career is."

"Excuse me?" I hissed out. "You know that my career is important to me, Jeff. I work my ass off, and I deserve to be on the news desk."

"Yeah, well, if you want a shot, then write the article."

"I can't. I told you that. Not until after the trial. We can cover it, and my memories of it could be a great closing piece for it."

"And not one person will give a shit, Maggie. It's now or never. Your choice, but if you don't write the article by midnight, don't expect another chance for a long time." His phone began to ring, and he dismissed me without another word as he answered and started talking to someone.

I left the room, feeling a mixture of numbness and anger. I didn't want to lose this chance, but how could I write the article and not affect the criminal case?

CHAPTER ELEVEN

GREGORY

I sure didn't expect our meeting to get pushed again, or for it to only last ten whole minutes when we were finally given an audience. This committee was willing to authorize over a million dollars' worth of medical supplies to be sent into a war-torn countryside but wanted to remain negligent of protecting it. They didn't have enough of a substantial threat to warrant a military escort at this time, hence the reason they had hired private security. Now that we had drawn up plans and gone over them in great detail, they wanted to hang us out to dry on the contract. They thought that civilian contractors currently working in the medical facility could handle the situation.

Maybe some civilian contractors could, but not the ones they were using. They were poorly trained and ill-equipped for the violent confrontations that they were bound to come across if word got out. Jake was pissed; although, to anyone who looked at him in passing, he was totally in control. He wasn't the only one that was fit to be tied, though.

I hadn't even gotten a chance to talk, and Jake had spoken for two fucking minutes before he was cut off and told that our help would no longer be needed. I thought Jake would lose his shit for sure, but he hadn't. He had clamped his jaw shut, nodded, and waited to be dismissed.

The entire way to the airport, his body had practically vibrated with frustration, and I was waiting for it to erupt. I knew it was only a matter of time, and the longer it took, the worse it was going to be. I watched him from the corner of my eye as we sat in the lounge at the airport, and he tossed back the third shot of whiskey in as many minutes. If he kept this up, I'd be carrying his ass to the plane, but at least he'd probably sleep the whole way home.

He slammed the shot glass down, and his phone began to vibrate on the bar; the office number showed up, and he pushed the phone toward me. His way of asking—no telling—me to take the call.

"Blaire here," I answered.

There was a pause. "Why are you answering Jake's phone?"

"He's busy; what's up, Alice?"

"How did it go?"

"All sorts of fucked."

"Aw, shit, what is he doing? Are you at the airport? Is he drinking?"

"Sitting in the airport lounge and Roger on the adult beverages."

"Dammit, Greg. Don't let him get trashed. He gets airsick when he drinks too much before a flight."

"Copy that." I chuckled slightly. "Did you need me to tell him something?"

"No, actually, I was trying to reach you, but you weren't answering your phone."

"Sorry, cops still have it, what's up?"

"Maggie Valor called looking for you. She asked me to have you call her as soon as possible. Said it was important to speak with you."

"Did she give you a number?"

"Yeah, I'll text it over once we get off the phone."

"Did she say anything else?"

"No, but she seemed disappointed that she couldn't speak to you right away."

"How long ago did she call?"

"Five minutes ago."

"Alright, send the phone number over; I'll give her a shout."

"Are you guys still on the flight I booked you?"

"Yeah, why?"

"Because someone will have to get his ass home. He's not going to stop drinking now that he's started."

I glanced at Jake; his face was void of emotion, which was pretty scary for a guy like Jake. "I can get him home."

"But then he won't have his car." She sighed. "I'll take an Uber to the airport and be there when you guys arrive. I'll get him home."

"You are a good woman, Alice. Too good of a woman to put up with our shit."

"Don't you know it! I should get paid more!"

"Little Alice needs hazard pay." I laughed. "I'll put in a good word for you."

"You do that; he might listen to you. He likes you."

"Ha! You could have fooled me. Send that number over Alice, and thanks."

"You got it, lover boy." I chuckled as I hung up, and Jake turned to me, brow raised. "Alice was looking for me." He nodded and turned his attention back to his beer. At least he seemed done with the shots for now.

His phone vibrated in my hand, and I saw the text. "Mind if I return someone's call?"

He shook his head and took a long pull off his bottle. Damn, there wasn't anything scarier than Jake in quiet mode. It pretty much freaked me out, and I decided not to tell him that Alice was going to be waiting to take him home. I wasn't sure what he would say to that.

I memorized the number for Maggie and then dialed it. She answered on the second ring. "Hello?"

"Maggie, it's Greg."

"Oh, I'm so glad you called. Is this your phone number?"

"No, it's my boss' cell. I don't have mine back yet and didn't have time to grab a new phone. Is this your work number?"

"No, it's my cellphone. The police released the phones this afternoon. I should have grabbed yours for you."

"That's okay; I can swing by the precinct on my way home. Is that why you were calling?"

"No. Um..." She paused. "Would you be able to meet me tonight? I need to talk to you about something."

"What time? I'm actually in Washington right now. Our flight is in about an hour. It's going to be a couple hours until we are back in town."

"Do you think you'll be back by say, eight?"

"Yeah, I should be."

"Okay, would you mind stopping by my house? I'd meet you someplace, but I need to be home for Mom tonight."

"That's not a problem; I can stop over when I get back. I'll swing by the police station, get my phone, and then send you a text to let you know I'm on my way."

"Perfect."

"Are you okay, Maggie? You sound stressed."

"I am stressed, and that's why I want to talk to you. It's about yesterday."

"Alright, but remember, I told you that we shouldn't be talking about yesterday."

"I know, but that's what I need to talk to you about, *not* talking about it."

Say what? "Well, I'll let you know when I can get there."

"Thanks, Greg. Have a safe flight, and I'll see you tonight."

"See you tonight," I echoed and hung up, looking forward to seeing her.

Jake grinned at me. "Booty call tonight?"

I laughed harshly. "No, far from it. Maggie wants to talk about yesterday."

"She's the hot blond that you were swooping in on from the front page."

"I wasn't swooping in on her; I was making sure she was alright. I told you, we go way back."

"Yeah, whatever."

"What the hell is that supposed to mean?"

He waved the bartender over and pushed his shot glass forward. Was this going to be the fourth or fifth?

"Nothing, it means nothing, Blaire. You live your life the way you want, and I'll live my life the way I want. Alex, Trevor, Mike, and Harvey can live the way they want too, and Alice! Alice, yeah, she can do whatever the hell she wants."

Well, damn—had I missed a few shots in there? It had been a long time since I had seen Jake going into a muttering tangent stage.

"You know what?" He looked at me, and I noticed that his green eyes were bloodshot and a little glassier than they should be.

"What, boss?"

"I don't want you to get a booty call from that lady, cuz if you do, you won't want to travel anymore."

I chuckled. "Where the hell did you get that idea? What makes you think that if I slept with Maggie, I'd stop traveling?"

"That's what happened with Alex and Trevor. Damn twits got whipped! Getting married, and, and, and, having babies and shit. It's stupid, and if you sleep with that woman, you'll be just like them." He pointed a finger at me before throwing back his whiskey.

"Jake, I'm pretty sure neither of those things is going to

happen. I have no intention of sleeping with Maggie, and as for getting involved with her, or anyone else, I have no plans. Maggie knows how I feel about that too, so I'm pretty sure she's not looking for a one-night stand. You're safe, boss; I'm not going anywhere."

He glared at me. "You better not, Blaire. I need you, man. I need you to keep traveling and help me with this company. You're important to me."

He might be drunk, but that was a compliment coming from him, and I appreciated it. Maybe Alice was right, and he did like me. "I'm here for you, Screamer. Whatever you need."

He grinned. "Did I ever tell you about the time that I scared the shit out of my drill sergeant in boot?"

"Uh, no, I don't think I have heard that story." For the next thirty minutes, Jake entertained me and half the lounge with stories of grandeur from boot camp. By the time we needed to head to our gate, we were both pretty wasted from the additional shots that had been sent our way from other patrons.

The minute the plane was in the air, Jake and I were both passed out. When we landed seventy minutes later, I had sobered up, but Jake woke with a massive chip on his shoulder. His normal disgruntled behavior amplified by ten. Poor Alice, she was going to regret coming out to get him.

When we got off the plane, Jake made a beeline to the nearest bar, then tossed back two more shots and a beer before he let me talk him into heading out through the security doors. I'd already sent Alice a few messages to let her know our status, and when we stepped through the exit doors, Jake stopped in the middle of the walkway and stared at her.

I shifted my gaze from him to Alice and felt my jaw drop— no way. Was there something going on between Jake and Alice? The two of them stared at each other with more heat than a damn volcano, but it only lasted a few seconds before Alice shook herself out of it and approached him.

"You're a mess," she said to Jake, taking his computer bag. "You could at least keep your tie straight and your shirt tucked in properly."

"What the hell are you doing here?" he growled toward her.

She got in his face, which was a bit difficult since he was about a foot taller. However, she yanked his tie forward so that his head had to come down to her level, and I bit back a laugh.

"I'm taking you home because I knew you'd be shit-faced. I wasn't going to let you drive or force Greg to have to deal with your sorry ass longer than he already has. Now, let's go. I assume you have a bag that was checked since you don't have your garment bag on your shoulder. Or did you lose it while you were drinking?"

I chuckled. "He checked it. He didn't want to bother with lugging it around."

"Of course, now we have to go stand around and wait for it." She shook her head as if she were exasperated.

"You want me to go get it? I can drop it off at his place later."

"No, go ahead and go, Greg. I'll do it." She sighed dramatically as we started to walk toward the escalator. "I'm getting paid overtime for this, and you are not."

Jake snapped. "I'm not paying you overtime to take me home."

"Oh, yes, you are." She rounded on him, getting into his face again. If I hadn't seen it, I would not have believed it. Jake literally backed up and dropped his chin to his chest. It was like his alpha had just issued a command, and I almost laughed out loud. Here Jake was, talking about Alex and Trevor being whipped, and he didn't even realize that he was right in line with them. He just didn't have the added benefit of a sexual relationship that they did. Unless—no, they weren't sleeping together. Or were they?

Huh, I'd have to talk to the guys and see if they knew

anything. When we reached the luggage carousel, I said my goodbyes, wished Alice luck, and headed out to find my truck.

By the time I got back to town, picked up my phone, and arrived at Maggie's, it was after eight. I parked in the driveway and studied the house. It looked the same, only a few minor differences since I was last here. Movement on the porch caught my eye. I hadn't noticed anyone sitting there, but an older woman stood and waved.

I climbed out and started up the short walkway. "Hello, Mrs. Valor. It's—"

"Gregory Blaire!" She grinned widely, and I was surprised that she remembered me. With how Maggie described her, I figured she wouldn't remember me at all.

"That's right; it's Greg Blaire. How are you?"

She came to the edge of the porch, her arms open wide, and I stepped in to hug her. "You sure have grown a lot for a young man." She pulled back and stared at me. "I'm not surprised that Maggie loves you so much. The two of you are going to be so happy one day when you get married, and your children are going to be just gorgeous."

The sound of the storm door opening captured my attention, and Maggie stepped out, looking mortified. I winked at her to let her know it was okay.

"You're right, Mrs. Valor. Someday, Maggie and I will be very happy together."

CHAPTER TWELVE

MAGGIE

I was mortified at the words that came out of my mother's mouth. Why couldn't tonight have been one of those times that she wasn't quite sure who anyone was? Sometimes that in-between place was so tough to deal with. Her ability to recognize people, but not put them in the right time-line, was brutal at times.

Thank god Greg wasn't upset and went along with it. Tomorrow my mother probably wouldn't even remember that she had seen Greg again. I could only hope.

"Mom, it's time for you to get ready for bed."

She grinned at me. "You just want Greg all to yourself. Alright." She tossed her hands into the air. "I'll just go hide in the bedroom. Just don't let your father catch you two messing around on the couch. You know he doesn't understand young love."

She leaned toward Greg. "Although, we were just like you two when we were young. We didn't wait for marriage either."

"Mom! Greg does not want to hear about your sex life. Oh, my god! Let's get you ready for bed."

Greg scrubbed a hand over his jaw, and I knew it was to hide the smile on his face.

"Oh, Maggie dear, Greg is a young man; his mind is always on sex."

I closed my eyes, stunned at my mom's comment as Greg chuckled softly. Like the disease itself wasn't horrible, the fact that my mother no longer had a filter just made it all the more fun to deal with.

"Let's go, Mom." I held the door open for her and peeked at Greg, who was now openly smirking as he stepped closer and leaned forward.

"You know, she's right. I do think about it quite often."

I glared at him. "Stop, do not encourage this."

He laughed a little more as he stepped into the house.

"Can you give me a few minutes to get her situated?"

"Take your time."

"I set aside a plate from dinner in case you didn't get a chance to eat, and there is beer in the fridge. Help yourself. I'm sure you know how to use a microwave."

"I appreciate it; I am starving."

"Alright, make yourself at home. I'll be back in a few minutes." I helped my mother get situated in her room, turned on one of her favorite television shows, and then told her I'd check on her later.

I expected to find Greg in the kitchen, but instead found him sitting on the front porch swing, his empty plate in his lap as he moved slowly back and forth.

"Wow, either you were starving or that took me forever." I took his plate as he laughed huskily.

"I was starving."

"You need another beer?" I asked him.

He held up his mostly full bottle. "No, I'm good."

"Okay, I'll be right back."

I left the plate in the sink and collected a beer for myself before I joined him on the swing.

"We used to sit here every Sunday night."

"Yes, we did."

"It seems like forever ago, but at the same time, it seems like only yesterday, too."

"I know. Trust me, every day is like that here. Some days she's really with it, others she mixes time up, and even I get confused about what is real or from the past. I'm sorry about what she said."

Greg took my hand. "Don't be. She's sick, Mags. You can't control that, and I know it's hard. I am rather humbled that she remembers me, though, and that she would have approved of us being together."

"Yeah, if things had been different."

"Yes, if things had been different."

"You know, after you broke up with me, she cried with me. I think she was almost as heartbroken as I was."

He sighed and started to pull his hand away, but I held on tighter. "I didn't say that to make you feel bad. I was just letting you know how much she thought of you."

"I bet she was angry."

"No, never," I told him, and when he didn't look at me, I let go of his hand and pulled his chin toward me. "She said to me that she knew it was gut-wrenching and that I probably thought that my heart would never heal, but that eventually, it would. And that one day I would understand your decision and how hard it had been for you. She knew that you had a higher calling —that you were destined to do more than just work a job but to immerse yourself into your career. Be one with it."

His brow furrowed slightly. "She said that?"

"Yeah, right here on this swing."

"Did you ever understand my decision?"

I let go of his face and turned to stare out at the street as a car passed. "I think so."

"You think so?"

"Yeah, I mean, I get why you wanted to join the military. Trust me, after 9/11, I wanted to join the military and go after the bastards, too. I think the hardest part was realizing that while you cared about me, I would never be your everything. How could I compete with your pride and love of country?" I laughed softly. "I really did forgive you years ago; I know I joke about it, but I did get over you."

"Did you?" he said, a brow cocked sexily.

I bumped my shoulder into him. "I did; it's you that has secretly been pining for me all these years."

He leaned his head back and laughed heartily as he put his arm along the back of the swing and squeezed my shoulder. "I have, I admit it."

"See, I knew it!" I leaned into him, putting my head on his shoulder. For a few moments, the two of us rocked back and forth, lost in our own thoughts.

"Not that I'm not enjoying this little moment, but it's been a long day, and I'm beat. What is it that you wanted to talk to me about?"

"Ugh, reality," I grunted as I sat upright. "I know you said that I shouldn't talk about what I saw, but is there any way around that?"

"Around what?"

"Around not talking about it?"

He shifted so that he was looking at me a little easier. "What is it that you want to talk about, Maggie?"

"The whole thing."

"I told you, discussing it with people could influence their memories of the events. It's best not to talk about it."

"I don't want to discuss it; I wanted to write about it."

"You mean for the paper?"

"Yes."

He shook his head. "No, bad idea. I know it would probably be great for your job, but if you do that, Mags, you're going to screw up prosecution. This town is too small for someone in the media to be giving details."

"Why?"

"Because if and when this goes to trial, it will be harder for them to find twelve people to serve on a jury that hasn't already formed an opinion of guilt."

"But they are guilty."

"I know that, and you know that, but you and I are not the justice system."

"Not that I need to debate this with you, but what about the freedom of speech and the press?"

"Yes, you have the freedom of speech, but you have to remember that anything that you say about that incident and make public won't be used in the trial, and the case could get thrown out without all the evidence. The defense only needs a shadow of a doubt to get the charges dropped. Do you want those men out on the street?"

"No."

"Then I think you'd be better off not saying anything. Why are you asking anyway?"

"Because my boss is an ass."

Greg's eyes darkened. "What did he do?"

"He pretty much told me that if I don't write an article about what happened inside, that he will make sure I stayed writing fluff pieces and romance columns. He said I had until midnight to write my account of what happened, and if I did, he would make sure it was front and center. If I got that space, I'd have my break, Greg, and they'd have to consider me for the news desk."

"That really means a lot to you?"

"Yes, it does. I love my job, but I want to report real stories, not this crap about how to know a man loves you and is worth dealing with his crap. It's all bullshit because we all know that men are jerks."

Greg started laughing. "Not all men, but yeah, most of them."

I grinned at him. "I know."

His cellphone vibrated, and he shifted on the bench to pull it out of his pocket. I turned away as he read a message and then chuckled.

"What's so funny?"

"Alice, our receptionist. She picked my boss up from the airport and took him home. He was pretty trashed, and she was letting me know that she left him alive."

"Is there a reason he got drunk on the way home?"

"The politicians that we were working with scrapped a detail that we were supposed to do to save a few bucks, but they are going to regret it."

"That sucks."

"Yeah, Jake was pretty furious, especially since we came up with the plan to get over a million dollars' worth of medical supplies safely into an area in Africa, and they have our plans, but don't want us to run it. They want their civilian employees to do it."

"But aren't you a civilian employee? I mean, you're not in the military."

"Yeah, technically, I'm considered a civilian contractor, but because we all have higher-level tactical training and military experience in wartime situations, we're expensive. They wanted to cut costs."

"So, they stole your plans, and now they are going to use people who aren't trained as well to do the delivery?"

"Yep, that's it in a nutshell."

"Is this public knowledge? I mean the medical supplies."

"It's not top secret or anything."

I tossed that around in my mind for a little while. "Greg, do you think your boss would mind if I wrote a story on that?"

"What?"

"Well, wouldn't your plan be proprietary information? I mean, if your company came up with it, then others shouldn't be able to implement it without your permission, right? They should be called out on that."

He stared at me for a minute and then began to smile. "Jake might go for that idea. He was pretty pissed today, and he is never afraid to make waves. Let me speak to him about it in the morning."

"Alright, you let me know. If I can't give my editor something that he wants, maybe I can give him something that he doesn't know he wants. God knows the media loves to bash politicians."

Greg got off the swing. "Mind if I hit your head before I leave?"

I must have looked totally stunned by his words because he barked out a laugh and grabbed my hand, pulling me off the swing.

"I meant, can I use your bathroom?"

"Why didn't you say that the first time?"

"I did."

"Yeah, okay. I think you said something about knocking my head around, not using my bathroom."

"Hit the head means go to the bathroom."

I stared at him with a duh look on my face. "I know that now, and yes, you may go hit my head."

I followed Greg into the house, enjoying the sound of his laughter, and watched him disappear toward the powder room before I took our beer bottles to the kitchen. I was about to rinse his bottle out when I paused and lifted it to my lips, running the smooth glass over my bottom lip for a moment.

I frowned at myself and jerked it away; what the hell was I doing? Greg was back a few moments later and paused at the edge of the counter. "Thanks for dinner. I appreciate it, Maggie."

"You're welcome. Maybe sometime you can join us while it's fresh."

"That would be nice."

"Would it?"

Greg stared at me thoughtfully. "Yeah, Maggie, it would be nice. I enjoy talking to you."

I stepped toward him, watching his shoulders roll back and tense as I grew closer. "I have enjoyed talking to you too, Greg."

His eyes flicked back and forth between mine for a moment, and I swear he started to lean forward, but suddenly jerked back and looked away. "Mags, don't."

I stepped closer to him, and he was now back up against the counter. "Don't what, Greg? Don't get close to you? Why? Are you afraid you might feel something for me? Don't you want to know if there is still a spark there from all those years ago? I do, why are you trying to avoid it?"

He stared down at me, his jaw tense. "It doesn't matter if there is a spark there, Maggie. It will never be anything. I can't give you what you want."

I snorted. "What I want? You have no idea what I want, Greg! Right now, the only thing I want is to see if kissing you is all I remember it being. Maybe all those nights I dreamed about it made me build it into some bullshit fantasy. I want to know if it is or not. I deserve that!"

I barely got the last word out of my mouth before Greg speared his hand into my hair and cupped the back of my head, bringing our mouths together. My fantasy was instantly blown to smithereens—every inch of my body burned as if a fuse had been lit on my lips and traveled right through my entire body.

His arm banded around my waist, and I clung to him. My body moved, but I couldn't focus on anything other than the way his lips and tongue were making me feel. He pressed me back against something cool—the fridge—but I didn't care as he pushed his body against mine, and I whimpered. One of his hands was on my face, holding mine to his as he ran his other hand down my side, brushing his thumb over my hardened nipple before he squeezed my breast, and my knees went weak.

"Oh!" a voice spoke from the other side of the room, and Greg and I jumped apart. He spun, putting his back to me as my mother laughed. "Did you kids forget that I was home? You shouldn't be doing that in the kitchen. Maggie's father might come home and see you, and he just won't understand."

CHAPTER THIRTEEN

GREGORY

*A*re you afraid you might feel something for me? The words echoed through my mind, bouncing from one side to the other until my head was a jumbled mess.

"It doesn't matter if there is a spark there, Maggie. It will never be anything. I can't give you what you want."

She snorted. "What I want? You have no idea what I want, Greg!" The anger exploded from her. The frustration she had buried all those years ago, mixed with the stress of yesterday and the need to know, tumbled out in her words. She was right. I wanted to know too; I was dying to know.

Since the moment I had seen her yesterday, the thought had been like a hammer banging in my mind. I'd forced myself not to consider what it would be like—it wouldn't be fair. But she brought it up; Maggie was pushing the issue, and damn if that didn't turn me the hell on.

I consumed her. I pulled her breath into my lungs to sustain me. Tasted her lips to feed my soul. Memorized the feel of her body against mine in those few brief moments so I wouldn't ever forget. Something in my chest cracked—was it the ice around my heart? No, it couldn't be.

When we were interrupted, my common sense crashed back over me. So hard that I almost stumbled as I moved away from her. I put her behind me to protect her from whatever threat had just walked upon us.

But it wasn't a threat; it was only her mother. The real danger to Maggie was me—it would always be me.

"I'm sorry, Mrs. Valor; I was just saying goodbye to Maggie and got a little carried away." I stepped further away from Maggie, turning slightly to speak over my shoulder. "I'll talk to you later; thanks again for dinner, Mags."

Maggie didn't say anything as I began to leave, and at the last second, I glanced back and found her staring at me, her lips swollen, her hair sexily mussed, her eyes wide in astonishment. It took every ounce of trained restraint to pick up my foot and take that next step forward—away from her—and then the next. By the time I got out to my truck, I was ready to hyperventilate.

I started the truck and pulled out of the driveway, changing direction quickly like the hounds of hell were nipping at my heels. That wasn't a fucking spark. That was a damn atomic bomb, and that woman had just blown up my entire nervous system. "Fuck!" I slammed my hand on the steering wheel as my hard-on ached like a mother.

I drove home, nixing the idea to go back a dozen times. Why had I done that? Why had I allowed her to get under my skin? Jesus, I'd need an exorcism to get her back out. When I parked at my house, I retrieved the mail and went inside, tossing it to the table without even looking at it and made a beeline for the fridge.

I cracked open a beer, guzzled half of it, and then slammed the bottle on the counter and went to my room, stripping my clothes off as I went. Two minutes later, I was under the stream of my shower; my hand wrapped tightly around my cock as I leaned back against the shower wall and recalled every fucking second of that kiss. The eruption was almost painful, and my knees shook as I finished. I bounced my head off the tile wall for a moment and then washed off. Maybe that would get her out of my system—or perhaps I would never get her out now —fuck!

~

I was at my desk the next day after lunch when Jake yelled into the main office section that we were having a meeting in the conference room in five. I leaned back and glanced at Trevor, who was seated at his desk, his fingers floating over his keyboard as he'd stopped typing and lifted his head.

"Think that is about that crap from yesterday?" Trevor asked.

"Probably. What else could it be?"

"Maybe another contract came through," Mike added as he paused by our cubicles. Mike was our technology consultant, a fucking whiz when it came to technology of any kind, but a bit twisted when it came to matters of the heart.

Trevor frowned. "I didn't know that we had another contract getting close to execution. Maybe we have a new potential client."

"Guess we'll find out," Alex said as he joined us from his office beside my cubicle. "Hey, Blaire, you want to go grab us coffee real quick?"

"Kiss my ass, Miller. You can get your own coffee from now on."

Alex lowered his voice, glancing down the hall. "Alice ordered a different coffeemaker yesterday. Should be here tomorrow."

"Thank god!" Mike commented as Harvey walked past and chuckled.

"You guys and your caffeine addictions."

I stood, staring after Harvey. "Hey, watch it, Harv. You're a little outnumbered here."

"I'll take my green drink any day."

Trevor gagged. "That shit is nasty. He made me one once on a bet. I almost barfed after the first sip, but he made me drink the whole damn thing. I felt sick for hours."

We all laughed as we gathered our notebooks and made our way to the conference room. Inside, we got seated around the table as we debated the merits of coffee versus green juice. There was no way Harv was going to win this one.

I heard Alice speaking to someone in the lobby, and then Jake passed the door. A few minutes later, Jake stepped in, Alice behind him, and trailing the group was Maggie.

I froze as Trevor and Alex both chuckled in my direction. What the hell was Maggie doing here? Maggie glanced over the group, her gaze barely skimming mine, but pausing with both Alex and Trevor as she smiled at them.

"Guys, this is Maggie Valor. She's a reporter with *The Rising Sun*. I know you know Greg, and I think you met Trevor Vaughn and Alex Miller the other day. The other two guys are Harvey Melton and Mike Johnson, and you just met Alice."

Maggie acknowledged everyone, and only then let her focus fall on me. Her face was devoid of all emotion, and I had no clue what was going on in her mind. What the hell was she doing here? And why was she giving me the cold shoulder?

"Maggie reached out to me late last night and said she was aware of the situation with the Med Scan clients and wanted to know if she could help." Jake directed his next words to me. "Thanks for that, by the way."

Was he serious or joking?

"How is Ms. Valor going to be able to help with that mess?" Alex asked.

"Maggie. Please call me, Maggie, Alex. I want to write an article on the trouble you are having. I've already done a little research on this, and I am aware that your proposal is proprietary information. If they were to implement any, or all, of your plan as it is laid out in your one hundred and eleven-page proposal, they would violate the original contract. They could be held responsible for punitive damages. I'm pretty sure that they could not do at least seventy-five percent of the delivery without using your proposal."

Alex turned to me, and I raised my brow. How the hell had she figured that out?

"What I want to do is write an article about how they are using your proposal to facilitate their project while hiring people who are not equipped to handle such a situation to save money and line their own pockets. The public would be outraged to know that they are willing to take a chance on losing all those medical supplies."

Harvey frowned as he spoke. "You're going to print that?"

"I'm going to draft the article, and then I am going to send it to the politicians that just nixed your contract and request a comment before publication. I already have the company here in the US ready to give me an interview about how much these supplies are needed."

"What do you hope to get out of this?" Trevor asked.

"What I hope to get is your company running the operation. I have a feeling once they see that you could sue them and that you have quite a backing on this, they might reconsider their decision to use the civilian contractors that they were telling you about. I don't think they will want the bad press, not with a humanitarian cause. I also hope to get exclusive rights to publish the story on how the medical supplies are transported and received."

"No," I said as Jake also responded.

"That would require you to travel with the shipment, Maggie."

She glanced my way, ignored me, and turned to Jake. "Yes, that is exactly what it would require."

"That would be dangerous for someone who isn't trained."

"What, trained to use a firearm? I am. I also have a carry permit and a loaded nine-millimeter in my bag. I am not a stranger to weapons, and I do not scare easily. I work well under pressure and think that I could be helpful to your company over there."

My brain was going to explode. There was no way she was going to travel with the shipment. No. Fucking. Way.

"Would you be willing to run through some safety training classes?"

"Absolutely," she said to Jake.

"Jake, can I speak to you—alone," I growled, and Maggie turned her chair slowly toward me. Behind that emotionless face was a smile waiting to explode out. What the hell was she doing?

Jake laughed slightly. "Sure, let's entertain your erratic thoughts in the hallway, shall we?"

I pushed out of my chair, glaring at Maggie the whole time I walked toward the door. She held my stare, never once showing emotion. Damn her, and damn, her poker face was better than ever.

I went straight to the lobby so we wouldn't be overheard as easily. "You can't let Maggie do that."

"Give me one damn reason."

"Because she's not trained, Jake. She'll get hurt or get someone else hurt."

"Are you worried about her getting hurt because she's a woman or because she's Maggie Valor?"

"What difference does it make?"

"It makes a lot of difference, Greg. Last night, you said nothing was going on with you two. At almost midnight, she calls me and wakes my drunk ass up, telling me that you told her about the project. How the fuck did she know about that?" He held a hand up. "Oh, wait, you went to see her the minute you got off the fucking plane—that's how."

"It's not what you think," I hissed.

"I don't care what the fuck it is, Blaire. She raised valid points, and she had a fantastic idea. We'll get this contract back on track, and if it requires her traveling with us, then so be it. I can assign you to watch over her pretty ass."

"Don't do that to me," I told him, my mind in a whirlwind.

"Why? You afraid you might get caught up on those sexy blue eyes and fall again? Well, let me tell you what. I think that might be a good idea."

"What?" I barked as I stepped back. "Last night, you told me to stay the hell away from commitment. Now you're telling me to get involved with someone—her."

"Yeah, *her*, not someone. That woman is willing to travel. She wants to write articles about what is happening behind the curtains with civilian contractors. She wants to see the world and help educate people. Do you know what that means? She won't care if you travel, because she will want to go with you. She won't want you to stay home and keep safe. She's getting too old to have babies, and she doesn't seem all that maternal anyway."

"Are you fucking crazy!" I said and winced as I realized how loud my voice was. "You want to let a woman travel with us? You have lost your damn mind, Jake."

"Not off the bat, I wouldn't. I would expect Maggie to go through our training, and if she isn't cut out for it, then we'd tell her it won't work. We should give her a chance, though." He stopped and shook his head. "No, not we; this is my company. I am going to give her a chance. I think it would be fantastic to have a reporter with us that can cover our stories, and maybe help us with locals in different parts of the world. Just imagine what this could do for our company."

"You really have lost your damn mind, Jake."

"Actually, I haven't, Blaire. I'm pretty focused on this, and I think it's one of the best ideas I have had in a while."

"Did she put you up to this?"

"No, I mean, Maggie suggested doing the transport, but I'm thinking long term here."

"Jake, don't do this to me, man."

"Do what? Put someone that you care about in harm's way, or put temptation before you?"

"Either! Both!"

"Suck it up, buttercup. Maggie is going on that mission if we get that contract back, and she's your strap." Jake slapped me on my shoulder and walked away, grinning.

CHAPTER FOURTEEN

MAGGIE

*A*fter Greg left last night, and I got my mother settled back in her room, I dwelled over what Greg had said regarding the proposal and client. I jumped online and did some research on the company he worked for, Safety Zone Security, and read the bios on the employees, the mission statements, and reviews from other clients. I searched for more on the internet and decided that what they were doing was a good thing, and I wanted to help.

Greg had called me from his boss' cellphone, so it was easy for me to hit the call button and get in touch with him. I just hoped he didn't get upset that I was calling so late. I believed that once I got him on the line and told him my idea, he might be willing to talk to me and let me see what I could do.

He had been groggy when he answered, but after a few minutes of conversation, he woke up and listened intently. A couple of minutes later, he was asking questions. Within fifteen minutes, he was sharing information with me. By the time we hung up, he had sent me the proposal and all the information that he had on the clients and organizations involved.

I was up until two researching, and then I grabbed a few

hours of sleep before I sat down with a strong cup of coffee and began to read the proposal. It outlined the materials it would be transporting, the number of people involved, the route that would be taken, and every other conceivable bit of information down to alternate routes and possible tactical disadvantages that they might have. Some of it I didn't understand, but most of it I did. It was a good proposal, a damn good proposal.

As I prepared myself to meet with Jake and the rest of his team, I tried to rein in my nerves. I had to come across as tough and knowledgeable, with the ability to do what I had planned. I could not react to Greg—at all.

I closed my eyes as the elevator began to rise. Since Greg had left last night, I had been trying to fight back the memory of that kiss. Holy crap, I did not want to think about that kiss.

That minute of passion had been more intense than any other moment of my life, and I knew that I had pushed Greg into it. I didn't want to have to push him into it. I wanted him to want it too. It had been incredible, and it made me realize that I was not over Greg—not by a long shot. I would never be over Greg.

Which sucked.

I didn't want to have feelings for him, just like he didn't want to have them for me. I knew he thought that he couldn't give me what I wanted, desired—deserved. I knew better, though. What could I do to prove to him that I was worth it?

The doors opened, and I stepped out, taking a deep breath as I recalled the thoughts that I'd had last night. I'd woken up this morning with the answer. I'd show him that I could live in his world. I might not be a trained tactical warrior like he was, but I could do some of what he did. I wanted to do it; I wanted to travel to the places that he went to and report the news. Share what these contractors were doing to better our country and other countries around the world.

Maybe they would let me do this one; perhaps they

wouldn't. All I could do was ask, and when I spoke with Jake at ten that morning, he seemed on board with the idea. In fact, he seemed excited about the possibility; now, if I could only get Greg on board.

When he asked to speak to Jake alone, I grew nervous. So far, I thought that things had gone well, but would Greg have the pull to get Jake to change his mind?

"Don't mind Greg," Trevor said as the door closed behind the men. "He's having a midlife crisis."

All the guys laughed. "Oh, is that what it is? I thought he was just having that time of the month," I replied with a smile that brought along more laughter.

Alex spoke up. "I like your idea, Maggie, and don't get me wrong, but do you think you're up to that kind of traveling? It will be a week or two of rough conditions. You'd be stuck with a bunch of men, not much in the way of privacy or luxury accommodations. We'll be tent sleeping, or in the trucks. Food is nothing to write home about, and you probably won't get a shower for several days."

"Even though I am wearing hundred-dollar pumps and dry clean only slacks, I do know how to rough it. While I might not have been in these types of situations, I have camped and done my business in the woods before. I'm not going to get freaked out by bugs or having to squat behind a tree. As long as you all keep the snakes away from me, I'll be okay. Snakes are a no-go for me."

Harvey chuckled. "Yeah, I'm not a fan of those bad boys either. I'll have your back if Greg decides he can't handle it."

"I appreciate that."

We all heard Greg's voice raise in the hallway. "Are you fucking crazy!"

Alice grinned at me. "Greg's not usually the uptight one."

The guys laughed, and then we all remained quiet until the door opened again. Jake returned with a smile on his face, and

Greg looked like he'd just ran his hands through his hair or had just woken up. He avoided eye contact with everyone as he took his seat.

"Alright, so now that we have that cleared up, Maggie, welcome, and we appreciate your assistance. The guys and Alice will give you anything that you might need, and there is a desk next to Trevor that you can use if you want to work here. That might be a better idea with some of our information."

"Absolutely. I'll let my boss know I'm working on a story and hang out here to get things going. That way, you can approve it before I send it out."

"Excellent." He turned to Alice. "Do you mind getting her set up? I have a few things that I need to go over with these guys."

"Sure," Alice replied, and the two of us left the room. Alice grinned at me as she closed the door. "Oh, I love that you got Greg all in a tizzy. He's going to be so much fun to work with today."

"You think?"

"Girl, that man is never quiet, so for him to sit there with his tail between his legs, and not only remain silent, but not look at anyone. Ha! He's all worked up and not sure what the hell to do."

I couldn't help but snicker. "Serves him right."

"I know this is not my business, but is there something going on between you?"

"I'll answer that if you tell me if you and Jake are an item."

Alice made a goldfish move, her lips flapping open and closed. "I don't know what you are talking about."

"Oh, please," I said as we stopped next to an empty desk. "You know I did notice the looks that the two of you were throwing at each other. Did you forget that I write a romance column?"

"No, seriously, nothing is going on between us."

"And nothing is going on between Greg and me either." The

conference room door opened, and the men came out. Alice and I watched them, and then Jake and Greg both stood there staring at us. Jake spun and disappeared down another hallway, and Greg turned and headed out of the office.

Alice and I looked at one another and started laughing. Yeah, so we both knew the answer to the question. Maybe there was something going on, but the two men that were involved were not willing participants. At least not right now.

"Let me know if you need anything," Alice said before she went back to the reception desk.

I dug out my laptop and all the notes that I'd taken and sat down to get to work. I called my editor and left him a message. All I said was that I was running down information for my column. He didn't need to know that my column was already written for the next eight days. Nope. And he didn't need to know that this wasn't for my column, but available for a prominent paper to buy.

I didn't have a buyer, but I did not doubt that if I submitted it to the *Times* or *The Washington Post*, I could have a spot immediately. If not them, there were a hundred political bashing sites that would grab hold of this and run with it. Not that I wanted to bash politicians, but I wanted the attention.

I worked for about two hours before I felt someone standing beside me. I looked up to see Greg, a cup of coffee in his outstretched hand. "Thought you might need one."

"Oh, yeah." I took it and immediately put it to my lips, swallowing the warm brew. "Thank you. I'm starting to drag a little. Didn't get much sleep."

Greg watched me for a moment. "I'm sure you didn't." He stepped back. "I'll let you get back to work."

I watched him head into a cubby catty-corner to me and get seated as he woke up his computer. He glanced back at me like he knew I was watching him and hiked a brow. I grinned and held up my coffee in a toast to him before I shifted so that my attention was back on my computer.

I was finished with the article and ready for Jake to look at it. Even though we were in the same office, I had been emailing back and forth with him all afternoon. I shot over the final preliminary article and leaned back in my chair, sipping the last of my coffee.

Greg was on the phone, speaking softly to someone. He was leaned back in his chair, his feet kicked out to the side and crossed at the ankle. He shifted his eyes to mine, and it was like getting shocked when you touched metal in the winter. The intensity of his gaze radiated down my spine, and he let his gaze drift from my face to my ankles and back up, the heat in his eyes growing with each inch. When his focus returned to my face, I was ready to start fanning myself. Was it hot in here? Was it the coffee? I looked away from him as my computer binged.

Jake had sent me a reply asking me to come to his office. I closed my laptop, tucked it under my arm, and stood. Greg was still sitting in the same position, and he once again let his eyes travel down my body. Only before they made their way back up, I hustled around the cubicle and toward the other side of the office. I was here for a purpose, and Greg was not that purpose.

Jake and I discussed the article for a few minutes, and he suggested a few tweaks.

"Alright, I think we have it. What now?"

"Now, I send it off, let them know it's going to be printed and ask them if they would like to comment on it."

"What do you expect to happen?"

"I expect that you'll get a phone call very shortly, and they will either want to slay you, or they will have had some major reconsideration of their decision." Jake chuckled.

"Send it."

"I have the email ready; I just needed your approval on the article."

"You have my approval." Jake leaned back in his chair and grinned. He was an attractive man, with intense dark-blue eyes and a shaved skull.

I attached the article, winked at him, and then hit send. He leaned up to his desk when his computer notified him of a new email and read what I had blind copied to him.

He glanced at his watch. "Let's see how long it takes."

"I give it thirty minutes," I told him. I closed my laptop and stood.

"Maggie, wait a minute. I wanted to talk to you about something else." I slipped back into my seat, uneasy for a moment as he eyed me carefully. "You seem like a woman who likes a little adventure."

I chuckled. "I guess."

"And you are serious about going on this mission delivery if we get the contract back?"

"Absolutely. I'll do whatever you ask."

"Why?"

"Because I want to report the success of it. I want to report on what your employees go through to help with the humanitarian needs. I might currently be a romance columnist, but that's not who I am. My goal has always been to report on politics, wars, humanitarian efforts, not how to keep a man. Oh, hell, no!"

"Would you be willing to go into a harsher environment and report on that too?"

I cocked my head. "Are you expecting things to get more dangerous?"

He shook his head. "No, I'm thinking about the future. I was wondering if you might be interested in becoming a field agent of sorts, and travel with the team. You could sell your stories freelance, help us land more business with positive reports, and eventually help more people."

I was shocked at his suggestion; it was so close to the line of thought that I had been having. "Jake, I would be very interested."

He nodded. "I figured you would be."

He told me a little bit more about what he was thinking, and I absorbed every word. I would most definitely do this. It would be an incredible opportunity for me. Maybe I wouldn't do it for long, but a couple of trips and I could get some street cred and land a bigger job with a primary news source.

"There is just one obstacle that you are going to have to overcome."

"What's that?"

"Greg."

I frowned. "Greg doesn't have any say in the matter."

"You are going to need to take that up with him. If you decide to do this, then you are his strap."

"Strap? What is a strap?"

"You will be attached to him, and he will be responsible for you. Some guys don't want the responsibility."

I thought back to the look Greg had just given me, and I began to smile. "Oh, don't you worry about Greg. I got him under control."

He started to chuckle, and then Alice's voice came over the speakerphone. "Jake, Oscar is on line one."

He glanced at his watch. "Eighteen minutes. Faster than either of us thought."

CHAPTER FIFTEEN

GREGORY

I needed air before I strangled Jake or turned into a complete asshole with Maggie. I hit the street and started walking. I had no place in mind to go, just a need to put one foot in front of the other and keep moving.

Jake was crazy to allow Maggie to go on that mission—operation, delivery, whatever the hell it was—if we did get it back. How could he allow that? How could Jake do that to me? He wanted to make her my strap? My responsibility? What an ass!

But if I didn't do it, who would? Harvey? Mike? Jake? Was Jake even going? I wasn't sure if he would put her under one of our part-time guys, but maybe he would if I refused.

I turned the corner, slowing my step as I began to realize that I was going to have to keep her with me. It was the only way to make sure she was safe. What would I do if she got hurt because I'd refused to watch her? Jesus, what would I do if she got hurt under my protection? The thought almost made me stumble.

No, if he wanted her to go, then I'd watch her. I'd protect her, but before she could go, I was going to make sure we tested her endurance and reactions. Get her to the range, see how she did on an obstacle course, not just firing from a line.

I knew that it wasn't standard practice for a press member to carry a weapon but working as a civilian contractor made things a little different since we weren't working for the military. Whether she was strapped or not, she needed to be appropriately trained and know how to protect herself if things went to shit.

I dwelled over that as I hit the next corner. Maggie had always been a strong-willed woman, eager to get into a debate and stand behind her beliefs. She never let me get away with anything when we were younger, and after last night's confrontation, it was apparent she was still like that.

I thought back to something else Jake had said when he'd been chewing my ear off earlier. He'd told me to go after her, get involved with her because she wouldn't want to sideline me. Was he right? In the past, I had avoided relationships because I didn't want to leave someone behind and not know if I was coming back, but what if that person was right there with me? If the two of us were sharing the same kind of life. Would she be able to accept that? Would she even want to do that? Could she mentally handle it?

Something close to excitement began to burn under my skin. What if Jake was right, and Maggie could do this? She could prove to us that she was fit to go, physically and emotionally, and then she kept going? Would Maggie and I be able to work with each other that way and have a relationship? Would she even want one with me?

After last night's kiss, I had to think that she might consider it, but before I got too excited about it, we needed to see if she could handle it.

On the way back to the office, I stopped at Cocoa's Coffee Café and picked us up coffee. The manager wouldn't let me pay, said it was the least he could do after yesterday.

Back at the office, I handed off the cup to Maggie and went back to my desk. I felt her staring at me, and I turned to see her toast me with her cup and then go to work. In the back of my mind, I was devising the perfect test plan for her while I worked on another proposal and caught up with an old buddy.

I was kicked back talking to Will, one of our part-timers who had just gotten back from a quick operation in Saudi Arabia, when I noticed Maggie looking at me.

Thoughts on what other kinds of endurance tests I'd like to do on her flew through my mind as I checked out every inch of her beautiful body. She knew that I wanted her; she knew it last night, so why not let her see it now? Maybe it would throw her off-kilter enough that she wouldn't pass the physical obligations for the trip. I could use it to keep her here and out of danger.

About an hour after Maggie disappeared into Jake's office, she emerged, and Jake called us all back to the conference room.

"Contract is back on," Jake announced as soon as we were all seated. "Thanks to Maggie."

Trevor gave her a high-five as Harvey did a little whoop.

"Alright, so when are we moving?"

"Wheels are up in ten days."

Alex asked, "And Maggie is going with us?" I'm glad he asked because I didn't want to.

"Yes, or we are going to assume she will be with us. I want you and Greg to put her through the paces. It's going to be a quick course, but I think she will be a quick study. This is only a level three operation, so if she knows the basics, I think she will be fine."

"Actually, can I have Trevor do it for me? I will be out of town tomorrow; remember I am meeting with High-Gen."

"Oh, yeah, shit. I forgot about that. Trev, you got a problem with that?"

"Nope, I'm good. I only have one contact I was tracking, and Harvey can keep an eye on it for me."

"Greg, you got anything in the fire?"

"Two, only one is important. The other one is a few months out."

"I'll take it," Mike offered.

"Alright, so Maggie, you up for this?"

"Yes, I am."

"Well, I suggest you go home, catch up on your sleep, and then get ready for a busy couple of days." Jake shook her hand and excused himself. Alex, Harvey, and Mike left too.

"Any idea what courses we should roll her through?" Trevor asked.

"Yeah, I have a few ideas, but Maggie, I have a question for you."

"Yes?" She lifted her chin as if daring me to do something.

"What are you going to do with your mom?"

For the flash of a second, her brow furrowed as if she were confused by the question, but it was gone so quickly, I wondered if I had imagined it. "I already have a plan for that."

"Yeah, what? Your neighbors gonna watch her while you are gone?"

"No. I appreciate the concern, but I have this covered, Greg."

"Alright, if you think that's not a problem. Can you meet us at our training warehouse at seven tomorrow morning?"

"Yes, what do you need me to bring?"

"Wear workout clothes; tomorrow will be a physical conditioning and self-defense day. Friday we will roll you through firearms and safety medical training. Monday and Tuesday, if you are still with us, we'll work through book stuff and policies."

"Alright, sounds like a plan." Maggie shook her hair back from her face and stood. "I'll see you both tomorrow."

"Night, Maggie," Trevor stated.

"Good night, Trevor. Greg."

"Mags," I replied as I leaned back in my seat and laced my

fingers over my stomach. She stared at me for a minute, then twirled around and was gone.

"And I thought things were hot with Davina and me; damn— you could get burned if you stepped between the looks you two give one another."

"That noticeable?"

"Um, yeah!"

"Are they as noticeable as the ones that Alice and Jake give one another?"

Trevor frowned. "What are you talking about? Alice and Jake aren't into each other."

I laughed. "They aren't? You sure about that? You might want to check them out a bit closer. When we got back to the city yesterday, you should have seen the blatant sexual interest in both their eyes. It almost made me feel like a peeping Tom."

"No shit?"

"Yeah, keep an eye on them. I don't think they have hooked up, but I think it's only a matter of time before they do."

"Damn, I never saw that one coming."

"Yeah, me either. Okay, I was thinking that we run Maggie through a fast track of the self-defense and physical challenge. Maybe get her started with a five-mile run, bring her into the gym and see what she can do with some obstacle course, and then put her through basic self-defense."

"Are you trying to kill her on her first day?"

"No, I want to see how she holds up, what her endurance level is. This might be a level three op, but it's going to be hot and dirty."

"Yes, I'm aware of the conditions, but are you trying to make it harder for her to succeed?"

I laughed and stood. "Trev, one thing you need to know about Maggie is that if she wants something bad enough, she's gonna get it. It doesn't matter what you, me, or anyone else does."

"Yeah, well, if that's the case, how come you two aren't together, because I'm pretty sure you're on her top ten list of things she wants."

"I doubt that." I pushed my chair into the table as he got to his feet. "I walked away from her and never gave her a chance to fight for me. When she says that I broke her heart, I have no doubt that I did. The day after we broke up, I returned to my unit and deployed a day later. She had no idea where I was or how to reach me."

"Shit, man, that was cold."

"Yeah, I know that now, but I wanted her to move on with her life. I wanted her to have everything that I couldn't give her."

"How did that work out for her?" He laughed as he slapped me on the back.

"She's divorced, taking care of her mother who has dementia, and not doing the job that she wants; what do you think?"

"I think you're in trouble, man. That's what I think, but damn, it is going to be fun to watch."

"Screw you, Trev." I laughed as we headed to our desks. "You going to be alright with her going with us?"

"I don't have a problem with a female on the team, as long as she can take care of herself. I don't think anyone else will either. What about you?"

I laughed a little. "I think I am damned if I do, damned if I don't on this one. Let's see how Maggie does over the next couple of days, and then I'll let you know."

"Sounds like a plan."

That afternoon, I finished my work and headed home. I was tempted to go by Maggie's house and talk to her, but I had a feeling if I did, we'd cross a line that we shouldn't be tempting right now. Although, I was interested in what she was going to do with her mom while she was away. I'd have to see if she'd talk about it tomorrow.

I was up early, dressed for a workout myself, and brought a change of clothes with me. When I pulled into the parking lot, I was surprised to see a car parked there already. Maggie opened her door, smiling my way as I turned off my truck.

"Okay, one point for you for being here early."

"You might remember that I was always the early bird when we were younger. It was me that was nagging you to get moving, remember?"

I laughed. "Yeah, I remember."

I told her to grab her things, and we'd secure them in the small warehouse.

"Do you do all your training here?"

"About seventy percent here. We can't do working range here because it hasn't been built yet, but we do the classroom, physical, medical, and less than lethal training here."

I was turning on lights when the door opened, and Trevor arrived with his duffel over his shoulder. "I didn't interrupt anything, did I?" he joked.

I wanted to smack him upside the head. I didn't want to think about the kinds of things he could have interrupted. I was already having a hard time not staring at the tight leggings and sports top she was wearing. I sure as hell hadn't missed the fact that she had some serious definition in her biceps either.

Before I could respond to him, Maggie did. "No, luckily, we haven't gotten started yet."

Trevor glanced at me, and I knew he was wondering if his comment had gone over her head until she spoke again. "We were waiting for you. I'm much more interested in threesomes these days."

We both nailed her with a look, and she put her hands up in the air. "I'm kidding! That was a joke."

I shook my head as I chuckled at her. "Alright, sassy pants, why don't you get stretched for a run."

"How far are we running?" she asked.

"Five, think you can do that?"

She spiked a brow. "Only five? I do at least eight every day."

Trevor snickered. "Yeah, let's stick to five because we are going to put you through a lot after that."

"Bring it on," she said as she leaned over and put her hands flat on the ground. My eyes zeroed on her tight buttocks, and I ground my teeth and turned away before I got myself all worked up.

It was going to be a long day.

CHAPTER SIXTEEN

MAGGIE

I hadn't slept much the night before. My mind didn't want to turn off, and I spent hours going over my decision time and time again to see if this was the right one to make.

When Jake had mentioned that he wanted me to join the delivery and hinted, rather boldly, that this could be something more, I suddenly envisioned a new future for myself. No more bullshit romance column, no more trying to prove myself to my editors and their bosses. If I traveled with Safety Zone Security, I could report on real conditions, real-world problems, and solutions. I could give some credit back to those who were making a difference.

The only thing that held me back from jumping in with two feet and holding on with both hands was my mother. If I made more than one trip, I'd have to make permanent arrangements for my mother in a nursing home. I wasn't sure if I was prepared for that—hell, I wasn't sure if she was ready for it. Yes, she was moving from the moderate decline to the moderately severe decline stage, and it would only be a matter of time before she would require more advanced assistance.

That's what I was dwelling over as I jogged between Trevor and Greg. I wasn't thinking about what they had planned for me today, or how incredibly sexy they both were, and I wasn't listening to the conversation that they were having about a client over the top of my head. Instead, my mind was playing back over a conversation I'd had with my mother many years ago.

"Maggie, sweetheart, you know how much I love you and appreciate you, but you did not need to put your career on hold just to come back and take care of me."

"Mom, I didn't put my career on hold for you. I am taking my career on a different path."

She pursed her lips and regarded me cynically. "You suddenly decided that you wanted to write about garden parties, kitchen remodels, and the hottest in home design?"

I couldn't lie to her; it was the last thing that I wanted to do, but the local architectural digest that I'd gotten a job with had an opening. The local paper hadn't been hiring anyone at the time, not even in the obituary section. I had decided to take the position at the digest with hopes that eventually something would open at the paper. At least I would have a job. "You know that I got tired of pulling knives out of my back."

My mom sighed. "Well, if you hadn't married a man who was as competitive as you were, you might not have had that problem."

"Mom, he is not the one that was stabbing me in the back."

She crossed her arms on the table. "Newspapers, like law offices, are still boys' clubs, Maggie. Women have to work twice as hard to prove themselves. It took me years longer to make partner than my counterparts."

"Yeah," I grunted. "I know."

She took hold of my arm. "Maggie, I need you to promise me something."

"What's that, Mom?"

"When this disease takes my mind, and I mean really takes my

mind, and you come to a point in your life where you need to decide if you should follow your career or care for me, I want you to go for the career."

"Mom—"

She put her hand up. "Maggie, listen to me, sweetheart. I've lived my life, and while it has been shorter than I anticipated, I'm happy with what I had. I don't want you putting your life on hold for me if something comes along that you honestly want to do and that can make you shine. You deserve to shine, Maggie."

"How can I just decide to walk away from you and put myself first? You never did that to me. One of the reasons it took you longer to make partner was because you put family first; you put me first. I can't just turn my back on you because I want a career."

"Yes, you can, Maggie. I'm giving you permission to do just that. I know that it might be years before this disease takes over my mind and my life, but I do not want it to take yours. I want you to put me into a nice home, come to visit me when you can, and I want you to live your life. I want you to find a good man, marry him, and live your life to the fullest."

"Mom, I can't just park you in a nursing home and walk away."

"I know it will be hard, sweetheart, and at times I'm not going to understand it."

"No, you're right. You won't. You'll be confused and scared and not know where you are."

"And I won't know those things even if I were here at home. When my time comes and God calls me home, your father will make sure that I understand that you did everything that I asked, and he'll remind me that I gave you permission to do that. I love you, Maggie, and I do not want you to hold back on life because of me. Jump and grab life with both hands and hold on. That's want I want you to do. Will you promise me that?"

I hesitated, but I told her yes, I would do that.

Now six years later, I was seriously contemplating that promise. Could I do that? Could I turn my back on my mother for my own personal agenda? Oh, I wanted to, but when push came to shove, could I be that selfish? I wasn't sure.

If Mom didn't have as many good days—well, more like hours—as she did, it might have been an easy decision, but she was still alright—sometimes—once in a while. Would Jake keep the option open for me for a little while?

Something told me that if I didn't take him up on this offer now, he'd find someone else to do it. Jake didn't strike me as the type of guy to be patient; he was crazy intense, and his mind was lightning fast.

I was going to have to see how this trip went. I'd already reached out to the head of the nursing home where my mother went for day-care programs. This wasn't the first time that I had put her into a facility for a short period. A couple of years ago, I'd gone on vacation with friends, and Mom had gone in for a week. Now I was working on scheduling her for up to two weeks. Maybe I could consider this a trial of sorts. See how she did, and how guilty I felt.

"Mags, you there?" Greg's deep voice broke through as he spoke my name.

"What?" I glanced at him quickly as we started to bank a turn, and Trevor dropped back behind us.

Greg chuckled. "I asked you how you were doing."

"Oh." I smiled at him. "I'm fine. I told you, I usually try to run eight to ten miles a day."

"That's good, shows you have stamina."

"Yeah, I do. You know, if you guys want to up the pace a bit, I'm good with that."

Greg held his hand out. "The pace is all yours. You set it, and we'll keep up with you."

"Great," I told him and quickened my speed a little bit. Neither of the two men had trouble keeping up, and before I knew it, we were back in the parking lot of the training facility for Safety Zone Security.

Trevor let us in, and Greg retrieved water. We took a few minutes to cool down, but before I had even stopped sweating, Greg and Trevor were setting up the obstacle course in the middle of the warehouse. It took them a while, and I took advantage of the time to stretch my muscles, breathe deeply, and tell myself I got this.

"You're going to run this a few times, and we are going to time you. We expect people to do it in under two minutes."

I scanned the warehouse floor. "That's easy."

Trevor snickered. "Yeah, maybe if you aren't wearing an extra fifty pounds."

"What?"

Greg reached into a closet and pulled out a military vest that had bulging pockets. "We'll be nice and take off ten pounds for you."

Well, damn. I wanted to tell Greg to leave it, but I wasn't sure I would even be able to complete the obstacle course with the forty pounds. I glared at the offending vest. "Let's give it a try."

Greg brought the vest to me and helped me get it situated over my shoulders. After a five-mile run, that I had kind of pushed to prove to them that I could do it, the extra forty pounds almost made my knees shake. Ugh, maybe I shouldn't have pushed it so hard. They could have said something about wearing a forty-pound vest!

Greg secured it around my torso, tightening the straps, and then he yanked on it to see if it was tight. I lost my footing and started to fall toward him, but I shot my hands out before I could come in contact with his body. My palms planted firmly on his very defined and sweaty chest.

"Sorry, didn't mean to do that quite so hard," he said huskily as we stared at each other for a moment, and then a smile exploded over his lips.

Yeah, he totally meant to do that. Didn't they say they were going to put me through the paces? If I knew Greg, he was going to make sure I failed so I couldn't go with him. He'd find some reason to show that I wasn't strong enough, fast enough, or fit enough to do it.

I was going to prove him wrong. I patted him condescendingly on the chest as I turned away. "Yeah, sure."

I shifted the vest around a little bit, rolled my shoulders, and walked in a circle, getting the feel of the substantial addition to my body weight.

Trevor approached. "We're going to put a helmet on you too. We don't need you bonking your pretty little head on something."

"Aw, thanks for thinking of my head as pretty, but I know you're lying your ass off, especially right now."

He laughed and winked. "I don't know. Women who work out are pretty sexy. Don't you think so, Greg?"

Greg was leaning against a support post a few feet away, and his eyes traveled down my body and then back up like they had yesterday. Damn him. He was totally trying to get me off my game.

"Definitely," Greg replied gruffly as his eyes locked on mine. I rolled my eyes and turned away from him. Let him ogle my ass as much as he wanted. At least, I wouldn't see him doing it.

Trevor took a few minutes to walk me through the obstacle course and explain what needed to be done: jump this, climb under that, pull this ten feet, push that fifteen, run around this, and so on. For the most part, it looked relatively easy. The hardest segment would be the wall at the end with a rope hanging down. It was only eight feet high, or so I estimated, but would probably feel more like sixteen feet by the time I got done with everything else.

"Alright, you are going to do this three times."

"Three?" I choked out the response and then laughed. "You guys really don't want me to go on this with you, do you?"

"Our feelings have nothing to do with this, Maggie," Trevor

said. "We want to see if you have the stamina to do it. Our days are long and hard, and we can't have someone with us that might hold us back. How about Greg and I do it with you?"

I was about to tell him not to bother, but Greg spoke up. "That's actually a good idea. It's been a while since I ran this. I'll go before you, Maggie, that way you can see the course in action."

"By all means, go right ahead, Mr. Competitive." I held my hand out, and he grinned.

"Let me grab another vest."

Greg went into the closet and returned with a couple of vests. He strapped his on, and I tried not to drool. The vest looked much smaller on him, but that was because his shoulders were broader and his back thicker. "You ready, Trev?" Greg asked after he got the vest secured.

"You aren't going to wear a helmet?" I asked him.

He laughed. "Fine, I'll wear a helmet too."

Not that I cared, but if I was wearing one, they should too. With his gear on, Greg stepped to the line, nodding to Trevor. "Let's go."

Trevor gave him a ready-set-go countdown, and he was off. My eyes stalked his every move as he vaulted over things, crawled under others, and hopped from one obstacle to the other, making it look effortless. Trevor and I walked along as he moved through the course and then toward the finish line as he reached the rope wall.

When he dropped to the other side and hit the finish line, Trevor called out his time. "One minute thirty-six."

"Wow!" I said in awe of his time.

"Wow? Was that a good wow or a bad wow?" He was breathing hard as he asked.

"That was a good wow. I'm not sure I'm going to be able to do it in under two."

"Actually, that was one of his worst times," Trevor commented. "You're getting old, Greg."

"Shut your mouth, Vaughn."

Trevor laughed and turned to me. "You ready?"

I inhaled deeply and sighed. "Let's get this over with," I told him as I put myself at the starting line. "I'm ready when you are."

"Okay, Maggie, give it your best. We'll let you do it three times, and count the best score."

"And if I don't make it under two minutes?"

Trevor smiled. "Let's just see how you do right now, alright?"

"Fine."

Trevor did my ready-set-go countdown, and I dashed off the line, mentally crossing my fingers that I did not embarrass myself.

CHAPTER SEVENTEEN

GREGORY

I half expected Maggie to complain about doing an obstacle course—but she didn't. I definitely thought she'd have something to say about wearing the weight vest, but she surprised me and kept her mouth shut. In fact, Maggie had been suspiciously reserved all morning. Where was her head?

During the run, she'd made a few comments, answered a couple of questions but, for the most part, did not take part in our conversation. I wondered if she was one of those people who liked to check out when they ran so that they weren't counting every footstep to the finish line.

I knew Maggie was listening to us because she'd chuckle every once in a while, but then slip back into silence—which bothered me. Maggie was never quiet, and I wanted to ask her what was on her mind. I wanted to ask her more than that, but I kept my mouth shut.

It was evident that Maggie did run often, and I never once heard her huff or act as if she needed to slow down. Once I told her to lead the pace, she'd picked it up nicely, and I wasn't the only one that noticed.

After we returned, we polished off a few bottles of water,

and then Trevor and I set up the obstacle course. We generally had everyone that went through our training run it at least twice, but I was pushing Maggie to the edge and wanted her to do it at least three times. I knew the obstacle course would be hard for her, especially the rope, but if she was as motivated as I thought she was, I had a feeling she'd get it done. Maybe not in under two minutes, but she'd finish. I'd never known Maggie to give up on anything.

Maggie darted off the line when Trevor said go, and she had no trouble popping herself over the two obstacles, even with the vest on. She got caught going under something, but readjusted herself lower and made it with only a short lapse in time. She pushed, she pulled, she ran, she tripped but caught herself, and when she hit the rope, Maggie tried her damndest. I could see her arms shaking, knew without a doubt that her legs were probably screaming at her, and I could tell that she was huffing. Her face was red, but she kept trying.

I glanced at Trevor, we shared a look, and then I jogged over to her side.

"Don't!" she hissed at me.

"Maggie, let me just help you get started. A little boost, and then you can finish it."

She grunted but didn't reply, and I lunged to the side to allow her to step on my knee and use it to get higher. She struggled for a moment, but then she finally grabbed the top, and even though she didn't want me to, I pushed her backside a bit to help get her over. Maggie slid down the other side, got to her feet, and crossed the finish line before slamming her back into the wall, sinking to the ground, huffing and puffing the whole way.

Her face was flushed, stray blond hairs stuck to the sides of her cheeks, and she see-sawed air through her parted lips. The woman had never looked more gorgeous to me, and I shook myself and turned away.

"What was my time?" Maggie finally asked after Trevor tossed her a bottle of water.

"Do you really want to know?"

"Yes," she snapped before she guzzled half the water from the bottle.

"Three minutes and twenty-seven seconds."

"I blame that on the wall. If I had gotten over that, what do you think my time would have been?" she asked him.

"You would have been over, but only a few seconds. You did excellent, Maggie; that wall just tripped you up."

"Stupid wall," she growled as she glared at it. When I laughed, she turned the glare to me, and I put my hands up.

"I was not laughing at you. I was laughing at the look on your face."

"Same thing." She sucked back the rest of the water. "How long do I get to rest before I have to do it again?"

"How about we let your muscles take a break, and we can try that again after lunch. We can work on some self-defense until then if that's okay with you." I answered, and she nodded, looking frustrated with herself.

Trevor helped her to her feet, and then he checked the vest he was wearing to make sure it was secure as I helped Maggie get hers off. "Oh, my god!" she exclaimed after the vest was off. "Let me run the next one without a vest and have no problem doing it in under two minutes."

I chuckled. "Yeah, that's not the deal."

"Just once." She batted her eyelashes at me.

"We'll see."

Trevor tossed the stopwatch to me, and Maggie stood by my side as Trevor ran the course, coming in two seconds faster than me. "I'll get you on the next round," I told him as he slapped me on the back.

"Yeah, we'll see about that."

For the next two and a half hours, we worked on self-defense drills intermittently as we discussed safety topics so we could rest between sets. By lunch, we were all starving, and when Maggie excused herself to the restroom, Trevor took a seat next to me at the table where we had some lessons laid out.

"She's in really good shape," Vaughn said.

"Yeah, she is."

"But you don't want her to go, do you?"

I sighed. "Not really."

"Why?"

"Would you want Davina to go?"

Trevor laughed. "Davina wouldn't want to go."

"But if she did, would you let her?"

"Hell no." He barked with a laugh, and I grinned.

"And why is that?"

"Because I don't want her to see the shit that we have to see, and I don't want to put her in harm's way."

"So, why is it wrong that I feel that way about Maggie?"

"Because Maggie wants to go. Maggie wants to see it and experience it and report it. I'm kind of with Jake on this, and I think it would be good to have someone along for the ride who can share what we do back here at home."

"And risk her life while doing it?"

"Greg, granted we have only been doing this for a few hours, but she has bypassed just about every other person we have ever trained on this stuff—male or female. It's like she's a sponge, and she's been waiting for this to come along. Now she has it, and she's gobbling it all down. Do you ever remember someone retaining the amount of information that we've given her this quickly?"

"Yeah, well, she has a photographic memory."

"Even better!"

I exhaled loudly. "I know, Trevor, but I'm still not happy with this. A woman like her shouldn't be traveling through what we do, or seeing the horror out there that we could face."

"I think maybe that's exactly the type of woman she is, Greg. Give her a chance. She might pass this, and she might not."

"I doubt she's going to pass the obstacle course."

"Yeah, and to be honest, it's unfair that she has to do it in the same amount of time that we do. She is smaller, and most women don't have the upper body strength necessary to get over that wall."

"Seriously? You think that she should have a different standard?"

"Don't women always have different standards?"

I glanced toward the bathroom. "Don't let Maggie hear you say that."

Trevor chuckled. "I won't, but Greg, what are you going to do if she passes everything?"

I clenched my jaw. "Try to find another reason for her not to go."

Maggie stepped out of the locker room, her eyes locking on to mine as Trevor replied softly, "Yeah, good luck with that."

∾

We took a leisurely lunch and then spent another hour talking over more safety information before I noticed Maggie staring over my shoulder at the obstacle course.

"You ready to give it a second try?"

"Yeah." She nodded slowly. "I think I am."

"Alright, then let's get your vest on you again and get you going."

"Can I try this one with only twenty-five pounds in the vest?"

Trevor and I glanced at one another, and he shrugged. "Sure, but it won't count toward qualifying."

"I know that. I think I just need to get through it once without help, and then I can do it with the full weight."

"Whatever you want, Maggie," Trevor told her.

I put the vest over her shoulders, and she held her arms out to the sides as I tightened the straps. I glanced at her face and found her watching me. My hands stalled for a moment as I tried to read what I saw in them. There was determination, but also a desire, and it rattled me to see that. I didn't want to desire Maggie.

The problem was that I did. So damn much so that I could practically feel her in my arms. I could imagine tracing my fingers over her firm body, and I could practically taste her on my tongue. I suppressed the shiver that tore through me and put distance between us, snagging the stopwatch out of Trevor's hands just so that I had something else to focus on.

Maggie was quick to start and moved smoothly through the course, only having issues with one task momentarily. When I glanced at the stopwatch, I was surprised to see her doing good on time. If she nailed the rope wall, she'd make it under two minutes.

Maggie jumped as she got closer to the wall and got herself up higher, but she struggled to get her foot position and lost precious seconds. I didn't help her this time, and after some serious focus, she managed to get herself up and over.

Yeah, she was fifteen seconds over the limit, but I was so damn proud of her for doing it on her own. We had quite a few men who struggled through the course.

She was huffing loudly as her chest expanded and released the air while I approached her. "You did great, Maggie."

"I didn't hit the time, though, did I?"

"Nope, fifteen seconds off, but you did a lot better this time."

"Stupid wall," she growled. "Do you make all the people who travel with you do this course in under two minutes?"

Trevor and I shared a glance. "No, only the ones that want to work with us."

Maggie bent down and put her hands on her knees, inhaling slowly, then holding it before releasing it again. She did this twice before she spoke again, and when she did, her breathing had slowed noticeably. Damn, I knew a lot of guys who couldn't calm themselves that fast.

"Why do I have to do this then? I'm not working for your company. I'm going so that I can shed light on the issues you all deal with."

"Maggie, your safety is important to us, and Jake wants to make sure that you can take care of yourself."

"Just Jake?" she barked back and raised a brow at me.

"No, not just Jake. I want to know you can take care of your-self too, Maggie. I can't have you go over with us and get hurt because you couldn't handle it."

"Let me ask you a question, Greg." She came to stand in front of me, the helmet sitting low on her head, and she tipped her face up; she was so damn cute at that moment. "I think you are well aware that I can take care of myself. I think you are looking for an excuse for me not to go."

"No, I'm not," I replied, and Trevor burst out laughing. "Shut up, Vaughn."

"Oh, come on, Blaire, tell the truth. You don't want her to go because you don't want to have a hard-on the entire time we are traveling."

I glared at him, and Maggie started to chuckle. "Oh, so that's the problem! You don't want me to go with you all because you want to sleep with me. Is that it, Gregory Blaire?"

"No."

"Yes!" Trevor roared, and I almost threw the stopwatch at him.

Maggie shifted closer to me. "You know, we can take care of that, Greg. Maybe if we sleep with each other, we'll stop wondering what it will be like. It's not like we haven't done it before."

I stared down into her pretty eyes; had she lost her mind? I didn't know about her, but I was pretty sure that having sex with her once would be nothing like it had been when we were teenagers. I also had a feeling that one time with her would never satisfy me. In fact, I was pretty sure a few years with this woman wouldn't be enough.

I think that scared me more than the thought of her traveling with us. As I stared down into her beautiful eyes, I realized that this woman still had a tight grip on my heart. Almost twenty years after I'd walked away from her to protect her, to allow her to have her life, I was finding that I'd never let her go myself.

Is that why every relationship I'd ever entertained had been doomed from the start? Because not one woman I'd ever met could hold a candle to the sexy, sassy, and smart-assed woman in front of me. My god! It was, and that realization was like a punch to my gut.

I swallowed as I stepped slowly back from her. "Sorry, Maggie, but that's not happening."

Before I looked away, I saw the disappointment in her eyes.

Maggie turned toward Trevor. "Do you have a problem with me going with you guys?"

"Um, not really."

"Not really? What does that mean? Do you think I could do it, or do you think I can't?"

"I think you could probably handle yourself, Maggie."

"Then what makes you hesitate to say I couldn't do the job?"

Trevor didn't answer right away, and when I glanced his way, the two of them were staring at me. Was I the reason he didn't want her to go? If I didn't have an itch for her, would he be willing to have her along?

I glanced around and didn't see the second vest. "Give me the damn vest so I can run this again."

Trevor shrugged off the vest and handed it over as I got ready. When he said go, I ran like my life depended on it. I told myself I was pushing to prove to him that I was better, but deep inside, I think I was running to see if I could outrun the past.

CHAPTER EIGHTEEN

MAGGIE

*W*hen I climbed in my car, I was both exhausted and elated. I had passed the obstacle course, but I'd had to do it an extra time. The third time, I had the forty pounds back in my vest, and I struggled again at the wall, but I got over it and missed the target time by ten seconds.

It had taken a lot of convincing to get Greg to let me do it one more time. Luckily, Trevor had talked him into it, and on my fourth try, I got one minute fifty-eight seconds. I had done it. I wasn't sure if I wanted to pass out or puke after I'd hit the finish line.

Trevor had helped me off the ground a few minutes later, gave me a high five and told me that he was impressed. Greg had given me the evil eye and walked away to start breaking down the obstacle course.

Now, as I drove home, every muscle in my body screamed. My legs ached, and my hands and shoulders hurt, but mentally, I was flying high. Greg couldn't block me from going if I passed everything, could he? I didn't think so, but I also didn't know what everyone else thought.

Right now, I knew that Jake was on board, and Trevor

seemed to be also. Although, I had a feeling that if it came up to a vote, he might back Greg. They were close, and they worked together. Plus, I'd learned that they had been together overseas for a time. I couldn't compete with that. I didn't want to. I didn't want to come between friends, but somewhere along the lines today, this opportunity became something more than a chance at something different. It had become a possible future, and now, I wanted it.

I wanted this job, wanted the opportunity to work with Trevor and Greg, and the rest of the men, too. I wanted them to accept me and give me a chance to prove to them that I could do this. I knew I could.

I arrived home with enough time to take a long hot shower and begin to prepare dinner before my mother came back. The aide from the nursing home walked Mom to the door, and that was a significant indicator of the kind of night we were going to have.

When Mom was feeling good, and her mind was clear, she'd let herself into the house. On days that she was confused and tired, the aide had to bring her into the house because Mom wouldn't recognize it or wouldn't remember that she lived here. Those days were few because she had lived here since before I was born. The house was deeply ingrained in her memories, but on those odd days when everything was foreign, so was the house.

I sighed as I turned the stove off, knowing that it was going to take a little while to get her settled. My stomach growled, and I silently admonished it to stop. I snagged a piece of broccoli off the counter that I'd been cutting and popped it into my mouth as I headed toward the front door.

"Hi, Monica," I said as I came around the corner, and my mother turned, a confused expression on her face. I smiled reassuringly at her. "Hello, Liz, I'm Maggie."

She furrowed her brow. Her hair was in disarray today. She must have been running her hand through it worriedly.

"Do I know you?" she asked in a small voice, so different than her usual tone.

"Yes, you do. You live here with me," I told her as I smiled gently toward her. "Come on in, and I'll get you something to drink while you sit in the living room and see if you remember anything."

My mother held her purse tightly to her chest as she passed me. Her head twisted back and forth as she took in everything on her way to the living room.

"How long has she been like this?"

"They said she was confused before lunch today. This afternoon she didn't want to do much, just sat around watching everyone."

It was going to be one of those nights. "Thank you, Monica. I appreciate it. You have a good night."

"You too, Maggie."

I saw her out and then went to find my mother. She stood in front of the fireplace staring at a picture of her, my dad, and me. If I had a dollar for every time that I found her staring at that photograph, I'd be able to afford a private nurse to watch over her.

"Do you recognize those people, Liz?"

"Well, I think so," she said tentatively. "I know that must be me, and I think this is you, right? It looks like it could be you as a little girl."

"Yes, that is you and me, and the man is my dad, your husband, Robert."

"Oh." She glanced around as if looking for any signs of him. "I'm your mother," She said it rather matter-of-factly. Somedays she denied it; today she accepted it.

"He is rather attractive. Is he here, your father?"

"No, Liz, he passed away several years ago."

She studied me, her lawyer cynicism shining through her eyes even though she wasn't herself. "Why are you calling me by my name if you are my daughter?"

I took a seat on the couch and leaned back. "Somedays you get a little confused, Mom. On those days, you don't always know who I am, and when I call you Mom, you can get a little defensive. I learned a long time ago to call you Liz when you aren't feeling like yourself."

She nodded tentatively as she began to look around. "And I live here?"

"Yes, you do."

"With you?"

"Yes."

"Where is your husband?"

"I don't have a husband, Mom," I told her.

She frowned as if she didn't like that answer, and I started to get off the couch, my legs aching from all the physical torment they went through today. "Would you like to help me cook dinner? I was just about to put stir-fry on."

"Do you mind if I look around?"

"Of course not, Mom. This is your house. If you want to see your room, it is up the stairs and the first door on the left. I'll be in the kitchen if you need anything."

"Okay," she replied, and as I headed back to the kitchen, I paused at the alarm panel and armed it. Not because I was worried that someone would break in. I was more worried that she would decide to investigate the outdoors and wander away. She had done that once but hadn't gotten far before a neighbor saw her and brought her home.

I was in the kitchen, the last of the ingredients cut and ready to go into the wok when the doorbell rang. I turned the stove off again and hoped that this was a quick interruption.

I disarmed the alarm and pulled open the door as my mother came down the stairs.

"Maggie Valor?" A man in jeans and a black t-shirt stood on the opposite side with a package in his hands.

"Yes, I'm Maggie Valor."

"Here, this is for you." He held the package out to me, and as soon as I took it, he spun and started heading back down the walkway.

"I don't need to sign anything?" I called as I glanced at the box. I turned it over in my hands, but there were no labels, no stamps, no nothing. There was something substantial inside the box that shifted as I moved it. I shook the box to see if there was a sound, but heard only the muted thud of the contents. "Who is this from?" I called to the man as he reached his car and climbed in.

"Who was that?" my mother said from beside me.

"I don't know. Some delivery guy."

"What is it?" she asked as I closed the door.

"I have no clue. I'll open it after dinner," I told her and carried it into the kitchen with me, setting it on the counter and going back to the stove. I was more interested in food than the mysterious package from a rude man.

Mom followed me into the kitchen and took a seat at the table. As I cooked, she studied every inch of the room. From time to time, as I stirred the food, I glanced at the box. Why were there no labels on it? Not even my name? It was starting to make me a little uneasy as I contemplated it.

I glanced at my phone, wishing that I had Greg's number to call him. He never had texted me when he said he would. What if I called Jake? Would he think I was paranoid? Maybe. Or maybe I could tell him I had a question for Greg or better yet, Trevor. Trevor wouldn't think I was paranoid, would he?

I picked up the phone and sent a text to Jake, asking him to have either Greg or Trevor call me because I had a question about something from today. A few moments after I sent it, he replied with a simple letter *K*.

I was just getting ready to put the food on plates when my phone rang, and my mother spoke up. "Um, I'm not sure what's in your box, but it looks like it's bleeding."

I glanced at the counter and saw the cardboard was dark. As I lifted the phone to my ear, I noticed that there was liquid oozing out from under the box.

"Hello?" I said absently.

"Maggie, it's Trevor. Jake said that you had a question."

"Um, Trevor, can you please call Greg and tell him that I need him to come over? I think it's an emergency."

"Are you alright?" Trevor asked, sounding immediately concerned.

"I am, I think."

"What's going on?"

"I had a package delivered a little while ago—and it's bleeding."

"What?"

I explained to him what had happened, and then what the box looked like. "Maggie, don't touch it. I'll call Greg. We'll be over in a little while."

"You don't both need to come. Maybe just one of you can check this out? Or do you think I should call the police?"

"No, let's see what it is before we get the police involved."

"Okay," I told him and hung up directly after. I backed away from the offending box as if it were poison, and turned quickly for the sink. I scrubbed my hands like I was about to go into surgery. What the hell was in the box?

"Who is coming over?"

"Um, friends of mine," I told her absently and wished that she wasn't here. I didn't know how this was going to go over. Usually, when she was in this state, I didn't have visitors come to the house because it confused her more. I didn't think I had a choice tonight, though.

I fixed our plates and brought them to the table. While we ate, the two of us kept glancing at the box.

"Do you think it is blood?"

"I have no idea, Mom."

"Maybe we should open it."

"I think we should wait until Greg and Trevor get here."

"Those are your friends? Do I know them?"

"Yes, they are my friends. You know Greg, but not Trevor."

"And how do you know them?"

"Because they work for a company that I want to work for."

"What do you do?"

"I'm a reporter."

"Like a news reporter?"

"Yes."

She looked excited. "Oh, do you get to work on those big stories?"

I laughed. "No, not yet." I didn't bother to tell her I only wrote a romance column. She probably would have laughed at me if I had told her that. As it was, she looked disappointed that I wasn't a prominent journalist. Yeah, well, stand in line.

The doorbell rang, and I wiped my mouth and went to answer the door. Trevor stood on the opposite side, and Greg was pulling up to the curb. "You guys are fast."

"Yeah, well, what you told me was a little bothersome."

"I hope I didn't pull you away from anything important."

"I had just finished dinner." He grinned as Greg joined us.

"Ah, too bad. I was going to offer you mine. I kind of lost my appetite," I joked with Trevor.

"You alright, Mags?" Greg asked as he came to a stop right in front of me.

"Yeah, just weirded out."

"Where is the package?"

"In the kitchen," I said, and Greg went to step around me. I grabbed his arm. "Greg, Mom's not in a great headspace today. She's pretty confused."

"No problem." He winked at me, and I followed Greg and Trevor back to the kitchen.

"Hi, Mrs. Valor," Greg said as he entered. "I'm not sure if you remember me or not, but my name is Greg Blaire, and this is my friend, Trevor Vaughn."

My mother studied them both. "I'm sorry, I don't remember you."

"That's okay," Greg said in a kind voice. "Sometimes I'd like to forget this meathead too."

We all chuckled, and then Greg glanced around, pointing at the box that had a nice little puddle around it now.

Trevor removed purple medical gloves from his pocket and handed Greg a pair of them as he removed a knife from his pocket. They were about to cut into the box when the doorbell rang again.

"What now?" I asked as I tossed my hands in the air. I turned back for the door, and my mother stopped me, leaning forward to speak quietly as she eyed Greg and Trevor. "You said you weren't married, but are either of them?"

"Mom, not now, okay?" I returned to the front door and pulled it open to find two police officers on the other side. Wow, did this have to do with the package that I had gotten? If so, who told the police? "Officers, what can I help you with?"

"Are you Maggie Valor?"

Aren't I the popular one today. "Yes, I'm Maggie Valor."

The officer stepped into my house, and I backed up. "Ms. Valor, we're going to need you to come with us."

"What?" The other officer took hold of one arm as the first one moved behind me, pulling my wrist back. "What are you doing?" My voice began to rise, and a second later, Greg appeared in the hallway.

"What the hell are you doing?" Greg growled, and the cop jumped slightly, his hand going to his gun.

"We're taking Ms. Valor in for questioning."

"Questioning for what?"

"I'm sorry, sir, we can't tell you that." Cold metal snapped around my wrist.

"Why are you arresting me? I didn't do anything wrong! What is going on? Greg, do something!"

The officer put his hand up toward Greg. "You can call down to the station and speak with Detective Highmore later."

"Wait! You can't take me away! My mother has dementia! She can't be left alone in the house."

"Can't your husband watch her?" one of the cops asked.

"He's not my husband, and she doesn't know him! You can't do this. I didn't do anything wrong!"

Trevor stepped around Greg. "Yo, Bigsby! What the hell?"

"Hey, Vaughn, sorry, we have our orders. Does her mother really have dementia?"

"Oh, my god! Do you think I would lie about that?" I hissed at the cop.

Greg approached the cop. "Yeah, she has Alzheimer's, and Maggie is her primary caregiver. What the hell is going on?"

"Come on, Bigsby, tell us something."

The cops looked at one another, and then Bigsby replied, "There is reason to believe that Ms. Valor was involved in the jewelry store robbery and kidnapping."

"What?" I shouted as my eyes nearly popped out of their sockets.

CHAPTER NINETEEN

GREGORY

I was just getting out of the shower when my cellphone rang. "What's up?" I asked Trevor as I answered.

"Did you see the text from Jake?"

"No, I was in the shower. Just got out. What's going on?"

"Maggie reached out to Jake, asked one of us to call her."

The last thing I wanted to do was to speak with Maggie right now, not after what I'd just finished doing in the shower. Hearing her voice again would put me right back in that sexually frustrated zone. "Can you give her a shout?"

"You are such a chicken!" He laughed.

"No, I'm starving. I bet you got home and had food waiting for you from your gorgeous fiancée, right?"

"Well, yeah."

"Yeah, so I didn't. I need food. Give Mags a call and see what she wants."

"Fine," he muttered and hung up. It wasn't five minutes later he called again.

"What did she want?" I asked in the way of hello as I dug around in my fridge, looking for something to eat.

"What's her address?"

I stood up straight. "Why do you want to know that?"

"Because I need you to meet me there."

"What's going on?" I closed the fridge.

"Maggie got a suspicious package delivered to her house. No label, no return address. Some guy showed up at her door, handed it to her, and walked away without a word."

"Okay, so what's in it?"

"She doesn't know, but she said it's bleeding."

"What?" I paused for one second and then put the phone on speaker as I rushed back to my bedroom. I grabbed socks and my sneakers, and while he was telling me what she had said, I put them on.

He was just finishing when I gave him the address, grabbed my keys and wallet off the counter, and rushed to the garage.

Who the hell was sending her things that bled? Had she pissed off a reader? Maybe someone had tried her romance advice and it hadn't worked, and now they were threatening her.

I arrived just after Trevor and in we went. I made sure to try and relax before I introduced myself to her mom again. Was it only the other day that her mother had given me a hug when I arrived and had thought that Maggie and I were still high school sweethearts? I could not imagine what that did to Maggie on a regular basis. Did her mother ever forget who Maggie was?

The counter was a mess; the dark blood was congealing around the box, and luckily Trevor had thought to bring gloves. We were just about to cut the box open when Maggie went to answer the door, and her shrill voice echoed down the hallway.

"What? What are you doing?"

I brushed by Trevor in a flash and went out to the hallway to see two cops trying to cuff Maggie.

Luckily, Trevor knew one of the guys and was at least able to get something out of him.

"How could they possibly think she had something to do with that mess? She was held captive just like I was."

"I'm sorry, sir, but I can't tell you any more than I have," the cop said to me.

"What about my mom?" Maggie was straining against the grasp that one of the cops had on her.

I stepped forward. "Maggie, you have to go with them."

"But what about my mom?" Her eyes began to water, and I cupped her face. The purple nitrile glove that I wore was so vastly different from her pale skin.

"I got her, Mags. Don't worry about her. You go with them; I'll take care of your mom, and we'll figure this out."

"Thank you. Greg, I didn't do anything," she said in a plea-filled voice.

"I know you didn't, baby." I brushed a quick kiss over her forehead before I stepped back, and they took her away.

"Is my daughter a criminal?" Mrs. Valor's voice seemed unusually frail.

"No, Mrs. Valor, Maggie is not a criminal. The police have the wrong information."

"Yeah, and we need to figure out what is going on. Maybe that box has something to do with it. Should we have told the cops about that?"

"No, not until we know what's inside."

As we went back into the kitchen, Trevor pulled out his phone and turned on the video so we could record what was inside the box. He took a video of Maggie's kitchen first and then the box as I began to cut open the sides.

I peeled back the edge carefully, wondering if something would go boom, but it didn't. Inside was a dead rat, and I growled, "Who the fuck sent her a rat?"

"Is there really a rat in there?" Mrs. Valor asked as she got closer, craning her neck to see.

"Yes, ma'am."

She peered into the box and wrinkled her nose. "What is my daughter involved in that she gets arrested and someone sends her a rodent?"

"I don't know, ma'am, but we will figure it out."

She sat at the table, and I found an extra-large ziplock bag to put the entire box into. Trevor searched under the sink to find cleaners, and the two of us cleaned the counter.

"What are we going to do about Maggie?"

"I need to get down there, but I'm not sure what to do with," I tipped my head to the side as I spoke softly.

"You go, I'll ask Davina to come over, and we can stay here with her. I bet Mrs. Valor will love to meet Devon."

"You don't mind?"

"Not at all."

Mrs. Valor was staring at her plate of food that looked virtually untouched.

"Do you want me to warm that up for you?" I asked.

"I'm afraid that I don't like eating alone." She frowned. "At least, I think I don't like eating alone."

I glanced at Maggie's plate. "How about I eat Maggie's with you? I didn't get a chance to eat yet, and I'm pretty hungry."

Mrs. Valor beamed at me. "That would be nice, but what about Maggie?"

"I'll stop and get her a sandwich on my way to see her. Trevor and his fiancée are going to stay here with you while I get things figured out."

She eyed Trevor as I put her plate in the microwave. "So, you're engaged?"

"Yes, ma'am," Trevor said and grinned. "And we have a little boy. You'll get to meet him in a few minutes."

She turned to study me. "And you? Are you married?"

"No, Mrs. Valor, I'm not."

"But you like Maggie? Don't you? You kissed her forehead before the police left with her."

I swallowed. "I do like your daughter. I like her very much." Maybe way too much, I said the last bit to myself as Trevor smirked at me.

"And does she like you?"

I forced myself not to look at Trevor. "I don't know. You'd have to ask her."

The microwave dinged, and I removed her plate before I began to warm up Maggie's plate. Trevor stepped out of the kitchen to call Davina, and when he came back, I was halfway through the plate of food.

"Davina will be over in a few minutes. She just finished bathing Devon."

"Okay, and you really don't mind staying here to keep Mrs. Valor company?"

"Not at all," he said as he took a seat on the other side of the table. "Go find out what's going on. Why do you think they suspect her of being involved?"

"I have no idea," I fretted. "I can't think of one thing that would suggest that she was involved, other than she's Maggie, and she is always getting herself in trouble."

"Well, hopefully, they will tell you something."

"Yeah, I hope so." I took my plate to the sink. "Mrs. Valor, it was nice to see you again. I'll make sure that Maggie gets home safely tonight."

"Alright, thank you," she replied and tried to smile at me.

What must be going through her mind? She didn't know any of us, or she did, but she couldn't remember us. What did she think of all of this? Of dead rats delivered in boxes without labels, and a woman who was supposed to be her daughter arrested? Or even of strange men being in her house?

I could not comprehend how confusing all of that might be

to her. As I drove toward the police station, I wondered how Maggie handled it day after day. On my way, I stopped at the deli and picked Maggie up a sandwich, a small bag of chips, a big chocolate chip cookie, a small bottle of orange juice, and a large bottle of water. I was starving when I had arrived at her house; I could just imagine how damn hungry she might be after today.

Inside the station, I waited behind another man who was talking to the desk sergeant through the thick glass. When he finished, I shuffled to the window. "I'm Gregory Blaire, I'd like to speak to Detective Highmore about the woman he is interviewing, Maggie Valor."

"If he's interviewing her, then he won't be able to speak with you. You can have a seat over there and wait until he's available."

I lifted the bag of food. "You are going to want to bring this food back to him right away. I know for a fact that Maggie has not eaten today and has blood sugar issues. If you don't feed her, you're asking for trouble."

He pursed his lips and pointed to the side door. I met him at the door and handed over the bag, where he immediately looked inside. "I'll take this back to him. Have a seat."

I wanted to push him out of the way and find Maggie myself, but I didn't. Instead, I took a seat and pulled out my phone as it vibrated to see a text from Jake.

Maggie was arrested? WTF?

I don't know the details. I'll let you know once I have them.

You do that.

It was about five minutes later when the detective came to the door. "Mr. Blaire, come on back."

"Are you done with Maggie?" I asked as soon as I was through the door.

"No, not yet. I'm letting her eat. Thanks for bringing her something. She actually just told me that she needed something to eat before her blood sugar crashed."

"Yeah, it's not pretty. Maggie has been hypoglycemic her whole life."

"How long have you known her?"

"Since she was fifteen. We dated in high school, but broke up after I joined the Marines and prepared to deploy overseas."

"Ah, so that's how you two know each other so well."

"Yeah, although that day of the robbery was the first time that I had seen her in nineteen years."

He studied me for a moment. "Did she act like she knew those men in any way?"

"No. Maggie was just as surprised and scared as the rest of the people in the café. She didn't act any differently. What makes you think that Maggie knew the two men?"

He watched me for a few seconds as if he was trying to decide on something. Finally, he sighed and pointed at a chair next to his desk.

"Forensics found her fingerprints on the vehicle driven by Len and Chuck."

"What?" I barked. "That has to be wrong. Why the hell would her fingerprints be on the vehicle? Wait, where on the vehicle?"

"On the driver's door, and inside the vehicle on the seat."

What the hell? How was that possible? Could Maggie be involved with those people?

"I know you haven't seen her in a while, but do you know if maybe she is in debt or needs money for something? Maybe she got involved with them because of that."

"Are you kidding? There is no way that Maggie would do something like that. No matter what her financial state, and I have no clue what her current state is, but I know Maggie."

"Alright, then can you think of a reasonable explanation why her fingerprints are outside *and* inside the car?"

"No," I said gruffly, "but I sure would like to learn the reason. My boss, Jake Taite, was considering hiring her to work for us.

If she's into something bad, the last thing he is going to want is her working for our company."

Damn her. What the hell had Maggie done?

"Okay, well, if you want to watch the interview, you can view it from the back room. I'm having a hard time believing that she's involved, but I don't have any explanation on the prints."

"Yeah, neither do I. I appreciate you letting me watch."

He showed me back to the room, and Maggie was just finishing her sandwich. The cookie and juice were already gone, but I had figured they would have been first so that she got the sugar into her system.

Det. Highmore settled into the seat across from her. "Are you feeling better now?"

"Yes, thank you so much. I was about to hit the floor, and it would not have been pretty."

I glanced under the table and saw her feet were bare. Damn, I hadn't even noticed that when they took her away.

"Alright, Maggie, I need to ask you how you were involved with Jefferson Lenard Bunker and Chuck Wiggis."

"I wasn't involved with them, Detective. I have never seen them before that day."

"Did you hire them to do the robbery for you?"

"What? No! I had nothing to do with the jewelry store robbery. Why would you even think that?"

"If you had nothing to do with it, can you please tell me how your fingerprints came to be on the car door, the handle, and the interior of the vehicle that those two men were driving?"

Her eyes went wide as she muttered, "Oh, shit!"

CHAPTER TWENTY

MAGGIE

$\mathcal{I}$ was extremely confused and afraid as we pulled up to the police station. The two cops told me nothing about why I was being brought in for questioning, or why they thought I could be involved with the robbery and kidnapping.

My mind was spinning as they parked inside a cinder block garage, and the door went down behind us. After the door was closed, one of the officers opened the back door and undid my seat belt. I stared at my bare feet as I put them on the cement outside the door. They could have at least let me put shoes on.

One of the officers took me by the elbow. His touch was firm, but not harsh as he led me to a door. A buzzer went off, and the door opened. I was brought into a room where there was a bench, a computer, a fancy camera, and another police officer. On the bench was an older man who reeked of booze and urine.

"Have a seat," my new cop buddy said, and I cringed as I sat as far to the right as I could. He squatted beside me and put a cuff around my ankle.

"Are you serious? I'm not going anywhere! You don't have to do that."

"It's for your safety and ours, ma'am," he said. "Now, stay here for a few minutes, and I'll let Detective Highmore know that you are here."

I lifted my foot as far up as it would go. "Yeah, like I can go anywhere."

The guy next to me chuckled.

The two officers that brought me in disappeared through another door. I stared at the dirty floor and my bare feet. Holy cow, I would never get my feet clean enough again. My stomach rumbled so viciously that the officer six feet away turned with a raised brow, and the drunk next to me cackled again.

I sure hoped that the detective let me eat something. How long did I have to be in their custody before they would feed me? If I didn't eat soon, I was going to crash. I was already starting to feel slightly light-headed, and soon, I'd start seeing spots and break out in a sweat. It wouldn't be long after that that I would pass out.

Maybe if I passed out, they would take me to the hospital, and I wouldn't have to deal with this mess. Although I was interested to learn why they thought I was involved. Had someone told them that I was? Did they capture Len yet? Maybe he said that I was involved, but why? What was Greg thinking? Was my mom alright? Was Trevor going to change his mind about me?

There was a clock on the wall across from me. It was white and black and had a secondhand that I watched go around and around as I counted the minutes, sixteen, seventeen, eighteen, and ran through a zillion questions in my mind. If I wasn't watching the clock, I was watching the officer as he worked on the computer in the corner of the room. The guy beside me was quiet, and when I glanced his way, he looked like he was asleep. I went back to staring at the clock, and the door opened again at twenty-three minutes. One of my arresting officers sauntered back in, smiled at me, and then uncuffed my ankle again. "Come on."

He took me through another door and down a hallway. Inside a small room stood a table and two chairs. He uncuffed one of my wrists and shifted the cuff to an eyebolt in the center of the table. I rolled my eyes.

"The detective will be in shortly."

"Thank you," I said to him as he left. Not that I had a reason to thank him, but it was just common courtesy to say it. He gave me a kind smile as he closed the door.

I shivered as I sat in the chair. I was only wearing a thin t-shirt and leggings, and it was freezing in the room. My body was going to rush through the last of my energy pretty fast to keep myself warm.

By the time the detective entered, my teeth were chattering. "Hello, Ms. Valor."

"Detective."

"Are you cold?" he asked.

"I'm freezing, and I'm starving. Your officers could have given me a chance to eat my dinner and put on shoes before they hauled me out of my house for no reason."

He stuck his head back out the door, messing with something in the hallway, and the air vent above my head stopped blowing straight down on me. Oh, thank god!

"There, that should make it a little more comfortable for you."

"Do you have a switch you can flip that will deliver food too? If I don't eat something soon, I'm going to pass out literally. I am hypoglycemic, and I haven't eaten in several hours. I was just sitting down to eat when your officers arrived."

"We'll get you something soon."

"It needs to be sooner than later; I'm serious that I'm going to pass out. I'm already dizzy and feeling sick to my stomach."

There was a knock at the door, and then it opened. The cop

outside ticked his head to the side as if he wanted the detective to join him. "Excuse me for a moment."

"Find me some food while you are out there," I told him, and he glanced back and closed the door without a word. A minute later, he came back with a bag and set it down on the table.

"Here you go."

"Holy crap," I said as I dumped out the contents of the bag. The bottle of water began to roll away, and the detective stopped it as I went straight for the orange juice and cracked it open with shaking hands. I guzzled half of it before I snatched the cookie. My hands were still shaking, and I had spots on the edge of my vision as my brow broke out in a sweat.

The detective took the cookie out of my shaking hands and tore open the package. I shoved the cookie into my mouth, scarfing it down as quickly as I could. I groaned as I swallowed and took another mouthful.

"I'm going to give you a few minutes to eat, and then I'll be back in."

I nodded to him, too focused on the food to care what he did. After he left, I finished my cookie, then unrolled the sandwich, and almost cried when I saw that it was turkey with swiss on a Kaiser roll with mayo and tomato. I flipped the bag of chips over and saw they were sour cream and onion. I laughed to myself because I knew who had brought me this meal.

The cops hadn't bought this for me, Greg had. Gregory knew that I loved turkey and swiss. He knew that my favorite bread was a Kaiser roll. He also knew that I would have needed a sugar fix and that I detested sour cream and onion chips—but he didn't. That's why he got them to let me know that he was here.

But if he was here, who was with my mother? That thought set my nerves on edge, but I knew that Greg would never leave my mother to fend for herself. She had to be safe. Maybe Trevor was with her. Hopefully, Trevor was with her, and she wasn't out in the lobby of the police station.

I was just finishing my sandwich and rolling up the deli paper when the door opened and Det. Highmore returned. "Are you feeling better now?"

"Yes, thank you so much. I was about to hit the floor, and it would not have been pretty."

He gave me a casual smile and nodded. "Alright, Maggie, I need to ask you how you were involved with Jefferson Lenard Bunker and Chuck Wiggis."

"I wasn't involved with them, Detective. I have never seen them before that day." Why did they think otherwise?

"Did you hire them to do the robbery for you?"

"What? No! I had nothing to do with the jewelry store robbery. Why would you even think that?"

"If you had nothing to do with it, can you please tell me how your fingerprints came to be on the car door, the handle, and the interior of the vehicle that those two men were driving?"

Suddenly it dawned on me. "Oh, shit!"

"Yes, oh, shit. Now would you like to explain?"

I winced as I cocked my head to the side. "There is a simple explanation, Detective."

"And I'm waiting."

"That day, I was walking to the coffee shop, and remember I told you that I had seen Len walking into the jewelry store. We crossed paths on the sidewalk."

"Yes, you helped build a composite sketch of him."

"Yes." I slapped my hand on the table. "After he walked past me, I looked to the curb to see their vehicle, and it was still running, but there was no one at the wheel. So I went over to the car and looked inside. When I didn't see anyone in the back seat either, I went around the car, opened the door, and removed the keys. I bet you found the keys in the back cargo area, right?" I waited for a reaction from him but didn't get one.

"I threw the keys back there. I almost threw them in the street, but I tossed them into the back instead."

"Why would you do that?"

"Because the guy gave me a nasty look, and I hate people that leave their cars running. It's against the law."

He laughed; he actually laughed as he shifted in his seat. "You really want me to believe that your prints were on the car because you were pissed off that the guy gave you a dirty look?"

"Well, yeah, but he left his car running! Isn't that against the law? It is against the law, isn't it?"

"So is entering another person's vehicle without permission. It could be construed as theft."

"But I didn't steal anything."

"You took their keys."

"No, I removed their keys and tossed them into the back. I didn't take their keys."

"You removed something that belonged to someone else to deny them of their property."

"No! I moved the keys to piss them off!"

"You do realize that because you removed their keys, you also removed their getaway vehicle, and that is why they came into the coffee shop. It was the only business open at that time of the morning."

I winced. "Yeah, I kind of figured that out."

He shook his head again.

"You believe me, right?"

"Ms. Valor, your answer is just crazy enough to be truthful. Yes, I believe you." He pulled keys out of his pocket and unlocked the cuff that was holding my right arm on the table. "I should warn you against getting into other people's business. The next time you see someone leave their car running, call the police. Don't get yourself in trouble."

"I will. I promise I won't do that again." I rubbed my wrist as I held my arm close to my chest. "Can I go home now?"

"Yes, Mr. Blaire is here. Stay here for a minute."

"Alright," I told him as I leaned back in my seat and stared at the chip bag, a little smile on my face. "I already knew he was here."

"Yeah, how so?"

"He knows I hate sour cream and onion chips, but he loves them. This was his way of telling me he was here."

He stared at the bag and then chuckled. "Smart guy. I'll be right back."

He left me in the room for a few more minutes, and I assumed he was doing whatever paperwork he needed to do to release me. A couple of minutes later, the door opened, and Greg came in, his brows low over his brooding eyes.

"Of all the stupid things that you could have done, Maggie. You almost got yourself into a lot of trouble."

"Yes, I know that."

"Why the hell didn't you tell them that you did that before?"

"I don't know." I shrugged. "I guess I thought I'd get in trouble for doing it."

His frown deepened. "You did get in trouble for doing it. You got arrested."

"No, I think I was detained, not arrested. They didn't read me my rights or fingerprint me."

He took my arm. "Come on, Mags, let's get you home. The detective said you could go."

"Who is with Mom?"

"Trevor and his fiancée are with her."

I blinked. "He brought his fiancée over?"

"Yep, and his son. I checked in on them a few minutes ago; everyone is fine, and your mom is having fun with Devon."

"Thank you, Greg."

"You're lucky we were there when the cops showed up," he said as we reached the front entrance, and the cop buzzed us out.

"Yeah, speaking of that. What was in the box?"

Greg glanced back over his shoulder and didn't answer until we were outside. "A dead rat."

"What?"

"Maggie, someone sent you a rat. Who else did you piss off?"

"No one!" I snapped as I crossed my arms over my chest. "I swear, I have no idea who would send me a rat."

He pursed his lips and then glanced down at my feet. Before I knew what he was doing, he bent down and scooped me up and over his shoulder.

"What the hell are you doing? Put me down, Greg!"

"I don't want you to cut your feet," he said as he started for the parking lot. His hand slapped against my backside.

"Ouch! Why did you just smack me?"

"Because you, Maggie Valor, are a lot of trouble, and you deserve a few spankings."

"I do not!" I hissed at him, and he swatted my ass again. "Damn it, Greg! Do not spank me again! Do you hear me?"

He laughed. I felt it radiate from his shoulder into my belly, and it slithered deep into my body, making parts of me unwantedly clench. Okay, so maybe not so unwantedly.

CHAPTER TWENTY-ONE

GREGORY

That woman was going to be the death of me. Why didn't she tell anyone about this earlier? More importantly, why didn't she just walk away from it in the first place? I knew that answer; Maggie couldn't help herself.

I hadn't seen this woman in nineteen years, but she hadn't changed one damn bit. She was as headstrong as ever, putting her nose where it didn't belong. She used to joke when we were younger that she had a nose for news, but I told her she had a nose for trouble.

I honestly didn't know whether to laugh at her or put her over my knee and spank her. As I took her out to my truck, I didn't have her over my knee, but my shoulder. I took advantage of the position to give her two swift smacks on the ass.

I knew if I could see her face, it would be beet red, and her eyes would be bulging with indignation. I carried her to the truck, unlocked it, and then began to lower her to the ground. Only as I put her feet down, her sinfully sweet body slipped over mine. My hands, which had been guiding her hips, pulled her closer to me. I should have been pushing her away—I knew it, knew I was asking for trouble—trouble that only Maggie could give me. Maggie's eyes went wide, but not because she was angry, no. I saw passion sparkling within them; my eyes locked on her parted lips.

She squeezed my biceps as she leaned forward, our lips only a few millimeters apart, so close that I could taste her breath. "Maggie." Her name fell off my tongue, just a heartbeat before my mouth was on hers. I pressed her back against my truck and plastered her body against mine. We kissed each other like we were drowning, as if we'd only find salvation in the other. The frustration of watching her move all day, or her determination, her grit inflamed me, and I was ready to tear her clothes from her body right here in the parking lot.

Someone laughed behind us. "Get a room before we need to arrest you two for public indecency." I pulled away from the kiss and turned to see two cops walking toward a patrol car, smirking our way.

"Get in the truck," I said to Maggie softly as I glanced down at her. Her lips were slightly red, her eyes glazed. "Let's get you home."

She nodded and climbed in without another word. We were almost home when she finally spoke.

"Thank you."

"For what?"

"For being here for Mom and me."

"You're welcome, Maggie. But I have a question for you."

She stared at my profile, and I peered at her momentarily. "Who got you out of trouble when I wasn't around?"

She crossed her arms over her chest. "I'll have you know that I didn't get in any trouble when you weren't around."

"So you saved this shit specifically for me? Isn't that sweet of you."

"Greg, I didn't do this on purpose. You know that, right? I admit that I went a little off the rails by taking the car keys out of the ignition, but I swear that is not my norm."

I chuckled. "Seems like the norm for the girl that I used to know."

"I'm not that naïve little girl, Greg."

"Sweetheart, you were never naïve. You have always had brass balls and a determination to do anything that you wanted to do. No one could ever pull anything on you."

"You really think so?" she asked after a moment.

"Of course I do, Mags. You were the strongest woman I knew back then, one of the strongest women I know now."

"Then you're going to let me go with you on this delivery."

"Maggie, you haven't finished the courses."

She laughed, and I glanced at her. "Seriously? Do you think that I'm not going to be able to pass the bookwork or firearms? Do you forget who you are talking to?"

"Maggie, I know that you can pass the tests, and you are probably a pretty good shot—most women who enjoy shooting are—but that doesn't mean that you should be going."

"Why not?"

I pulled my truck to the curb in front of her house. "Can we not do this right now? We need to go in so we can let Trevor and Davina go home."

"Fine, but then you are going to answer the question, Greg."

"Yeah, we'll see."

Maggie knocked on the locked door, and we waited. Trevor peered through the window and let us in. "How is she?" Maggie asked as soon as the door cracked.

"She's fine, sleeping actually. How are you?"

"I'm fine. Trevor, I can't thank you enough."

Trevor put his hand on her shoulder and smiled down at her; if I didn't know how much he loved Davina, I would be jealous as hell. "Davina and Devon did most of it. Come on, let me introduce them before we get out of your hair."

Davina was putting Devon into his car seat when we came

into the living room. "Maggie, this is Davina, and our little guy, Devon."

Maggie glanced at the baby, smiled slightly, and then touched Davina's arm. "Thank you so much."

"You're welcome. I'm glad we were able to help. Your mom enjoyed playing with Devon and went up to bed about thirty minutes ago."

"I'm going to go check on her. Thank you again. I owe you one."

Maggie squeezed Trevor's arm as she walked past him and then raced up the stairs.

"What happened?"

"You're not going to believe this," I said with a chuckle and then told him what Maggie had done and how the cops thought she was involved.

Trevor laughed. "Jesus, she's a trip."

"Yeah, she is. Thanks again for helping us out."

"Us?"

"Her, okay, smart-ass."

He slapped me on the back. "I'll talk to you tomorrow, and we'll discuss that rat problem at the range. Maggie's still up for training tomorrow, right?"

"Yeah, probably more than ever right now," I muttered and saw them to the door.

In the kitchen, I pulled out a beer and twisted the top off, guzzling half of it as I leaned back against the counter. Maggie entered the room and came directly to me, pulling the beer out of my hand and drinking the rest while staring me in the eye. Damn—

I forced myself to stand still, torn between putting space between us or removing what little space we had.

"Why not, Greg?"

"Why not what, Maggie?"

"Why don't you want me to go?"

"Because I don't think it would be safe for you."

"Bullshit!" she hissed and leaned slightly toward me. "You don't want me to go because of what's between us."

"There is nothing between us, Maggie."

One of her eyebrows hiked high, making her look so damn sexy. "You're going to go there, Greg? You're going to try and lie to me and tell me that there isn't something going on between us?" She set the bottle down, stepping between my legs and brazenly putting her palm over my groin. Fuck. Me. "If there is nothing going on, why are you already getting hard?"

"Maggie, don't do this."

"Why, Greg? I know you want me. I want you too. Why shouldn't we?" She rubbed her hand over my now throbbing erection. "We're adults, Greg."

I tried to stand up straight, but she pushed me back. "You're not getting away until you talk to me, Greg."

"Maggie, what do you want?" The question came out gruffly, and her eyes ignited with fire.

"You! Isn't that obvious?"

I closed my eyes, hiding behind my eyelids, trying to find a way out of this. I knew that if I stepped over this line and kissed this woman again, I wouldn't stop—not this time.

Maggie's chest pressed against mine; her lips brushed over my neck as the fingers of one hand flitted down the back of my neck, and the other hand pressed against my hard-on. "Admit it, Greg, you want this. You want me."

I ground my teeth, fighting it with everything I could until she slipped her hand lower and cupped my balls, pressing the heel of her hand against my shaft.

"Admit it, Gregory Blaire, you want me as much as I want you."

"No—more, sweetheart. So damn much more!" I wasn't aware that the words had left my lips until I saw the shock in her eyes as I speared my hand into her hair and pulled her toward me.

The kiss was explosive, and a second after it started, I was ridding her of the damn tight little t-shirt. I left her lips only long enough for the material of hers and mine to pass over our heads. I yanked the cup of her bra down so I could get to her breast, and I sucked the hard peak into my mouth as she wrestled with the button and zipper of my pants. I moved on to her other breast as she tugged at my jeans to get them off my hips.

I nipped her nipple, and she whimpered, her knees almost buckling, and I put my hands to her waist and peeled down her leggings and panties in a few swift pulls. I lifted her to the countertop, jerking the pants off her legs and throwing them to the side before latching back on her breast. Her hands were in my hair, then clawing at my back as she arched toward me.

She reached between us, grasping my shaft, and a shiver tore down my spine. I jerked her hand away, afraid that with as excited as I was, it would be over before it started. I fucking needed to taste this woman. I dropped to my knees, pushing her thighs further apart as I dove between her legs. She pressed my head closer, arching backward until she hit her head on the cabinet.

I devoured her, lost myself in her taste and the sounds that poured out of her mouth. I took her to the top, held her tightly as she fell over, and then I was on my feet, filling her as she clung to me and brought our mouths together. I rocked into her as she tensed around me, and we shattered together in an awe-inspiring moment.

For a few seconds, we held one another, and then she leaned back and said, "I told you."

"Yeah," I replied as I shifted away and bent to grab my pants that were around my knees. "And just because we had sex, it doesn't mean that I'm going to let you go. Just the opposite."

Her mouth flopped open. "What?"

I zipped my pants and looked around for my shirt, grabbing Maggie's leggings off the floor and tossing them to her. "Exactly what I said, Sweetheart. Just because we had sex, it doesn't mean you are going."

"Greg, you can't stop me from doing this if I pass everything."

"Yes, I can."

"Why would you do that? I just proved that you want me."

I spun around on her and got in her face. "You proved that you are a good seductress, Mags. You're a beautiful woman; of course, I wanted to have sex with you. Jesus, you're fucking gorgeous, Maggie, and sexy as hell. That doesn't mean that I want to work with you—travel with you. In fact, it means the fucking opposite. You're a goddamn distraction, Maggie. You could get one of the other guys, or me, killed."

Maggie jerked back, startled by my outburst. "I would not be a distraction."

"Oh, really? Do you think that after that little dick tease, I could possibly resist not thinking about screwing you every which way I could? Come on, Maggie, be smart. Before this, every damn time I looked at you, all I could think about was being in you and having you scream my name. Now that I've had you, tasted you again, you think that is going to stop? Fuck no! It's just going to be worse."

I yanked my shirt over my head and glared at her. I knew I was a total asshole for this, but I couldn't stop myself. I was laying my fear at her feet, and I hated myself for it.

"I can't do my job if all I'm thinking about is how to get you naked, or wondering how many of the other guys want to do that themselves. You're not going, Maggie, and that's final."

I didn't give her a chance to respond as I spun around and hightailed it out of the house. The memory of her shocked face, beautiful naked body, and angry-as-a-viper eyes followed me out of the house and all the way home.

CHAPTER TWENTY-TWO

MAGGIE

*W*hat just happened? I mean, what-the-living-hell just happened?

The front door closed; I heard his truck start, and then it accelerated away from my house, and still, I just sat there in shock.

Damn him! I jumped off the counter, trying to untwist my leggings and panties and then shoved my legs in before yanking my shirt over my head and punching my arms through the holes. I went to use the bathroom and then came back and sanitized every counter in the kitchen, pausing when I got to the counter where the box had been. Where did it go? Had Greg thrown the rat out? A rat—why a rat?

For about two seconds, I thought about calling Trevor, but I didn't want to bother him again. I still didn't even have Greg's phone number. Damn him! I was going to have to wait until tomorrow to find out more about the stupid rodent.

I armed the alarm and went up the stairs to my room. The entire time I seethed over what Greg had said. Did he seriously only see me as a woman to screw? Was that all I was? Did he not feel anything for me? Was I a total idiot to want him to feel something for me? My god, I was. I was a fool.

I stood in the shower, so frustrated with myself that I wanted to scream. I had forced the issue tonight. If I hadn't been so brazen, hadn't pushed Greg into responding to me, maybe I could have found a way to get him to change his mind. Was it going to be possible to change it now?

I tossed and turned for a while and finally fell into a deep slumber until my alarm went off. As soon as I opened my eyes, thoughts of Greg flashed into my mind, but I shoved them away. I had no time for him today, and I was going to prove to him that we could be adults and work together even if we were attracted to one another.

After pouring my coffee, I took another hot shower to ease my stiff muscles and was thankful that today wasn't going to be as physical as yesterday. We were going to the range this morning and then doing some classroom work after lunch. I hoped that we could cover everything quickly and get done earlier than yesterday. I needed to make an appearance at the paper.

My boss had sent me several annoying text messages about the fact that I didn't do the piece on the hostage situation at the coffee shop. I think he still wanted me to do it, but I wouldn't. Greg was right. I would rather see the two men locked up than to build my career off something that could result in them getting free.

After I got my mom off to her day program, I collected the gear I would need for the range and left. In the car, my mind fell back on the package I'd received the night before. Who would send me a rat? I didn't think that I had any enemies, but I guess one never really knew that unless they were confronted by one.

Rats signified sneaky creatures that went behind your back. People that you once respected but no longer did because they had become disloyal to you. Who had I been disloyal to? I could not think of a single person that I had wronged, especially one where I might have gone behind their back. Was I overthinking this? Had someone killed the first animal they came across and sent that to me as a warning? My hands clenched the steering wheel as an eerie feeling slipped down my spine. Was someone threatening to kill me?

No! That was absurd. Who would want to kill me? No one, that's who. It had to be a random incident. Some kid was playing tricks, wanting to scare me. Yeah, well, that wasn't going to work on me. I'd have to speak to my neighbors and see if anyone else had something similar happen.

I put the stupid dead animal into my mental closet and realized as I fought to close the door that it was starting to get a little full. When I'd opened it to store the rodent inside, memories of last night with Greg tried to explode out, but I'd caught them and wrestled them back. I was going to have to start dealing with some of those things or I'd run out of room for good.

A few minutes later, I pulled into the range lot and gathered my gear. I had my rifle bag in my left hand and my range bag in my right. I'd brought my handgun and my father's hunting rifle. I hadn't shot that in a while, but I did know how to use it. When my father was alive, he had taken me hunting, and I'd taken down a few deer in my day.

I had always enjoyed using the rifle, but these days I didn't have much of a chance to train with it. It wasn't like I had plans to climb in a tree stand anytime soon.

I found Trevor inside the building at the counter, speaking with an employee. I glanced around as I approached him, but I didn't see Greg anywhere. There had been several trucks outside, although I hadn't looked at them carefully to see if any were his. I told myself that I didn't care. If I kept telling myself that, maybe it would become true.

"Morning, Trevor."

"Hey, Maggie. I need your license, and if you have your carry permit with you, that will help too." I pulled them out and passed them over to the man waiting. He leered at me slightly, and I forced myself not to roll my eyes.

"How are you today?" I asked.

"Doing well, what about you? Did you get any rest last night?"

"I did." I laughed. "I actually slept well. I think the fact that you all kicked my ass yesterday might have had something to do with that."

He chuckled and glanced over my head, nodding to someone that I assumed was Greg. When Alex paused next to me, I did a double take and then looked behind him. "Hello, Alex."

"Hi, Maggie."

"What are you doing here?" Trevor asked as he turned and leaned back against the counter, arms crossed.

Alex's gaze shot toward mine quickly and then to Trevor. "Blaire had some things come up. He asked me to cover for him today."

I clamped my jaw shut, forcing myself not to react, and that lasted a whole two seconds before I snapped, "What a chicken!"

Trevor laughed. "Ah, man, what happened after I left your house last night?"

"Wait—" Alex put his hand up. "Why were you at her house?"

"That's a long story," I told Alex. "And one that has no business in today's course of events."

Trevor was frowning, but then he shrugged. "Okay, you're right. Let's focus on what you need to get through."

A few minutes later, the paperwork was done, and we were given a key. Trevor explained that the key was to a training area, not open to the public, and I followed them down a hallway to a dark-gray door. Trevor reached in and turned on a few lights.

"Maggie, why don't you get your stuff out so I can see what

you have. I'm going to have Alex help me bring in our gear. We'll be back in a few minutes."

I nodded and watched the door close. I glanced around; there was a small classroom area with four tables and eight chairs. There was a whiteboard on the far wall and a large glass window that opened up to a range area. I set my bags down and went to check it out.

On the far end, targets hung, and there were lines painted on the cement ground at different intervals in different colors. There was a partial wall built on the far side, with a door in the middle, and two large metal barrels randomly set on the range. I assumed they were for concealment fire.

I glanced back at the door and wondered what Trevor and Alex were really talking about out of earshot. Had Greg not come today because of last night? Had Greg told Alex about what happened? I didn't think so, but what *had* he told him?

I was almost done setting my stuff up when the door opened, and Alex and Trevor returned, both with their arms full of stuff. Okay, so maybe Trevor really had needed Alex's help to retrieve all the gear. "Wow, you could have asked for help."

Alex chuckled. "That's okay. I needed the workout. I've missed the gym this week."

I took a seat while they got things together, and then Trevor and Alex looked over my guns, showed me a few of theirs, and asked me safety questions. It didn't take us long to load up our magazines, and they gave me a vest to wear and had me load up on ammo. They also told me I was using a different gun and fit me with a thigh holster. Then Alex helped me get an earpiece secured into my ear and showed me how to control volumes with the headphones I would be wearing over them.

"I can hear you on the range; why do I need to wear these?"

"Because when we are on the job, this is how we talk when we are separated. We can be in different rooms or different cars and still stay in touch. This will give you a chance to try it out, start to get used to it."

It didn't take long to get used to it or to hearing their voices whispered into my ear. I wondered briefly what Greg's voice would sound like through the earpiece, but I dismissed that quickly.

We worked on the range for about three hours, and while it was work, it was fun. I learned quite a bit and tried some different firearms. It was obvious that I knew my way around a gun, and even when they got my adrenaline going, I was still consistent with my shooting. Both Alex and Trevor appreciated that, and I could tell they were impressed. Would Greg have been? Who knew—who cared?

After we finished, Trevor and I went to a deli on the way back to the training facility. Alex had begged off, saying he had a meeting he had to attend and that I was in good hands with Trevor.

Trevor and I had just gotten our food and taken a seat when he gave me a long look. "So, you going to tell me what the hell happened last night after I left?"

I stopped, my mouth wide open, my sandwich almost to my mouth. "I'm not sure what you are talking about."

"Bullshit, Maggie. When I left, Greg was in a decent mood, and you two seemed to be getting along."

"What makes you think that we aren't getting along now?" I stuffed my sandwich into my mouth.

"Because Greg isn't here."

I shrugged my shoulders, wiped my mouth, and then finished chewing. "I thought Alex said he had something else to do."

"Yeah, that was a lie, and you know it."

"Sorry, I can't help you there," I told him.

"Maggie, I'm trying to help here. I know, and I'm pretty sure you know, that Greg doesn't want you to go. He doesn't think you'll be safe, although this is going to be one of the safest ops we've ever done."

"Yes, I am very aware that he doesn't want me to go."

"Did he tell you why?"

I took another bite and chewed methodically as I mulled over how to respond. "Yes, Greg told me that I was a distraction and not only to him, but the other guys wouldn't need my kind of distraction."

"Your kind of distraction?"

"Yes, because I'm a woman."

He laughed. "Because you are a *beautiful* woman, and Greg wants you for himself."

I pointed at him. "That he does *not* want. He specifically said that last night. Of course, that was after—" I stopped and shoved a chip into my mouth as his eyes went wide.

"You slept with Greg."

I pursed my lips. Crap! "We most definitely did not sleep. We had sex, quick and dirty, and in the kitchen no less. Then he threw a fit and stomped out of the house."

I expected Trevor to back his buddy, but he laughed and said, "You got under his skin! That's awesome. I mean, I knew you were already there."

"You did?"

"Yeah, it is obvious that Greg is really into you, but he's scared to get involved with anyone. I've known the man for like fifteen years, and he's never been in a relationship with anyone that lasted more than a week." Trevor blinked and then started laughing.

"What's so funny?"

"Nothing. I just remembered something Greg told me years ago. You know, he used to carry your picture around with him."

"What?"

"Yeah, when I first met him, we bunked together while we were in a training class, and he used to take your photo out

183

every night and look at it. I completely forgot about that until now."

"Maybe it wasn't me."

"It was you. I have no doubt. Greg told me he let you go so that you would move on and have a great life."

"Stupid," I said. "He could have given me a great life."

"Maybe, or maybe he needed to get to this point in his life before he realized that's not only what he needs, but wants."

"I don't know about that, Trevor. Besides, he's going to do everything he can to keep me from going on this trip."

"Yeah, but I think you should go. Jake thinks you should go, and now that Alex has seen you shoot and heard about your day yesterday, I'm pretty sure he will be on our side."

"So, you'll back me on this? You won't side with him?"

"No, I think you can carry your weight."

"Will I be a distraction to you?"

He shook his head. "No, not me. I might think you are a beautiful, sexy woman, but there is no way I would think more than that. Even if I didn't have Davina in my life, as far as I'm concerned, you, Maggie Valor, are taken."

I laughed. "I am far from taken."

Trevor grinned at me. "You had sex with Greg last night and got him so flustered that he ran away with his tail between his legs. Trust me, girl, once he gets his head out of his ass, he'll realize that he screwed up and will come crawling back to you on his knees."

"Yeah, and if he does that, I might just make him stay there for a while."

Trevor laughed and held up his soda cup. I tapped mine to his. "You are my kind of girl, and if Greg pushes the issue of you not going because he doesn't want to be responsible for you, I have your back."

"Thanks, Trevor. That means a lot to me."

CHAPTER TWENTY-THREE

GREGORY

I slept, but it took a while to get my mind to calm
down and turn off. I was up earlier than I wanted to
be, so I decided to hit the street and get in a run. As I moved, I
tried to work through the frustration that I felt at myself. I had
acted like a complete ass last night, and I couldn't believe that I
had told her that I wouldn't be able to concentrate with her
around—that she would be a distraction. I had meant it, but I
shouldn't have said it the way I had.

I didn't do distractions. I'd trained to shove that shit deep
down inside and focus. To focus on what my mission was, what
the operation was, what the ultimate goal was. I should have
been able to put her out of my head. I should have been able to
pretend like she was no one to me, just another civilian
contractor we were escorting. There had been a few women
who had traveled with us recently, and I'd been assigned to
oversee them. Several had been attracted to me. A couple had
even managed to get into my bed for a few hours.

Those women had been distractions, but only momentary
ones. After we parted ways, I never thought of them again, just

as I'm sure they didn't think of me either. Was Maggie thinking about me today? What names was she calling me if she was?

Maggie—she was still as much trouble as she always was. Damn her for trying to get even with that guy because they had looked at her wrong. What kind of woman did that? And the rat, what the hell did she do to get a dead rat delivered to her house?

The rat reminded me of the counter, and that prompted the memory of her sweet, sweet body at my mercy. I almost stumbled as I ran, thinking of her crying out as I shifted deeper into her.

Yeah, Maggie and I had sex when we were teens. It was pretty vanilla back then. The most outrageous thing was having sex in a car. Otherwise, it was on the couch, the floor, and maybe once in a while in her bed. The missionary position was the norm unless we were in my car, then she was sitting on my lap. Oral sex was occasionally tried out too, but neither of us was great at it back then.

I guess as it went for sex between teens, it was pretty good, but last night. Gee-zus! Last night put every single one of those previous escapades to shame, and it had only lasted ten minutes, maybe fifteen at the most, but it had been incredible.

Maggie had grown into one fine woman. Her body was firm and toned, her ass tight and round, her breasts small and perky. She had the perfect athletic body, and I could imagine working that body out to its limits. I knew without a doubt that Maggie was no prude. She would be a wild cat in bed if we ever got there.

The problem was, I didn't know if we should get there. Jake had suggested I go out with Maggie because she might not have an issue with me traveling, but what if she wanted to go on every run that we made? Some of them were too damn dangerous—shit, there were some I didn't even want to go on.

As I finished my run, I got caught on that last thought. What if I didn't go? Would Jake give me shit if I didn't do this one? Would he fire me? I didn't think so. He probably wouldn't be too happy about it, but I didn't think he'd fire me if I told him I wasn't going.

If I didn't go, then one of the other guys would be tasked to watch her. I knew that Harvey, Trevor, Mike, and Alex would all be great candidates, although Mike and Harv were single. Even Jake would be okay; it was his idea that Maggie join the group anyway. Maybe he should be required to watch her—that might teach him a lesson.

What about Rob, Brett, Drake, Cliff, Bill, Wyatt, and Joe? They were all the part-timers that we brought in to do operations as needed. All of them were single, and all of them total fucking dogs—well, Drake and Wyatt weren't as bad, but they were still single.

To be honest, I wasn't sure if Jake had decided which PTer's were running this job. I knew that the proposal stated that there would be between eight and ten people. If Maggie went, then that would leave us with nine spots. Five FTer's, not counting me, and four PTer's. I could remain back here and watch over things.

That was actually a good idea. Alice and I could hold the fort down, and I could give up my spot to one of the other guys. I'm sure they could use the money. With that decided, I arrived home and called Alex while I was filling my water bottle.

"Hey, how are things with Maggie? I heard about last night."

"That was a shitshow," I replied.

"Trevor said she got questioned by the police."

"Yeah, Maggie decided to stick her nose where it didn't belong, but she managed to get it cleared up."

"That's good. Trevor said she did well yesterday."

"She passed."

He laughed, echoing my words. "She passed."

I so did not want to talk about Maggie. "Yeah, hey, I have a favor."

"What's that?"

"Can you hook up with Trevor today and help him at the range? They are going there first thing this morning."

"I have a meeting at one."

"Trevor would only need your help at the range, and she's an experienced shooter, so she will probably run through things quickly. They probably won't be there past eleven."

"Why aren't you going?"

"Because I forgot I needed to get a blood test done today."

"You'd rather get your vein pricked than spend a few hours behind the trigger? Are you ill?"

I chuckled; he knew me well. "No, routine shit for my physical that needs to be done ASAP."

"Why can't you hit the lab and then go to the range?"

"Because I'm asking you to do it."

"Are you avoiding Maggie?"

I hesitated just a fraction of a second too long. "No."

"Bullshit." He sighed. "Look, I'll help Trevor out because I'd like to see Maggie in action, but you need to get your head out of your ass. She's going with us, and you're going to need to deal with that."

"Yeah, maybe."

"Maybe, my ass. Jake already said that she's going. If she can hit employee time with forty extra pounds on her, she's fit enough to go. Especially if she does a good job today. He's totally into this idea of a reporter joining our team."

I didn't want to debate it with him. "You're going to help Trevor?"

"Yes, I'll help him."

"Okay, thanks. I'll catch you later." I hung up before he could say anything else. Yeah, I knew it was suspicious, and I knew I wasn't fooling him, but I didn't care.

I showered, made myself breakfast, and then headed to the lab. I wasn't joking about needing a blood test; I did require one. I just hadn't needed to get it today. It was a good excuse, though.

After the lab, I went into the office. Alice was in an extra foul mood when I stepped in. "Where the hell have you been?"

I stopped on a dime at her tone. "Getting a blood test. Is there a problem?"

"No, Jake found out that Alex isn't here today and wanted to know where he was. No one seems to want to answer their damn phone today! Is there something wrong with your phone?"

I pulled it out of my pocket and saw the three missed calls. "Sorry, it was on silent and not vibrate."

She grumbled under her breath for a moment. "Go see Jake. I'm tired of dealing with his crap today, and it's not even ten."

I started to step away, but paused and shuffled closer to her desk. "You okay, Alice?"

"I'm peachy, Gregory. Go talk to your asshole boss."

"Blaire!" My name echoed down the hallway, and I grunted and went to see what his major malfunction was.

"Your highness," I muttered as I stepped into his office.

"Jesus, where the hell have you been?"

"Screamer, is there an emergency that you need me for? Did someone die? Is the world going to hell? Did a client back out of a contract?"

"No, what the hell are you talking about?"

"I'm talking about how you are losing your fucking mind because I'm not here, and you've got Alice so pissed off she almost took my head off when I stepped inside the door."

"That's not my fault."

"Did you lose your shit on Alice? Because I would bet you a hundred bucks that you lost your shit on her, and that's why she's ready to murder the first person who crosses her."

"I might have demanded her to find you or Alex."

"Alex is at the range with Trevor."

"Why aren't you there?"

I sank into the chair across from him. "Because I had to get a blood test."

"That couldn't have waited?"

"No, my doctor wanted me to get it done ASAP."

The muscles in his jaw ticked as he clenched his teeth a few times. "Trevor said she did good yesterday and that she'll be an asset on the trip."

"An asset? He did not say that."

"Yeah, actually, he did." I frowned, and Jake leaned back in his seat. "Why don't you want her to go? I mean for real?"

"Because Maggie is a distraction that we don't need. She's nosy as hell, and she constantly gets herself in trouble. It's not just me that I'm thinking of here. She will be a distraction for everyone because we would constantly be watching and waiting for her to do something stupid. Last night, she got brought in for questioning because one of the guys who did the robbery looked at her wrong that day right before they pulled the heist. She got pissed off, went inside their getaway car, and hid the keys. That's why the cops wanted to talk to her. They found her prints in the car and thought she was involved."

Jake laughed. "Bold."

"Yes, bold and stupid. Jake, trust me, Maggie Valor is trouble with a capital T. She has been that way her whole life. Why do you think she is working as a romance advice columnist and not at the crime news desk? Because she gets herself in trouble, that's why."

"You know that how?"

"I know that because I know Maggie."

"What are you going to do if I decide she is going anyway?"

"I'm going to tell you that I'm not going. I'll give my position away to one of the PTer's, and they can run it. Besides, if you are going, and I know you want to, then it makes sense to have one of us back here at the office. I can cover everything that needs attention while you are away."

He inhaled loudly and released it slowly as he glanced around. "I had thought about that."

"Then I'll stay back. If you want Maggie to go, then you take her."

"You care about her." It was a statement, not a question.

"Not how you think. Maggie drives me nuts and not necessarily in a good way."

"Bullshit!" Jake laughed. "I'll think about it, but I'm just going to tell you now that I think you're a wuss for not going."

I stood up. "You think what you want, Screamer, and while you're so interested in other people's business, figure out a way to make it up to Alice."

"She's fine."

"She is far from fine, Jake. You owe her at least an apology."

"Fine, whatever."

"You know, I'd watch it if I were you. One of these days, Alice is going to tell you to go to hell and walk out. She's the glue to this place, man. You know that, and she knows that."

"We'd be fine without her."

I glanced at the open door, hoping that her radar ears couldn't hear us. "For your sake, I hope she never hears you say that, and you know as well as I do that we would not be."

"Yeah, alright, I know that. I will come up with something."

"You do that. In the meantime, I'm going to go check with Mike and see if he heard from my client yesterday."

"I think he did, and I think there was a question."

"On it," I stated as I left his office. Alice was not at her desk, so I went straight to Mike's, which was on the other side of Alex's. Mike had an office because he needed more space than the rest of us for all his techno-toys and gadgets.

I took a seat in his guest chair. "Heard there was a question with the client."

"Yeah, what are you doing here? I thought you were working with your girlfriend."

"She's not my girlfriend."

"Does she know that?"

"I did not come in here to talk about Maggie; can we just stick to work, please?"

"Fine," he grunted.

As Mike and I talked, in the back of my mind, I wondered if Maggie was into some of the kinky shit that Mike was. Would the two of them get along? I gripped the arms of the chair tightly and then forced myself to relax. It didn't matter to me what she did or who she was with.

I was just thankful that Jake had given me the green light to stay here. At least I think I was—fuck!

CHAPTER TWENTY-FOUR

MAGGIE

"Can you come over tonight?" I asked Heather as I rushed up the steps to the building that housed the newspaper.

"Sure, what time?"

"Eight? Unless you want to come for dinner."

"No, eight will work. I have a few other things going on after work."

"Alright, I'll see you then." I opened the door to the paper and prepared to hang up on Heather, but she stopped me.

"Wait! Did you really get arrested last night?"

I stopped in the middle of the lobby. "Where did you hear that?"

"Donna mentioned it, said Tobin told her after he heard it from Sarah, whose brother is a cop."

"No. I was not arrested," I snapped.

"You weren't?"

I sighed; it wasn't her fault that my life was going off the rails. "I'll explain it tonight, Heather. I gotta go."

I hung up before she could respond and wondered what I was going to be walking into when I got up to the third floor. I'd already received three voicemails and six text messages from Jeff about being arrested. How had they heard that?

After lunch with Trevor, the two of us had gone back to the training center and worked on some other safety protocols. It was simple stuff. Well, simple if you had common sense, and we got through it quickly.

I glanced at my watch and winced. It was almost three. Okay, maybe not as quickly as I had hoped. I rushed to the elevator and waited for the car to arrive. When the doors opened on the third floor, I practically exploded out of it. I glanced nervously toward Jeff's office and then made a beeline for my cubicle, hoping to at least be able to hide there for a few minutes before I was demanded to make an appearance in his office.

"Where the hell have you been?" Jessica, a co-worker, said as I slithered into my desk. She looked both ways in the narrow aisle between our cubbies and then rolled her chair into mine. "Did you seriously get arrested?"

"No, I did not get arrested. I was brought in for an interview."

"But you were handcuffed!"

"How the hell do you know that?" I asked her.

"Because I saw the picture!"

"What picture?"

"The picture that they are going to run in the evening edition and post online at five!"

"What?" I squeaked.

"If you weren't arrested, Maggie, you better go talk to Jeff!"

"Yes, you damn well better talk to me. Where the hell have you been, Maggie Valor?" Jeff growled as he rounded the corner and almost bowled over the top of Jessica in her chair.

"I told you I have been working on a story."

"Does your story have anything to do with being arrested?

Were you released on bail? I couldn't find any charges filed on you."

"Oh, you'd like that, wouldn't you?" I taunted. "No, I wasn't arrested, and I wasn't charged because I didn't do anything. I met with Detective Highmore because he had more questions."

"We have a photograph of you in handcuffs."

Who took that damn picture? "I was not arrested, Jeff."

"What were they questioning you about? Was it a false arrest? We could do a story on that."

"No, it was not a false arrest. I was *not* arrested, Jeff!" I threw my hands into the air as I lifted my face into the air. "I was not arrested!" I shouted so that everyone else listening could hear. "I was detained to answer a few questions."

I turned around and glared at Jeff. "You do know what detained means, right? Or do I need to explain that too?"

"Of course, I know what detained means, Maggie."

"Well, that's good," I said sassily. "I was brought in to answer a few more questions about the robbery. Something got distorted, and I had to clear it up. It was all a misunderstanding."

"What was the misunderstanding?"

I tugged my bottom lip under my teeth and glanced away. "I can't tell you."

"What the hell are you talking about, Maggie," he screamed. "Why can't you tell me? This is a newspaper, goddamn it! We report the news! You were smack-dab in the center of the biggest story we've had in months, and you refuse to talk about it. Do you know what this could do for your career?"

I burst to my feet and got in his face. "And I told you that I was not going to talk about that because it could screw up the chances of those dirtbags being prosecuted. I'm a witness, a victim in this case. I cannot give the details until after the hearing. I could influence potential jurors."

He shifted back, glaring down at me. "So what the hell have you been working on? I know for a fact that you haven't been watching over your column. You have over a hundred comments online that haven't been answered, which is bad even for you. You're slacking on your duties; I should fire you."

"Then fire me, Jeff! I told you I was working on a story."

"What story?" He put his finger into my face, "And you better not tell me it has anything to do with politics." I tried not to wince, and he glared at me with bulging brown eyes. "I told you that unless you did this article about the robbery, you weren't getting near the news desk with a ten-foot pole."

I straightened my spine and rolled back my shoulders. "You know what, Jeff? You will not dictate what kind of articles I am going to write anymore."

"Of course I can, I'm your boss. Or did you forget that, Maggie?"

"Oh, I did not forget that you are in charge of some people, but as for being my boss, you are *not* my boss anymore. I quit!"

He shifted back as if I had slapped him—I should have. A moment later, he began to laugh. "You quit? Where do you think you're going to find a job, Maggie? Do you think anyone else around here is going to hire you? Not a chance in hell."

"Don't worry your elephant-ass-head about me," I snapped at him before I turned back to my desk and started collecting my possessions.

"My what?" Jeff sputtered. "What are you doing?"

"I just told you I quit. I'm gathering my stuff, and then I'm out of here."

"But you have a column to finish!" he seethed, and the vein in his temple began to bulge. The man was going to have a heart attack right here if he didn't calm down. "You can't walk out in the middle of a series."

"You wanna watch me?" I snapped.

"Maggie, you didn't give your two weeks' notice."

"I think you'll live."

"It won't look good, you just walking out of here like this. It will only be harder for you to get a job."

I laughed. "Like you are worried about me getting a job. Give me a break, Jeff."

"Fine, I'll accept your resignation, but you have to finish your series at the very least. It's doing well for the paper, and we can't just stop it in the middle."

"Alright, I'll finish the series, but only because I already have them written," I told him as I opened one of my drawers and started digging through it for my personal items.

"Then what are you doing? If you're going to stay until you finish that, why are you still packing?"

"Because I can do that from home, Jeff. I do not need to be here. I will send the rest of my columns to you tomorrow, and then I'll oversee them, but then I'm done. So find yourself someone else to write stupid romance advice that doesn't work!"

He grew quiet for a moment, and when I peered his way, he had his eyes closed. That was when I noticed that Jessica was still squashed between us, her chair pushed back as far as it could get in my little cubby, her eyes wide with excitement. The only thing missing was a bucket of popcorn in her lap.

"Jeff, please move so Jessica can get back to her desk."

He startled like he hadn't even seen her, and his cheeks started to pinken. He stepped out of the way, looked at me and opened his mouth as if to speak, and then turned and walked away, shaking his head.

"I can't believe you just quit," Jessica said as she rolled herself backward toward the aisle. "That was awesome. I wish I could do that. What are you going to do now?"

"I already have another stick in the fire. I'll let you know how it pans out soon," I told her as I went back to packing my things. Maybe I should have been more upset over the fact that

I'd just quit my job. The problem was, I wasn't. In fact, I was trying really hard not to break out in song and start dancing.

A few people stopped by, said a few words, wished me well, and then went about their business. Forty minutes later, I was carrying my copy paper box filled with my favorite pens, a couple of pictures, some files, notebooks, and an eclectic assortment of bobbleheads that people had given me. I'd return my ID badge once I was officially done with my column, just in case I needed to come back for some reason.

On the street, I paused and looked back at the building. I'd had big dreams when I started here a few years ago. I knew it would be hard starting over, but I had been excited about the future. That future hadn't taken me very far, or in the right direction, but I had a feeling that this one would—maybe, hopefully—oh, my god! I just quit my job!

I turned slowly, struck by the sudden decision, and began to walk away. What the heck did I just do? I know it wasn't a great job, but it had been a paycheck—a little paycheck—and insurance. It had been health insurance! Holy crap! I was getting close to forty. Wasn't that when your body starting going to hell? Wasn't that when I was going to need my medical insurance the most?

The whole way home I was trying to keep from panicking, and I was just pulling into my driveway when I got a phone call from Jake.

"Hey, Maggie, how are you?"

"Hi, Jake, I'm doing alright. What can I do for you?"

"Well, I've talked at length to Trevor, Greg, and Alex." He sighed loudly.

I gnawed on my bottom lip as he paused, a bad feeling growing in my gut. "And?"

"And I'm not sure if it's going to work out, at least right now."

My entire body went stiff. "What? I thought I had passed everything. I thought that you were on board with this."

"I am Maggie, or I was. I love the idea of having a reporter along for the ride, but this might not be the right time."

I clamped my eyes closed, telling myself that I was not going to cry about this. "Did Greg talk you out of it? Is that what happened?"

"No, Maggie, that's not it."

"Then why not? You're the one that thought this was such a great idea. What has changed?"

"I still think it's a great idea; I just don't think now is the time."

I heard a woman's voice on the other end of the line. "Look, I'll talk to you soon, Maggie. I have to take another call."

"Okay—" I started to say, and the phone went dead. I glared at the phone, and the urge to cover my face and sob tore through me, but I forced myself to get out of the car and go inside.

I pushed it all to the side and started dinner. With the chicken in the oven, the pasta cooking, and the veggies ready to warm, I signed on to my computer and started reading the comments on my column.

Jeff was right, I did have a ton of comments, and I had barely scratched the surface when my mother arrived home. I watched the aide bring her halfway to the door and then wait for her to get inside.

I was about to check on her when she stepped into the kitchen. "Something smells good."

"Chicken and pasta. How was your day?"

Her lips puckered as she contemplated that. "I think it was a good day."

"I'm glad to hear that." She seemed to know who I was today, and we had small talk over dinner, and then she helped me clean up. She was heading up to her room to watch her favorite show when Heather rang the bell.

"Come on in. What do you want to drink? Beer, wine, or tequila?"

"Holy crap! Are you offering tequila? You only do that when shit has really gone off the rails."

I snorted and reached into the cabinet where I kept the bottle. "Oh, yeah. I'm offering tequila. Now, let me see if I can get this all correct. A few days ago, I ran into my high school sweetheart, who, by the way, is more gorgeous than he was at nineteen—if that is possible. Then I was held captive by two psychos, and luckily freed after about an hour."

I retrieved two shot glasses and set them on the counter with a bang. "Then I argued with my ex after I got offered a position and was then handcuffed—not in a good way—dragged to the police station and accused of being involved in the earlier robbery. But before that, I had a dead rat delivered to my house, from only God knows who. Then after the police station, I had incredible sex with my ex right here in the kitchen before we got into another massive fight."

Heather's eyes were wide, and she shot a quick look around the kitchen as I continued. "Today I was fired from my job—or I quit—I'm not sure which one happened first, and then I lost the other position I'd been offered—probably because I'd had sex with my ex. Plus, Mom is changing daily, and I never know who is coming into my house each evening."

I poured tequila into the shot glass and pushed one toward her. Her mouth still hung open, but she lifted the glass to her lips, threw it back, and then set it down. "Start with the sex, and then you can explain everything else."

The doorbell rang again. "I swear to god, this house has become Grand Central Station." I tossed back my shot and then went to answer the door. As I approached it, I hesitated. What if it was another delivery person and they brought me another rodent? I peered anxiously around the curtain and saw it was Greg.

Without thought, I ripped open the door. "You have some nerve showing up here."

"Whoa, back down, tiger. I came over to explain and apologize."

I glared at him. "I'm not in the mood for this tonight, Greg. I've had a hell of a day." I turned and walked away from the door and back to the kitchen. I heard the door close and his footsteps following. I poured myself another shot and threw it down the hatch before I glanced between Heather and Greg.

"Greg, Heather. Heather, Greg." I poured another shot as Heather leaned toward me, lowering her voice in a stage whisper.

"Is this the ex?"

"Yep," I muttered.

Heather turned and looked him up and down, and Greg shifted slightly as he if were uncomfortable with her scrutiny. He glanced at the counter, noting the shot glasses and tequila. "Hello, Heather. I'm sorry. I didn't mean to interrupt your girls' night. I can hang out in the other room until you guys are done."

"Oh, no, please stay," I told him and grinned. "Go ahead and apologize, might as well do it in front of Heather. It will save me from having to explain it to her later."

CHAPTER TWENTY-FIVE

GREGORY

*W*e all gathered in the conference room to discuss the op. Even though I wasn't going, I was still part of the discussion. The private cargo plane that was transporting the supplies was next Saturday. It would leave on Monday. The travel time was going to be about thirty hours, with two stops for refueling and changing pilots. It should take two days to transport the supplies if everything was in place and working in their favor, a day there to make sure everything was okay and help unpack things, then another two days to return to the airport. The trip would finish with a commercial flight back to the US that would take them another thirty-six hours with layovers.

If things went on schedule, they would be back in ten days.

"You sure you don't want to go, Greg? I can hang back here at the office," Mike said.

"Nope, I'm staying back."

"Just can't trust yourself around her, can you?" Trevor joked.

"She has nothing to do with this," I replied as I leaned back in my seat and laced my fingers over my stomach.

"She has everything to do with this," Alex said, pointing a

finger at me. "But I get it. If it wasn't for having Lexi in my life, I might have been interested."

"I'm not seeing anyone," Harv said with a wide grin.

"Keep your fucking hands off of Maggie," I growled, and everyone laughed.

"Yeah, guys, keep your hands off her; he has already called dibs." Trevor smirked my way.

"What the hell does that mean?"

"It means, you've already tapped that. Maggie told me all about it."

"She did not!" I spouted abruptly and then laughed.

"Oh, yeah, she did!"

The guys all busted my balls for a few minutes, and the more I tried to deny it, the harder they beat on me.

Finally, Jake wrangled them back in. "Alright, guys, we all know she's off the market, and Blaire over there can deny it all he wants. I will watch out for her."

The door opened, and Alice poked her head into the room. She was in a much better mood now, and I wondered if Jake had finally apologized to her. "Gregory, there is a detective here to speak with you."

Trevor started laughing. "You going to be arrested now?"

"No, douchebag, I'm not," I said as I got to my feet. "I'll be right back."

In the entry, Det. Highmore was waiting, and we shook hands. "Do you have someplace that we can talk privately?"

"Yeah, sure, come on this way. Alice, if they finish, let Alex know that I'm using his office for a few."

"You got it," Alice called out cheerily. Damn, whatever Jake did for her must have been fantastic. She was like a different woman.

I closed the door behind the detective and told him to have a seat as I rounded the desk. "What's up? Did you guys catch Len?"

"Not yet, but we discovered some rather disturbing news."

"Yeah, what's that?"

"Len and his cousin owed money to a cartel, quite a lot of money, and that robbery was a last-ditch effort to try to settle the debt."

"Damn, did Chuck tell you that?"

He shook his head. "He had told us a little bit, but we put the pieces together after he was killed."

"Wait. What? Chuck's dead?"

"Yeah, the prison says it was suicide, but an inside source says there was a hit put on him."

"So they are looking for Len too, then, huh?"

"It's a little worse than that, Greg."

"What do you mean, it's a little worse than that?"

"They are going after all the hostages."

Every nerve in my spine prickled as I tensed. "What are you talking about?"

"They are targeting all the witnesses. Five of them have already turned up dead."

"What? When?" My stomach dropped to my knees.

"This morning, that's why I'm here. At first, no one connected them, but I happened to walk into a discussion and saw a picture of one of the victims. I had interviewed him, and when I started digging, I realized they had all been in the coffee shop or the jewelry store."

"But how did they know? As far as I know, there hasn't been much press on it. How do they know who was in there?"

He frowned. "I'm pretty sure they paid someone for that information. Right now, we are looking into everyone involved in the case and auditing the files to see how that information was accessed."

"You think it is someone in your department?"

"Sadly, yes."

"So, what are you doing?"

"Right now, we are letting everyone know to be very careful. If others get killed, we might be able to put the rest in a safe house."

"You're going to wait for others to be killed before you do that?"

"Let's hope not, but yes. The bosses think that maybe they only knocked out a few to scare the others into not talking. I disagree, and that's why I'm warning people."

"Shit." I leaned back, rubbing my jaw as I mulled this over. "Hey, did anyone get any weird packages delivered?"

He shook his head. "I don't know, why?"

"Because Maggie had one delivered last night. No label, no return address. A nondescript guy came to the door, asked her name, handed her the box, and then left."

"When was this?"

"Right before your boys showed up to bring her in."

"Why didn't she tell me about that?"

"Because when she came in, she didn't have any idea what was in the box. Trevor and I opened it after she left."

He grew thoughtful. "Okay, I'll have to have officers check with the others, go back and ask family members about the ones that are deceased."

"Alright, what do you want me to do?"

"Keep Maggie safe. She's the only one that can ID Len positively."

"Maggie is supposed to be going out of town in a week for about ten to fourteen days."

"What? No, she needs to stay in town, but stay safe. We have to have her ready to testify at a preliminary to make sure the charges stick. If she even thinks of leaving the area, we'd have to take her into protective custody."

"Can't that wait until she's back? Two weeks isn't that long."

"Yeah, and what if she's hurt while traveling?"

"What if she's killed here?"

"Sounds like you need to keep her safe."

"I thought that was your job?"

"Yeah, well, as I said, they aren't convinced that the deaths are connected. They were all different, some at home, some out. One was a freak car accident, another drowned in a tub."

"What do I need to do?"

"Keep her safe. You work security. You are probably better able to handle this than most cops with your background."

"And in the meantime, what is your police force going to do?"

"Try to find Len and bring him in. See if he'll give up the cartel members for a plea. If he doesn't, we are going to need Maggie to put him behind bars. I'm going to need both of you around."

"Wait!" A thought occurred to me. "I think Len might already be dead."

"Why do you say that?"

"Because remember Len took photographs of all the ID's of the people inside. Then there were the four of us that didn't have ID's, and we were put in the bathroom. Are those other three alive?"

"I'd have to check to confirm, but I think so."

"I think the cartel might have his phone. If they do, then they have all the addresses of the people that were inside. It might not have been someone at your station."

"I'd like to believe that was how it was done. I'll confirm that information; in the meantime, will you be able to watch Maggie?"

I laughed. "She's going to hate it, but she's going to be stuck with me for a while. I'll keep her safe. Keep me updated."

"You got it, Greg."

I showed him out and returned to the conference room. "Maggie's not going."

"What?" Jake barked.

"I said, Maggie is not going. There is something bigger going on than a dead rat being delivered. Several of the other witnesses are mysteriously dead. That dead rat last night, Trevor, might have been a warning."

"Shit, but wouldn't it be better if she was out of the country?" Alex asked.

I shook my head. "Yeah, probably, but he said that if she tries to leave the country, they will take her into protective custody. They need her to stay put to be able to ID Len when they find him. Although I have a feeling that he's already dead."

I went on to explain to them my thoughts and what the detective had asked me to do. "So, Jake, you need to tell Maggie she can't go, but don't tell her why. If she knows what is going on, I'm not sure what she will do."

"And you're going to be protecting her?" Harvey asked.

"Yeah, I don't think I have a choice in the matter," I muttered.

"You could go on the trip in my place, and I'll watch Maggie," Mike said, and I nailed him with a hard look.

"Over my dead body!" I hissed his way, and everyone laughed.

"Yeah, that's what I thought." Mike smirked.

That's why a few hours later, I was pulling up in front of Maggie's house and carrying a backpack with me. I had a feeling that Maggie was going to balk at this, but I wasn't going to give her much choice.

She was in an Alice mood when she answered the door, and I wondered what the best way was to calm her down. I followed her back to the kitchen and found another woman sitting on a stool at the counter.

"Greg, Heather. Heather, Greg," Maggie said, and her friend leaned forward.

"Is this the ex?"

"Yep," Maggie replied dryly.

Her friend turned and checked me out. I needed to figure

out how to talk to Maggie without her friend here, but I had a feeling that was going to be harder than it should be.

"Hello, Heather. I'm sorry. I didn't mean to interrupt your girls' night. I can hang out in the other room until you guys are done."

"Oh, no, please stay. Go ahead and apologize, might as well do it in front of Heather. It will save me from having to explain it to her later."

I glanced at her friend and then focused on Maggie as I shifted forward slightly and set my backpack on the counter. "Maggie, this is not something that your friend needs to be involved in. This is between us."

"She's my best friend; I tell her everything."

"You always did like to share everything with your friends," I retorted. "But for her safety, you need to keep this quiet."

Maggie laughed as she put the shot glass to her lips again. "Her safety? Why? You planning on breaking her heart too?"

"Maggie, cut it out. This is not about us. This is about the incident and the rat."

"What did you find out?" She glanced at my backpack momentarily before she poured herself another shot.

"We can talk about it after Heather leaves."

"I don't want her to leave," Maggie said. "It's not good for the two of us to be alone together."

Yeah, no shit! "Heather, I'm sorry to butt in here, but I really do need to speak to Maggie, and it would be safer for you not to be around her right now."

Heather studied me and started to get off the stool. "Is she in danger?"

"Yes."

Heather turned to Maggie. "I'm going to go. If he says you are in danger, then I am going to believe him. You can fill me in on everything next time."

"Heather, you don't need to go," Maggie said and glared at me.

"Yeah, I think I might need to leave. I think you two have some things you need to discuss."

"Yeah, like how he talked Jake into not letting me go on this trip!" Maggie raised her voice, pulling her shoulders back. Damn, if that didn't turn me on to see her spun up that way. I had always loved it when she fought back against me when I tried to push her into something.

"I didn't have anything to do with that, Mags."

"Bull—shit!" she yelled. "You had everything to do with that."

Heather went around the counter and hugged Maggie. "Mags, maybe you should slow down on the shots. Listen to what he has to say, and call me later."

Maggie scowled at me over her shoulder the whole time. As Heather stepped away, she glanced at me. "Take care of her."

"I will, Heather."

I walked Heather to the door, and she paused before she stepped out. "Is she really in danger?"

"Yes, very much so."

"Keep her safe, please."

"I will," I told her again, and then Heather was gone.

Maggie was pouring herself another shot when I stepped in, and before she could pick it up to drink it, I snagged it out of her reach and tossed it back. "No more alcohol. I need your head here."

"Why?" She rolled her eyes.

"Maggie, your life is in jeopardy. Five other people who were in the café with us are dead. That rat was a warning that they are coming after you."

She stared at me, and I saw the words shifting through the alcohol haze that was trying to take over her mind. "What?"

I hadn't planned on telling her, but I realized that she needed to know the truth. I stepped closer. "Your life is in danger.

210

Detective Highmore came to see me today; he wants me to stay with you and protect you."

"Stay?" she asked, and her gaze cut back to my backpack. "You mean to stay, as in sleep here?"

"As in be beside you and make sure you are safe, Maggie."

Maggie practically jumped back a foot. "There is no way in hell that I am going to let you sleep in this house! Not after you just ruined my career!"

CHAPTER TWENTY-SIX

MAGGIE

"*R*uined your career? What the hell are you talking about, woman? I'm trying to save your life, not ruin your career. One has nothing to do with the other!"

I lunged forward, grabbing his shirt and practically smashing my nose into his. "I'll have you know that you did totally ruin my career. I quit my job at the paper! I was going to be working for your company, and now I'm banned from that! It's all your fault!"

I saw the desire in his eyes, witnessed his pupils dilate, his nose flare. I was turning him on, and strangely enough, I was totally turned on myself. If I didn't watch myself, I'd end up naked and back on the counter again. Oh, please!

Greg took me by the shoulders and urged me back. "Maggie, Jake isn't letting you go because the police don't want you to leave the area right now. This has nothing to do with me or him."

I frowned. "Bullshit!"

"I'm serious, Maggie. Detective Highmore came to see me this afternoon. He told me what's been going on. He said that you need to stay in town because you are the only eyewitness that can ID Len. When they find him, they are going to need you pretty quickly for the preliminary hearing."

"Are you trying to tell me that Chuck won't testify against him? I thought they were going to try and get Chuck to flip on Len."

Greg's eyes shifted off to the side, and he sighed as his chin dropped to his chest momentarily. Whatever was about to come out of his mouth was not good. "Chuck is dead."

"What?" My voice squeaked, and suddenly, the anger I had at Greg went up in smoke, and I was thankful that he was still holding my shoulders. "What do you mean, he's dead? And wait, did you say other people were dead too?"

The alcohol was hiding some of his words, but I fought to clear the fog out of my mind.

"Yeah, look, let me get you a glass of water, check the house real quick, and then I'll explain."

"Check the house for what?" My voice began to rise again, and he pursed his lips.

"Maggie, get yourself a glass of water and have a seat. I just want to check the doors. Is your mom home?"

"Yes."

"Alright, what is the code to your alarm?"

"Why?"

"Because I want to arm it."

I told him the code and watched him walk out of the kitchen and down the hall toward the front door. A moment later, I heard the alarm pad beeping, and then his footsteps echoed back to me as they grew further away. I shivered. Who was dead? Was it a coincidence? Or was it all related?

I did as Greg told me to do and poured myself a glass of water, along with one for him, and set them both on the table. I was about to sit down when I glanced up at the window and then rushed around the table and yanked the curtains closed.

My heart thudded a little harder as adrenaline rushed

through my veins and began to burn the alcohol off. Why had I drunk all those shots? Why? Oh, because I'd been planning on wallowing in the misery caused by my high school sweetheart.

I put my face in my hands and heard Greg arrive back in the kitchen. "Oh, good, you closed the shades. I did that in the rest of the house too."

"Sit down and explain what the hell is going on, Greg." I lifted my face out of my hands as he took a seat. "You said other people died. Who died, and how?"

"Five right now, I don't know who, but they were all at the café. The detective said that Chuck supposedly committed suicide in jail, but an informant said it was a hit, and there were hits out on everyone who was there that day."

"Why? Why would Len want to kill all of us? Just to stay out of jail? Doesn't he know that his sentence is just going to get longer and longer until he rots in a cell?"

"I don't think it's Len that is responsible for the killings. I have a feeling that Len might already be dead."

"What?" I stared at him, trying to figure out what the hell he was talking about. "If Len is dead, then why do they want the rest of us dead?"

"Because Len was involved with a cartel, and he owed them big money. He did the jewelry heist to try and square things up."

"Only the jewelry heist went wrong."

"Yeah, and I'm pretty sure the cartel is trying to clean up loose ends, which means everyone who was there that day."

"But we don't know anything about them. We don't even know for sure that it is the cartel that is killing people. Do we?"

"You're right, we don't, but they also don't know if Len or Chuck said anything in the café about what they were doing or who it was for. They'd want to silence everyone to keep it all quiet."

"Did the detective say that?"

He shook his head. "No, that's my theory."

I lifted my glass and paused. "Yeah, well, I don't like your theory."

"I know," he said, and for a few minutes, we were quiet. "Jake only canceled you going because of what is going on right now. If you had tried to leave, the police would have taken you into custody so that they knew where you were for the preliminary hearing."

"They would have arrested me to keep me safe?"

"They would have put you into protective custody. I figured that you'd rather put up with me for a little while than have to do that. I wasn't sure what would have happened to your mother if that had happened."

I rubbed my hands over my face; it was still tingling from the alcohol. "Oh, my god! My mother! What if they do something to hurt her?"

"We can protect her, Maggie, but she's going to need to stay here in the house with us."

"What if I can get her moved into the nursing home early? I was already making plans to have her in there while I was traveling. A few days early shouldn't hurt. Maybe it will protect her."

"It might, especially if they don't know about her, but they probably already know about her."

"What do you think I should do?"

"I can't answer that, Mags. That has to be your choice."

I grabbed Greg's hand. "Greg, I can't have her hurt in this. I don't think she should be here."

"Then tomorrow, let's see if we can get her moved into the nursing home."

"Okay, but what are we going to do?"

"You and me?"

"Yeah."

"We're going to hang out, stay out of trouble, and see if the cops find this guy."

I laughed. "You know, I expected you to say that we were going to come up with a plan and find these people."

Greg chuckled. "No, Maggie, my days of looking for trouble are over. I just want to make sure you are safe. Plus, I think I owe you an apology."

I peaked a brow. "You owe me an apology? For what?"

"For what I said last night, for how I treated you. I should never have said or done any of that."

I didn't want him to regret last night. Yeah, he said a few things that had hurt, but the sex had been incredible. So incredible, I was already wondering if we might be able to do a little more of it while we were stuck here at my house. I pushed away from the table and stood. "You don't need to apologize for that, Greg."

I started to step away, and he grabbed my wrist. "I do, Maggie. You deserved better than that. I treated you harshly, practically forced myself on you, and then verbally attacked you."

I threw my head back and laughed. "Did you not notice that I was a willing participant, Greg? You hardly had to force anything."

"It shouldn't have happened, Maggie."

I cocked my head, searching his face for a sign of a lie, but I didn't see one. He actually believed that it shouldn't have happened. I stepped around him and grabbed the back of the chair so I could shift it.

"What are you doing?" he asked, but before he could figure it out, I was climbing onto his lap, our chests almost touching as I stared into his surprised blue eyes. "Maggie, get off my lap."

"No. You didn't force anything last night, Greg. I wanted you as much as you wanted me. I still do."

He swallowed, and I watched his Adam's apple bounce. I ran my hands over his shoulders, brushing my fingers against the short hair at the nape of his neck. "Maggie, get off my lap."

"Why? You want me, Greg. I know you do."

"Of course, I want you, Maggie, but this isn't a good idea."

"Why is that? Because you can't give me what I want?" I leaned forward, resting my chest to his, and brought my mouth close to his ear. "You can give me what I want, Gregory."

"Maggie, please get off my lap." His voice was hoarse as if he were struggling.

I nipped at his ear, then flicked the tip with my tongue, and his hands spanned the sides of my waist. "I want this, Greg. I want you."

"I'm going to ask you one more time, Maggie. Please get off my lap."

I kissed along his jaw, then back to his ear, and down his neck as I pulled his face to the side. He sucked in a sharp breath, and his hands tightened on my sides as he shifted his hips up against me, holding me tightly against him.

"Maggie." His voice was slightly strangled, and I clamped my teeth down on his neck. A second later, my feet were touching the floor as he stood and shoved me away. "No! Maggie, I told you I couldn't give you what you wanted! This is not going to happen again. It was a mistake to have let it happen last night."

"You are so full of shit, Greg! I'm tired of hearing that you can't give me what I want. You don't even know what the hell I want!"

"Yeah, well, whatever it is, I can't give it to you."

I growled my frustration as I spun away from him. "I'm going to bed. There is a blanket on the back of the sofa. You can sleep there."

He grabbed my arm and pulled me to a stop, and I was hoping that it was to say he was wrong, and he did want me. "You'll have to work from home. You won't be able to go into the paper."

I laughed, and it was a bit hysterical sounding even to my own ears. I think part of it was fueled by unrequited desire, the other, fear of what was happening in my life. "Work? Ha! I don't have a job anymore. I quit today, remember? Good night, Greg."

I yanked my arm out of his grip before he could say another word and rushed from the room. Let him turn the rest of the lights off. I needed to put distance between us as tears began to fill my eyes.

In my room, I went straight to the bathroom and turned on the shower. As I stripped off my clothes, the tears began to fall, but it wasn't until I was under the stream of water that I bowed my head and sobbed into my hands.

My life spun around in my mind, twisting and twirling like a tornado about to unleash fury. People had been killed; who was next? The rat was a warning; was I next? I wanted Greg with every ounce of my soul, but he pushed me away. My mother— my mother—if something happened to her because of me! I shuddered, even though the water was hot. Now I didn't have a job, but that was almost the least of my worries. If I didn't have a life, what good would a job do?

I stood in the shower and cried for a few minutes. I never was a huge crier. If I got to that point, and it was rare, I'd explode, sob for a few minutes, and then suck it back up. I washed and conditioned my hair, shaved my legs, and then got out and did my nightly moisturizing routine on my face. Being almost forty, I was starting to see fine lines creeping up around my eyes.

As I rubbed in my moisturizer, Greg's face came to mind, and the many creases around his eyes. His years of being out in the sun, playing havoc with his skin. Unlike mine, which irritated me, his were attractive, and more than once, I'd noted them when he laughed or smiled.

Did he notice mine? Did he care? What did he think that I really wanted? Was he talking about marriage? Kids? My career? I honestly didn't have any idea what it was that he thought I wanted. Maybe I could find a way to ask him. Not tonight, but maybe tomorrow when the sun was up and I wasn't still buzzing.

I climbed in bed, rolling to my side and trying not to think about the man downstairs. What was he doing? Was he lying there thinking of me? Was he thinking about someone else? Wait, was he involved with someone else? Was that why he didn't want to get involved with me? Is that why he said that it had been a mistake?

Maybe that was the reason. Maybe Greg was seeing someone, and my showing up in his life had thrown him off-kilter a bit. I smiled to myself as I closed my eyes.

When Greg and I were young, there wasn't a girl around that could have gotten him away from me. I had never once worried about him cheating on me. I knew without a doubt that I was his everything, which is why it had hurt like hell to be replaced by Uncle Sam.

But Greg was back, and if he were with someone else, I'd find a way to remind him that I was the girl he loved and that he could still love me.

CHAPTER TWENTY-SEVEN

GREGORY

*W*ell, fuck! I put my hands on my hips and scowled at the floor after Maggie raced from the room. The woman had no clue what she did to me, and pushing her away from me had been hard as hell.

When this was over, the two of us needed to sit down and discuss this. I had to make Maggie realize that I wasn't good enough for her and that she deserved better. She needed a husband who could cater to her every whim, fill her house with children.

She sure as hell didn't need a guy who was going to be gone half the time and who had no interest in having children—zilch, zero, none! It wasn't that I didn't like kids, I did. I just couldn't imagine bringing a kid into this fucked-up world. Besides, I was a selfish son of a bitch and wanted to do what I wanted when I wanted it.

That's one of the reasons I hadn't been in a meaningful relationship since I was nineteen. A few dates with a woman and they were already talking about the future. They would start talking about how fun it would be to take vacations and spend all kinds of time together. Didn't they know that I just wanted to have a few laughs, screw them, and then go? I didn't want to think about vacations or when I needed to meet parents. And bullshit chatter with friends—um, no!

My idea of a vacation was to sleep for days, maybe sit on my buddy's boat and fish for hours while I drank one beer after the next and then slept some more. Maybe having a hot chick with me who liked to get on her knees would be okay for a few days, but no longer than that. I sure didn't want domestic bliss and responsibility. I was almost forty, and I didn't see that changing any time soon. Call me a crass asshole, I didn't care. I was who I was.

I grabbed a beer out of the fridge and went around to double-check the windows and doors again, turning a few lights off on my way. I dropped my backpack on the floor next to the couch and toed off my shoes. Before I sat down, I removed the gun from my inner waistband holster and set it on the table.

I stared at the stairs, wondering if I should go up and apologize to Maggie. *Yeah, right!* My inner demon snickered. *You only want to go up there so you can jump in bed with her. Come on, let's go! I'm up for it, and so are you.*

I tore my eyes from the stairs. The last thing I was going to do was listen to that dark, twisted part of myself. Nope. Maggie deserved better. Instead, I messed around with my phone, answered an email, and drank the beer. About an hour later, I was dozing off when a soft noise had my eyes flashing open. Every part of my body remained still, except for my hand. That tightened around the gun under the pillow behind my head.

I tried to search the shadows as I heard another sound—a shuffle, maybe? Was that Maggie? Her mother? A mouse? Or was someone else in the house? Another noise outside the window had me springing upright, the hair on the back of my neck rising as I listened.

There was a scuffing noise down the hall. Had someone gotten past me? Did I check the windows in the kitchen? I was on my feet, moving a second later. I peered around the corner toward the kitchen. The hallway was empty, the light from outside casting a long shadow from the front door toward the kitchen. Another sound came from the kitchen and I rounded the corner, my gun out in front of me as I walked silently on my bare feet.

I paused at the entrance to the kitchen and listened. It was quiet for a moment, and then the sound of something touching down on the counter. I peeked around the corner. Maggie stood on the other side of the room, bathed in light from the water dispenser on the front of the fridge. I released the tense breath I'd been holding and let the gun fall to my side as I stepped around the corner.

I took two steps before I froze again, and Maggie almost knocked her glass over. A loud sound right outside the window had her spinning toward it and stepping backward. If I didn't do something quick, she was going to walk right into me.

I stepped behind her, put my hand over her mouth to stifle the scream that I had no doubt was going to erupt from her mouth, and whispered, "Mags!" into her ear to let her know it was me as I aimed the gun toward the window.

She had sucked in a breath to let loose a scream but didn't when she realized it was me. Instead, she latched on to my arm and pulled it from her mouth as we took another step back in unison.

A cat shrieked outside the window, and then another one, and the hair rose on both our arms, but a moment later, the sounds moved away. It was only animals.

I stepped around Maggie and went to the back window, peeling back the shade carefully and checking the night. One of the cats sat in the middle of her back porch, cleaning itself. Maggie made a squeaking noise behind me that I attributed to the stress.

"It was just a couple of cats," I said, and I turned around and froze.

On the other side of the kitchen, a man held a knife to Maggie's neck. The whites of her eyes glowed as she went up on tiptoe to avoid the blade at her throat. She grasped his wrist as she tried to pull his hand away, panic on her features.

How had that fucker gotten behind me? "Let her go," I said as I pointed the gun at him, and he shifted a little further behind her. "Let. Her. Go."

"You think you can hit me before I slice her throat?" he said, his voice slightly accented, which made sense if he was a hitman for a cartel.

"I have no doubt I can hit you before you do that." Maggie shifted her body. I gave her the merest of glances and a slight nod that I hoped she could see in the dark.

That position that she was in was one that we had just trained her for. Maggie closed her eyes as soon as I shifted my head, and then a split second later, she jerked to the side, leaving his head wide open. I fired one shot, and he went down, taking Maggie with him.

She screamed as she went back and squirmed out of the dead man's grip. I pulled her to her feet. "Go, call 9-1-1," I said as I pushed her behind me and then reached over to turn the lights on.

Maggie looked around my shoulder. "That's the guy that brought me the box!"

"Are you sure?"

She nodded, and I told her again to call the police. I kept the gun on him as I kicked the knife out of his hand and then bent down to check for a pulse. I had little doubt that he would have one; his brains were all over the wall behind him.

Maggie was talking quickly behind me, and then I heard another voice, and I looked up to find Mrs. Valor standing at the foot of the steps, her hand holding the lapels of her robe to her chest. She was staring at the man on the floor, then lifted her eyes to mine. "Life sure has gotten more interesting since you came back to town, Greg."

~

*T*hree hours later, the police were closing the door behind them, and Maggie and her mother were upstairs packing. Det. Highmore was called in. He told us that Len's body was recovered earlier tonight and that the dead guy in the kitchen could directly tie this whole thing to the cartel. He had been on their radar for a while. It could have also put a higher price on our heads, and now we were being moved.

"I don't know," I told Jake. "Or how long."

"Damn it, this couldn't have happened at a worse time."

"I know, I'm sorry."

"Don't worry about it. Keep that woman and her momma safe. We'll cover this. Get back when you can, and if you can keep Alice updated, do that."

"I will; I might be able to work off-site."

"If you can, do that. At least maybe cover emails and shit. Be safe, and tell Maggie I said hello."

"You guys have a safe trip too."

I hung up and found Maggie coming down the stairs with a suitcase, her mother right behind her. Maggie looked a little shell-shocked, her face almost as pale as the medical gauze around her neck, but her mother didn't seem any worse for wear as she stared at the mess down the hallway.

"You okay, Sweetheart?" I asked as I approached her.

She tried to nod but then shook her head. "No, I'm not."

I pulled her into my arms, holding her close to me as I kissed the side of her head. That incident had given me a significant scare. The memory of the knife to her throat was ingrained to the back of my skull. When Maggie had jerked her head to the side, the tip of the blade sliced under her jaw. Luck-ily, it hadn't gone deep and missed any major arteries or muscles. The paramedic that had shown up had put a little skin glue on it and a butterfly bandage and said it would heal without stitches.

"I need to get Mom's medication," she said as she pulled away. Her eyes were downcast as she made her way down the hall and stepped over the mess that was there. The detective said he'd have a cleaning service come in and take care of the biohazard issue. How long would it take to clean from her mind?

Fifteen minutes later, we stood at the door, and Maggie glanced back at her house and shook her head. I walked her and her mother out to my truck while the police officers watched us.

I called Mike on the way back to my place, and he was waiting when we arrived. "Here, I have a laptop and a dispos-able phone for you to use. I'm gonna check the truck for tracking devices, and I'll keep an eye on the ladies while you grab your gear."

"Will only take me a minute; I already have my go-bag ready."

"Take your time." Mike slapped me on the back after handing over a backpack. I hustled into my house and was back out in less than five minutes.

Mike was standing at the passenger side door, talking to Maggie. I tossed my stuff into the back, under the bedcover, and met Mike on the passenger side. Maggie looked whipped, huge circles under her eyes.

"Keys to the place are in the front pocket. Me and the guys are the only ones that know where you'll be. I'll reach out to your detective tomorrow and let him know that if he needs you, he should call me." He held his hand out, palm up. "Your phone."

I gave him my phone and noticed that he had another one in

his other hand. Must have already collected Maggie's. "Thanks for the help, Mike."

"You're welcome. Now get on the road. The truck was free of trackers, and I assume you were watching your six on your way here."

"I was, it was clear."

"Well, then get on the road. You have a hike. My number is on the phone, send me a text when you make it to the cabin."

"I will." I clapped him on the shoulder. "I appreciate it. I owe you."

"Yeah, you do. I am missing out on some serious beauty sleep."

"You need all you can get," I joked as I went around to the drivers' side and climbed in. Maggie still had her window down, and she glanced at me and then Mike as he put his hand on the windowsill.

"You guys take care. I'll talk to you soon."

We said goodbye and got on the road. The drive was over four hours before we bumped down the dirt road to the small cabin. I was surprised that Maggie had stayed awake the whole time. When we arrived, we carried in our gear and the cooler of food that Mike had stowed in the back for us.

The cabin was sparse and tiny, but clean. We got everything inside, and Maggie got her mother situated into the smaller bedroom while I put supplies away. When she finished, she stared at the other bed for a long time before she came to stand in front of me.

"Please do not let me sleep alone tonight."

Her eyes looked haunted and exhausted. I cupped her cheek. "I'll stay with you if you want, Maggie."

She took my hand from her cheek, kissed my palm, and then led me back to the bedroom. She kicked off her pants, snaked her bra out of her sleeve, and then crawled under the covers. While the cops had taken my one gun, I had others, and I set one on the nightstand, removed my pants and shirt, and climbed under the covers after I turned the light off.

Maggie shifted over the mattress to affix herself to my side, and I held her. Neither of us spoke as we lay there, and slowly we both began to relax as sleep edged in on us.

I tried not to think about how good she felt in my arms and tried to focus on the fact that she had almost been killed tonight instead. I wanted to be angry—on edge, alert. But having her head on my chest, her breath brushing over my skin, calmed me in a way I hadn't been since I'd joined the Marines. Not long after she fell asleep, I drifted off myself.

CHAPTER TWENTY-EIGHT

MAGGIE

The entire way to the cabin, I'd replayed the night—over and over again. I'd come down to get a drink of water and had the sudden need to check the windows again myself. Plus, my firearm was in my purse, and my purse was on the kitchen table.

The noise outside scared me but not as much as Greg slapping his hand over my mouth to stop me from screaming. I was just getting over that scare when suddenly another arm banded around my chest, and a shiny blade reflected off the ambient light in the room.

For a moment, I wanted to panic, to meltdown, scream, maybe bawl like a baby, but the recent training exercises that I'd gone through began to flash through my mind. What did you do in this scenario? Ah, yes, get the eye of your help. Let them know you were ready. Don't panic, and then move!

I had felt the blade slice under my chin as he began to fall backward. I didn't think about my injury again until I was on the phone to 9-1-1. When something hit my arm, I looked down and found blood dripping off my chin. I'd turned and called Greg's name.

"It's not as bad as it looks, Maggie. You're going to be alright." He had held me close, kissing my head, and then my mother was in the room, and the cops were there, and we were all separated. The paramedic tended to my wound, and I was questioned. Det. Highmore arrived and asked more questions, and then they were moving the body. I couldn't believe it was the same guy who had brought the dead rat to me. The cops found that he had gained entry through the window in the laundry room.

When Greg finally came to me and told me to go pack, I didn't question it. My mother was already gathering her things, and I was thankful that she was in rare form tonight and lucid.

With everything together, we'd left the house, gone back to Greg's, and watched as Mike went around the truck with a device in his hand. He put some things into the back of the truck, and then asked for my phone right before Greg joined us.

When we had gotten to the cabin, I'd been too tired to think, much less give a crap about where we were.

Now the sun was up, and I was still lying over Greg's chest. His arms wrapped around me tightly, his hand on my hip. Every once in a while, his fingers would twitch. I didn't want him to wake up and move away. I wanted him to keep sleeping for a while so I could enjoy this. Memorize this moment before he disappeared from my life again.

I realized that as much as I might care about Greg, and want to force the issue, he needed to come to me. When he was ready, he would, but I had to stop pushing it and wait. I didn't want him to be with me just because I was forcing him.

"Big sigh," his husky sleep voice said, and I lifted my head.

"Did I sigh? I didn't even realize it."

He chuckled, and his hand rubbed up and down my hip for a moment. I rested my head back down, and his hand continued to move. His hands were rough, and the stark difference between his fingers and the soft skin on my hip was stimulating.

I let my fingers trace slowly over his chest; his hand shifted lower, and he brushed his fingers down over the curve of my buttock, coming sensually close to a spot that was suddenly screaming for his attention. I ran one finger around his nipple and watched it peak. Oh, how I wanted to flick my tongue over it, tease it a bit.

I shifted my knee further over his thigh, boldly moving it higher toward his groin, and he made a croaking noise in his throat. His left hand cupped the underside of my thigh and shifted my leg so that it covered his erection. He moved his hips against my leg, his hard erection making my breath come faster. The hand that had curled around my hip slipped lower, dipping under the edge of my panties, and delicately touching my most sensitive flesh.

I gasped, suddenly needing him to touch more. He brushed his finger along my center, then paused to press his thumb to the little nub as my body quivered. I pressed into his hand, and he rubbed more as he slipped a finger into me and groaned as he realized just how wet I was for him.

He rolled me to my back in a sudden move and kissed me once before he gently kissed my chin and the covering over my injury. He slipped a hand down my rib cage to under my shirt and lifted it to expose my breast. He stared at it for a long moment, and I wondered if he was disappointed they weren't bigger.

A moment later, he murmured, "Fucking perfect," as he took one into his mouth. I arched my back, holding his head to my chest as he suckled my breast and then moved to the other. He pulled at my panties, and I was right there with him, removing mine, and then tugging on his boxers. I yanked my shirt over my head, and Greg reared back and let his gaze drift down my body. One hand slowly followed his perusal, and then he kissed me intensely before his mouth followed the path of his hand.

Greg moved down my stomach, nipping at my hip bones,

running his tongue around my belly button, and then licking right up my center as he spread my legs wide, pushing my knees out, and lifting my ass off the bed so he could cover my sex with his mouth. A finger slipped in and stroked me as he took me higher. A second finger joined the first, and as I was beginning to thrash on the bed as the intensity began to grow, he added a third finger, picking up speed, and I threw my head back as I tried to hold in the scream of ecstasy.

He licked at me, entered me over and over again, and didn't stop until I started to whimper and push his head away. He chuckled as he removed his mouth and fingers, and then before I knew what he was doing, he flipped me to my stomach.

I was a rag doll as he rubbed himself against me, and then he lifted me to my knees, and without hesitation, he plunged forward. I pushed back against him, meeting him in the middle each time as our bodies slammed into one another. He kissed my spine and reached around to touch my bundle of nerves again. I shoved his hand away and replaced it with mine.

He growled behind me, "Yeah, touch yourself, Maggie. Come with me, baby. Come with me."

His command made my touch electric, and it didn't take long for me to stop holding back. In a small part of my brain, I was aware that my mother was under the roof with us, and that if she were awake, she would probably be pretty confused. I didn't need to add scared by the animalistic sounds after last night.

I buried my face into the mattress to muffle the noises, and right after I came, Greg did too. His fingers gripped my hips so hard I wondered if I would have bruises, but I didn't care. I would welcome any mark this man left on me, including the injuries I would have on my heart after he left me again. It was worth it.

Greg stopped moving and curled around my body, pulling

me with him as he went to his side on the mattress and kissed the back of my neck. "Jesus, woman."

I laughed. "Is that a good Jesus, or bad?"

He went up on an elbow and leaned over me, pulling my face toward his. "That was an amazing Jesus. You are so gorgeous, Maggie, and your body, damn, I'm barely done, and I'm almost ready to go again."

I stared at him, wondering if he was saying that because we'd had sex or because he really thought that.

"Yeah, well, your body is pretty fine too for a man who is almost forty."

He laughed and lay back down. "You know that when I came in here last night, this was not what I intended to happen."

"I know," I replied softly.

"You aren't upset?"

"No, why would I be? Not sure if you noticed it or not, but I happen to enjoy sex."

"I just didn't want you to think I was using you."

I shifted to look at him. "Are you?"

"What?"

"Using me?"

His brows lowered, and his forehead lined. "No, Maggie. I care about you."

I nodded and then sat up and threw my legs over the side of the bed as I found my t-shirt and pulled it over my head. I needed to put space between us before he started to apologize and say it should never have happened.

"Maggie, I have a question I need to ask you. I probably should have asked you earlier. No, I definitely should have asked you earlier."

"What?" I threw him a look over my shoulder.

"Are you on birth control? We've had sex twice, and both times have kind of been spur of the moment."

I started to laugh as I collected my underwear off the floor.

"Don't worry, Greg. I'm not going to rope you in with an unwanted pregnancy."

"So, you're on birth control?"

I retrieved my jeans and stuffed my foot into one leg, wondering what he was going to say when I finally answered him. Maybe he wouldn't see me as such a perfect person now. "No."

"You're not? Maggie, shit, you should have said something." He sat up in bed, pulling the sheet over his waist.

"Oh, relax, Greg. I won't get pregnant. It's not possible."

"What do you mean, it's not possible?"

I turned to stare at him. "To be honest, that's none of your business. All you need to know is that it's not possible."

"Maggie—"

I put my hand up to stop him. "Greg, stop. You've already told me that you aren't interested in a relationship with me, so you don't have the right to ask me personal questions. We had sex twice. It was awesome, both times, but you're right. That's all it is, just sex."

I turned for the door as my knees began to buckle. I barely made it out the door before I leaned back against it and put my hand over my face.

I don't think I had ever lied so much in my life. It was so much more than sex. It was like his body, his mind, knew exactly what to do to mine to please it. Like it was built for mine, and mine alone.

Suddenly, a sound caught my attention, and I lifted my head. The front door was open. I glanced around quickly and found the coffeemaker was not only on, but almost full. I moved toward the front door and heard a squeak. I peered out, seeing my mother sitting on the far end of the porch, rocking on an old porch swing, a blanket over her shoulders and a coffee mug in her hands.

I went to pour myself a cup and then joined her outside. "Good morning. How are you today?"

She grinned at me from behind her mug. That alone was odd because she had stopped drinking coffee a few years ago. Every once in awhile, she'd pour herself a cup, but not often. "I'm probably not as good as you are."

I felt my cheeks begin to warm. "I don't know what you're talking about."

"Oh, please, Maggie. The walls in this cabin are not thick in the slightest. Made me rather jealous."

Maybe I should have kicked Greg out of the bedroom and let him come out here first.

"Yeah, well, don't be."

"Why is that?"

"Because we were just working off stress."

"I think it's more than that, Maggie. I know that you and Greg never were able to keep your hands off one another." She pursed her lips. "I'm a bit confused about how and when he came back into your life, and why we are here. Wherever we are."

I chuckled. "You don't remember last night?"

"Everything is a muddled mess in my mind, Maggie. Nothing makes sense." She looked so sad, and I went to sit beside her.

"I know it doesn't make much sense, Mom. I wish I could fix it, fix you, and make you better."

"Oh, Maggie, I know, but this is not your problem. Tell me, Maggie, how often am I lucid?" She turned to me. "Truthfully."

"Not very often, Mom. Sometimes you can go for a week or two without knowing where or who you are, and sometimes you are good for a few hours. It has been a long time since you were with me for a full day."

She sighed and sipped her coffee. "Yeah, I think I knew that."

"It's okay, Mom. You still have years ahead of you."

"Don't bullshit me, Maggie." I laughed. "Why is Greg back? Did he finally come back for you? I knew one day he would, and he'd tell you that he still loved you."

"No, that's not it, Mom. We just ran into each other." The door opened, and Greg stepped out, a mug in his hands as he turned toward me. For a long moment, we stared at one another, and then he yanked his gaze to my mother.

"Mrs. Valor, how are you today?"

"I'm fine, Greg, but I'm starving. I'm sure you two worked up an appetite too."

His eyes widened, and I saw the blush stealing up his neck. "Well, let me see what I can find to make for breakfast."

He disappeared into the house, and my mother turned to me. "You are blind if you do not see how much that man loves you, Maggie Sue Valor."

CHAPTER TWENTY-NINE

GREGORY

The fuck that was just sex. I stared at the closed door. How could Maggie say that was just sex? I flopped back on the bed and stared at the ceiling as my fist hammered the mattress beside me in frustration. Damn, that woman. I swear she was a vixen; her sweet little body just had to touch mine to inflame it, and I couldn't think straight.

What did Maggie mean she couldn't get pregnant? I should be happy to hear that. We could have all the sex we wanted and not need to worry about using anything. Frustratingly, I wasn't pleased about that. I didn't like the idea that Maggie couldn't have children. Had she been pregnant before? Had some random complications ruined her pregnancy and any chance of having kids? That thought stabbed through my chest, and I threw the sheet back and got out of bed.

After I was dressed, I slipped into the bathroom and then poured myself a coffee. I could see Maggie and her mom on the swing talking, and I joined them on the porch. The moment I stepped out the door, all I wanted to do was drop to my knees in front of Maggie and beg her to explain why she couldn't have kids. Why did that bother me so damn much?

Instead, I rushed my sorry ass back inside, mortified that her mother seemed to know we'd had sex and started rummaging around in the kitchen for something to fix. Mike came here quite often, so there was an excellent selection of canned and boxed goods. A peek in the fridge showed eggs, bacon, a pound of hamburger, cream, orange juice, a few condiments that wouldn't spoil anytime soon, and the bottom shelf was stocked with beer. I wondered if it would look bad if I downed a couple of those real quick.

The door opened, and I peered back to find Mrs. Valor stepping inside. "Did you sleep alright?" I asked her as she went to the coffeemaker and began to pour more.

"Yes, I slept better than I expected to." She turned and glanced around the cabin. "This is a cute cabin; Maggie's father would have loved it here. The lake is beautiful."

"It is nice. I've come up here a couple of times with Mike."

"It was kind of him to allow you to borrow this." She studied me carefully, and it began to make me very uneasy.

"Would you prefer eggs or pancakes for breakfast?"

"I'd prefer you to tell me what you are doing with my daughter."

I turned to face her. "Excuse me, Mrs. Valor?"

"Oh, cut the Mrs. Valor crap, Greg. You have known me for over twenty years. I think by now you can call me Liz and you can be straight with me. You broke Maggie's heart when you went away. I understood why you did it, and part of me appreciated that you did it. I hated the thought of her sitting around, waiting for you to come back and not living her life."

"That's why I ended it, Liz. I wanted Maggie to have a good life and not wait for me. I knew I wanted to do twenty years in the military, and I didn't want to put her through that."

"And now? What do you want with Maggie?"

I slipped into a chair at the table. "To be honest, Liz, I don't know. I didn't expect to see Maggie again. I thought she was living in Atlanta, and I assumed she was happily married with a horde of kids."

She dropped her head and put her chin to her chest. "Yeah, well, things don't always go the way you want them too." She pulled the chair out across from me and took a seat.

"Yeah." I chuckled. "I am very aware of that."

"Do you love Maggie?"

"Liz, I haven't seen Maggie in nineteen years. I care about her; I will always care about her, but I can't say that I love her." I paused. "What I can tell you is that Maggie might be the only woman I have ever loved. There has never been anyone like her in my life since I walked away from her. Not one serious relationship."

"Do you want a relationship?"

"No," I said immediately, and then my eyes strayed to the door. "I don't know."

"Well, Greg, I can only give you my opinion. I think there is a reason that you never got involved with another woman. I think that you gave Maggie your heart when you were seventeen years old, and you never took it back. I think that Maggie tried to go on with her life, but she couldn't because she was still holding out hope that one day you might come back."

"Liz, I can't give her what she deserves."

"Deserves? Gregory Blaire, what are you talking about? The only thing that Maggie wants is a man who can be there for her. She's a very strong woman, and she doesn't need a man to do stuff for her. She needs a man to love her and be there for her, that's it. She needs someone to share her life with."

"What if I'm not good enough for her? I've got nothing except a job and my father's house. What do I have to offer her?"

"You have your heart, Greg." She reached over and patted my hand. "That's all Maggie wants. She doesn't need anything else, and I'd like pancakes, please."

I chuckled at her abrupt change in topic. "I can do pancakes."

"I'm going to shower and get dressed while you cook. Give Maggie a few minutes of peace. She's been through so much, and this thing between you is a bit overwhelming. If it makes you feel any better, I think she doesn't feel that she is enough for you either, and with the added burden of me, it makes it even harder, but that doesn't mean that she isn't willing to try."

She set her coffee mug beside the sink and disappeared into the other bedroom. I sat there for a few moments, then pulled out the notebook from my pocket. In the back were the photographs of Maggie, old and new. Could Maggie and I have what we once had?

I shoved the pictures back in the notebook and got busy cooking breakfast. Liz had just turned off the shower when I took the last pancakes off the griddle and put them on the plate to stay warm in the oven until everyone was seated. The bacon was already on the table, orange juice was poured, and there was still enough coffee for everyone if they wanted more.

I popped my head out the door and didn't see Maggie. My heart began to race as I stepped further out. "Maggie!" About three hundred yards away, I saw her down at the dock. I closed my eyes as I tried to rein in the fear that was on the verge of exploding through me.

I carefully walked barefoot over the rocky driveway to the grassy area and then toward the dock. Maggie sat at the end, her feet dangling over the edge; a breeze lifted her bright-blond hair and danced it around her shoulders. She turned and looked over her shoulder when she felt the vibration on the dock from me.

"Hey."

"Breakfast is ready." I put my hand out to help her up. She looked at my hand, and for a moment, I thought she would push it away. Instead, she slipped her hand into mine, and I pulled her to her feet. Once she was standing, she let go of my hand, but I wrapped an arm around her waist and pulled her forward.

Her blue eyes went wide as she stared up at me, and for just a moment, I stared deeply into them. I needed her to understand something. "That was more than sex, Maggie. *You* are more than just sex to me."

Her features softened, and a hint of a smile slipped over her lips. I cupped her cheek as she responded, "Thank you, and I'm sorry for saying that."

"Did you mean it? Is it just sex between us for you?"

"No." She shook her head. "It's more than sex for me too, Greg."

I leaned forward and kissed her tenderly. "I don't know what this is, Maggie. Since I walked away from you all those years ago, I've never wanted more from anyone. It's like when I said goodbye, I closed the door to my heart and locked it. Part of me wants what we used to have, only at a more adult level."

She chuckled. "Do we have to?"

I rubbed my knuckles over her cheek. "Sometimes. You know I'm not one to admit fear, but there is part of me that is afraid that I might disappoint you, Maggie. I'm not the young boy that I once was. I'm a grown man with extreme views, and I'm set in my ways."

She took my face in her hands. "Greg, you could never disappoint me. You are amazing. You went from a confident and sexy young man to a very confident, powerful, sexy man. And we've always had different viewpoints on things. That is what made our relationship so great. We could disagree and still find common ground. I'm not interested in a ring, or even a promise of forever."

"What are you asking me for, Maggie?"

"I'm asking for a chance to get to know you and for you to get to know me. You think you might not be much, but I'm an out-of-work reporter that just can't seem to get herself on track for reporting real news."

"Why are you out of work?"

"Oh"—she stepped back, laughing as she took my hand and

turned us toward the cabin—"I got a little pissed at my boss, and he threatened to fire me, so I quit instead."

"Maggie," I started to say something, but she stopped and put her fingers over my lips.

"Please don't ruin the peace we have between us right now and tell me I'm trouble. I know that I'm trouble. I've always been trouble, and I always will be trouble. Just leave it alone."

I took her face in my hands, and the words I love you brushed over my mind, but I managed to keep them in. It was like time stood still when it came to how I felt about her. Suddenly, all the emotions I'd had for her years ago filled my very soul, and I knew that I didn't want to let her go. "Sweetheart, I want us to get to know one another. I can't promise you anything more, but I want to try."

"I'll take that." She hesitated. "What about your job?"

"What about it?"

"Would you have a problem if I worked there and traveled with you?"

I frowned. "Maggie, is that something that you really want to do?"

"Yes, I have always wanted to report on important issues, and I think it would be a perfect way for us to build a relationship."

I chuckled. "I'm not sure about that. It's dangerous and stressful and sometimes boring as hell."

She grinned cheekily up at me. "But if I'm along for the ride, it wouldn't be quite so boring. I mean, I could always see what trouble I could get into."

I kissed her. "Yeah, I bet you could. I think that we would have to discuss it a little more. I get why you want to do that, and I know Jake thinks it will be great and he might be right, but I'm going to need a little time to get used to the idea."

"But you aren't saying no?"

"No, I'm not saying no. I'm saying we will discuss it once this mess has been cleared up."

I curled her against my chest and held her for a long moment. "Thank you, Greg."

"You're welcome, and don't think this conversation is over. We still have things to discuss, but right now. Let's eat. Your mother should be dressed now."

When we got back to the cabin, Liz was standing in the middle of the room, looking around.

"Mom, what are you looking for?"

She turned to us, her eyes bouncing back and forth between us as if she was unsure of something. Maggie sighed softly beside me as she dropped my hand and stepped forward.

"I'm waiting for the bus, but I don't see it. Did the bus come already?"

"Liz, there is no bus today. Let's eat breakfast."

"I already ate breakfast; I want to get on the bus. I don't know this place."

"No, you didn't eat yet, Liz," I said to her. "You took a shower while I made breakfast. I'm Greg, a friend of Maggie's. How about we all sit down and eat the pancakes I made?"

"I don't like pancakes; I like eggs."

"Liz, you love pancakes," Maggie told her. "We have them every weekend."

"Who are you? Do I know you? I don't think I have ever seen you before. I want to go to my room."

Maggie closed her eyes and then walked into her mother's room. A moment later, she returned with a picture in her hand. "Liz, here is a photograph for you. This might make you feel better."

Liz took the picture and stared at it for a long time, her eyes constantly moving as they shifted over every pixel of the image. "Who is this man?"

"That is your husband, Robert, and my father."

"I'm not married."

"You were married, Liz."

"I don't remember him. Why don't I remember him?"

"Because you have Alzheimer's, Liz. You forget some days and get confused on others, but this picture always reminds you that you are with family."

She lifted her eyes to me. "Are you part of the family?"

Maggie glanced my way and then smiled. "Yes, Liz. Greg is part of the family."

I drew closer to them and put my arm around Maggie. "You might be confused, Liz, but you're safe."

She nodded slowly as she dropped her gaze back to the picture and then looked at Maggie. "You said that I like pancakes?"

"Yes, you sure do."

"Okay, then I'll have some pancakes."

CHAPTER THIRTY

MAGGIE

*I*t had been a long time since my mother called me Maggie Sue, and tears crowded my eyes. At that moment, my mother was one hundred percent with me. Her words, the look in her eye, the feel of her hand on mine meant so much.

I threw my arms around her as tears began to fill my eyes. "I love you so much, Mom."

"I love you too, dear. I wish life were easier for you. I'm sorry for making it so hard."

I clung to her harder. "No, you don't. I would do anything for you."

My mother pulled back. "Would you really do anything for me?"

"Yes, of course!"

She collected my hands and held them between us. "Then Maggie, it's time for me to move into the facility. I know that my lucid times are few and far between. Even I can tell that I have huge gaps missing from my life. It's not fair for me to ask you to continue to put your life on hold. You deserve to have more, do more, be more."

"Mom, how can I do that when I can take care of you?"

"Because I'm telling you that it's okay, sweetheart. I love you so much for everything that you have done for me, but it's time for you to return to your life." She glanced at the door. "To build a life with him."

"I'm not sure he wants one."

"He does but be patient. You are both hardheaded, but you'll get there."

My mother had gone inside a few minutes later, and I decided to walk down to the dock. Could I put my mother into the nursing home? Hadn't I just two days before been planning on doing that if I took the job? Yes, but would Greg be able to deal with me working with him?

It might come to a toss-up between the two of them: the job versus the man. In a perfect world, I wouldn't have to choose.

With the trouble that I was currently in, maybe it was a better idea to get her settled into a center. Then at least she wouldn't be caught in the middle of this mess. Who knows how long we were going to have to hide. This place might be a beautiful little cabin, but I wasn't sure it was big enough for Greg and me together, much less large enough for my mother and her different levels of clarity.

I felt the wood under me vibrate and turned to see Greg. When he put his hand out to me, I felt like this was more significant than just him helping me off the ground. It was as if he were lending me a hand to move forward in my life, but would it include him?

When Greg wrapped his arms around me and stared down at me, I felt like I was on the precipice of something—a life-changing moment. "That was more than sex, Maggie. *You* are more than just sex to me."

I stepped off the cliff. Greg and I needed to take it slow, but we would get there. I had no doubt. From the way we felt, to how things might go if we worked together, we'd have difficulties and struggles, but we could do it.

As we stepped back into the cabin, I stared at my mother, once again lost to me, and knew that she had given me a gift today. It was time to accept her permission and move her to a home. A place where they could keep her safe, and I could visit with her, but still have my life without having to worry every moment of the day.

Over breakfast, it was a struggle to keep from crying, but I managed to make it through. I was washing the dishes when the cellphone that Mike had given us began to ring, and Greg retrieved it and took it outside. Mom sat on the other side of the room, staring out the window, waiting for the bus. She had a long wait.

I dried my hands on a towel and went to join Greg outside. As I reached him, he put the phone on speaker and put his arm around my waist and pulled me to his side. "Maggie is here, and you're on speaker now."

"Maggie!" Jake's voice bellowed through the line. "Girl, Greg said you were trouble, but man!"

Greg chuckled as I responded, "I like to keep people on their toes."

"Yeah, we see that. Well, I was just confirming with Greg that it's a no-go for you to travel with us this time because of the situation that you're in. The two of you need to stay safe and off the radar for a while."

"I understand," I replied.

"But that in no way will keep you from traveling in the future. I already told Greg that if he has a problem with it, he can staff the office, and I'll go with you." A few people laughed in the background.

"Yeah, well, we'll talk about it later. One issue at a time," Greg said before he kissed my brow.

"Hey, guys, it's Trevor. I spoke to Detective Highmore today. He said that after last night's events, the problem might be going away. The word on the street is that the contract on the witnesses has dissolved. He isn't one hundred percent sure, so he doesn't want you guys around for a while, and he's suggesting to most of the other witnesses that they take a vacation, but it looks like the danger might be gone."

"That's good to hear," I said. "Any idea how long we have to stay under the radar?"

"He said at least a couple of weeks, so whatever you guys need, you let us know, and we'll take care of it."

I gnawed on my bottom lip for a moment. "Trevor, I might have to take you up on that. Before all of this started happening, I was getting my mother ready to do a respite at the nursing facility that she does a day program with. I think it might be better for her to be there. Is there any way you could help me make those arrangements and maybe get her transported there?"

"Absolutely! You text over phone numbers and contacts, and Davina and I will take care of it for you."

"In the meantime," Alex said, "Can you two stay out of trouble?"

I laughed. "We'll try, Miller."

They discussed a few other things, and I let Greg take it off speaker as I sat on the swing. When he got off the phone, he came to sit beside me. "You sure you want to do that with your mom?"

"Yes," I smiled at him. "This morning when she was here with us, she told me it was time for her to go. She knows she is getting worse."

"You know I'll help you with anything that you need with your mom."

"Thank you, Greg. I appreciate that, but I think it's time. She will be safer, and they can care for her better there."

"Hey, no one can care for her better than you, but you know them, I don't."

"True, but you know what I mean. She will be alright there. For a long time, I couldn't even think about it because I felt guilty, but she wants me to do it."

"If that's what you want."

"It's not what I want, but it is what I need to do."

Greg put his arm around my shoulders. "There is something else that you need to do."

"Yeah, what is that?"

"You need to tell me why you can't have kids."

I inhaled sharply and then released it slowly. "Do you want kids?"

"Not particularly," he replied. "It has never been a huge want on my list, and I kind of think that with as messed up as this world is, I didn't want a child to have to navigate it."

"Are you just saying that, or do you mean it?"

He pulled my face around to his. "I mean it. But if you want kids, then it might be a discussion we can have later."

"No, I don't really want kids. I thought I did once, and then I got pregnant, and it was a nightmare pregnancy. Problems from the start with both the fetus and me, and I ended up having an emergency delivery at five months, and they did a partial hysterectomy."

"So you can't have kids even if you wanted them?"

"Nope. Does that bother you?"

"No, as long as it doesn't bother you."

I shook my head. "No, I got over it a long time ago, and then I was taking care of Mom, and that was almost like having a child again. It was enough."

"Alright, do you have anything against a cat?"

I laughed. "You like cats?"

"Yes, I do. Got a problem with that?"

"No, I do not."

"Alright, so no kids, only cats."

"Maybe a dog sometime in the future."

"Maybe."

I laced my fingers with his. "You know, earlier you said that when you left me all those years ago, you had locked up your heart. I think you left your key behind."

"You do, huh?"

"Yeah, I think maybe I'm your key, and I can help you get the rust off your heart so we can unlock it again." I turned to study him, and he stared deeply into my eyes.

"I'm not sure you need to work on the rust, Sweetheart. I think you've already got the key in the lock. You just need to give it a solid turn."

"Yeah?"

"Yeah."

"I want to learn who you are, and fall in love with you again, Greg. Is that weird?"

"No, because, quite honestly, despite how much trouble you are, that's what I want too, Maggie."

I laughed. "I'm not that much trouble."

Greg pulled me so that I was sitting on his lap, and he curled his fingers around my neck and led my face toward his. "You are a lot of trouble, Maggie, but you're my kind of trouble."

I laughed as he brought our lips together, and I wrapped my arms around his neck. I was looking forward to learning about this man and falling in love with him all over again, and truth be told, I was really looking forward to getting into trouble with him too.

THE END

While Greg and Maggie still have a few things unresolved, they did get their Happy-For-Now ending. Make sure to check out Unexpected Storms, when Greg and Maggie will be back along with the rest of Safety Zone Security as Harvey needs to step up his groove as Ali sashays onto the scene.

THE UNEXPECTED SERIES

I hope you enjoyed Unexpected Trouble, if you did, please consider leaving a brief review. It's the best way to tell an author you enjoyed their book!

If you haven't already, make sure to check out the rest of the Unexpected Series.

Unexpected Packages, Book 1

Lexi Miller restarted her life five years ago and has been living a regimented routine ever since. With a great job and a best friend who tries everything to get her to break-out of her boring life, it's not until her birthday present arrives at her door, opened by a stranger, that things finally start to get interesting.

Alex Miller is ready for his second career after retiring from the military. He's excited to start training contractors in safety issues and getting to know his daughter after being away for so many years.

When a package addressed to him shows up on his doorstep,

he is kind enough to deliver the box to the rightful owner. When Lexi opens the door, Alex quickly realizes that he's found the beautiful woman he has been catching peeks of as she comes and goes from the building.

From misunderstandings to new beginnings, Alex and Lexi come together, but a business trip threatens their future right before Valentine's Day, and neither is sure they will ever be reunited.

Unexpected Arrivals, Book 2

Trevor Vaughn loves his job, his women, and his bachelor lifestyle. Sadly, for him, all of that might change when Davina Daniels walks into his office pushing a stroller.

The problem is that Trevor doesn't have any idea who Davina is. After she explains that he is the baby's father, he finds himself clueless as to what to do next.

After begging for her help, Davina and Trevor begin to form a friendship that will bring them together in time for their friend's wedding and a single night of steamy romance.

It's after their moments of bliss when words are misspoken, strangers show up, and baby Devon is raced to the hospital that their newfound romance is put to the test. Will Trevor and Davina find a way back to each other, or will the storms continue to crash down over them?

Unexpected Trouble, Book 3

Big things are happening at Safety Zone Security, and before a client meeting, Gregory Blaire heads down to Cocoa's Coffee Café to grab some much-needed caffeine. Running into his high school sweetheart was almost the last thing he excepted, but the jewelry store heist that went wrong tops even that.

As hard as Maggie Valor works to build her career as a

serious journalist, she's stuck as a romance advice columnist, and she'll do just about anything to change that. When Maggie runs into Greg and then gets taken hostage, her mind is torn between the story and the man who broke her heart.

With Maggie putting herself in the way of danger, stepping into Safety Zone Security to help with a client, and then pushing to join an operation, all Greg can see is trouble. Now the police are questioning her, a thief is out to get her, and the only thing Greg can do is take her on a delivery operation to keep her out of more unexpected trouble.

Unexpected Storms, Book 4

Ali Davidson is ready for a serious relationship; only the conventional methods aren't much help in finding the right man for her. Could being a contestant on the May I Have This Dance television show help her find love on the dance floor? Her friend and producer, Holly Melton, believes it will be the perfect way to find a connection.

Harvey Melton works long hours and travels a lot, but while burning time off from work, his sister begs for his help. Harvey would do anything for his sister, including dance on her silly television show.

Ali has to decide between her three dance partners, which two she will ask back for a second dance, and then choose between them to explore a relationship. With Ali trying to make her decision between the two final men, she has significant distractions in her kitchen.

When more patrons get sick, and the threat of the restaurant and her reputation are on the line, Holly steps in to get Ali help and enlists the guys at Safety Zone Security. When they show up, Ali is surprised to see Harvey, and the attraction between these two is undeniable and stormy.

Coming Soon:
Unexpected Desires
Unexpected Ties

Check out Chapter 1 of Unexpected Storms

"Hey, man!" I stepped through the front door at Maggie Valor's house and clapped hands and shoulders with Greg Blaire, a friend and co-worker at Safety Zone Security. "It's about time you came back to the real world!"

"No doubt," he said as he let me go and shut the door behind me. "Come on in, everyone is out back."

"How does it feel to return from a five-week exile?" I asked him. Maggie and Greg had been off the grid that long after they had been held hostage during a robbery. A few of the hostages had turned up dead, and someone had come after Maggie, but luckily Greg had been there and took the guy down.

It wasn't the guys involved with the robbery and kidnapping that had been worrisome; it was the cartel that those guys had been working for. They hadn't wanted to be given up by Chuck and Len, so they'd killed them, and several other witnesses too. Then anyone who was left was asked to head out of town.

A couple weeks ago, a few came back, not Maggie or Greg, but a couple other people, and so far, their lives had not been threatened and there had been no signs that the cartel wanted any further retribution. Hence the reason Maggie and Greg finally came out of hiding.

"It feels great, and it sure is nice to be back at home."

"Home?" I glanced around. "This is home now? Are things going that well for you and Maggie?" When the two of them had gone into lockdown, Greg had been doing everything he could to keep distance between himself and his former high school sweetheart.

Greg frowned at me. "You know what I mean, Harv, home as in back here."

"So you and Maggie aren't living together now?"

"I didn't say that." He chuckled and slapped my back. "Go get yourself a drink; I have to grab something from the kitchen."

"Alright, I'll see you out there." On the back deck, Alex and his pregnant wife, Lexi, were seated on a gliding love seat, and Trevor had his squirming son, Devon, on his lap, while his fiancée, Davina, helped Maggie with something at the food table. Alice was over there too, along with Mike and two pretty women that I didn't know. Mike was laughing at something that one of the women had said.

Standing off to the side, talking shit to one another was Jake, our boss, along with Drake, Wyatt, Joe, and Brett, who were all part-timers with our company. I made the rounds, saying hello to everyone, and Greg tossed me a beer as he came back out of the house.

A few minutes later, Greg had his arm around Maggie when he called for our attention. "Thanks to all of you for coming. While Maggie and I had a great time being on vacation for a full five weeks, we are very happy to be home and to have you all here."

"You guys married yet?" Jake called out with a laugh.

"No, we are not, and we aren't in any rush to do that either." Maggie didn't look the least bit upset by his words as she smiled up at him. "But we did reconnect nicely after nineteen years, and I know I feel like I know her better than I ever did. I'm pretty sure she knows every single one of my bad habits now, and she is still willing to stand here beside me."

Brett whistled loudly as Wyatt joked, "Damn, anyone who can put up with his shit, and I mean that literally, is good in my book."

Laughter and a few crude jokes about bathroom etiquette went around the group for a few moments.

Maggie was laughing, a huge smile on her face. "Do you know how many times I got yelled at for putting the toilet paper on wrong?"

"Wait!" Trevor snapped. "Don't tell me that you put it on so it hangs under?"

"Of course I do, doesn't everybody!" Maggie replied in laughter.

"No way!" Jake called out loudly. "Even the patent office has it on record that it has to hang over!"

"But that's crap!" Lexi joined the conversation. "Just because when they did a drawing of toilet paper, they had it hanging over, that doesn't mean that is the end-all way to do it."

Alex barked out a laugh and pointed at Lexi. "But that's how *you* hang it!"

She shrugged. "I know, but that doesn't mean there is a right or wrong way to do it."

"I'll remember that the next time you growl at me for putting it on wrong," Alex joked.

The debate continued for a few more minutes before Greg put his hands up to get everyone's attention. "Alright, we can finish this debate later. There is something that Maggie and I wanted to share with you."

"Well, if you aren't getting married, are you having a baby?" Davina asked. Maggie and Greg looked at one another and held each other a little tighter as Greg shook his head.

"No, no babies in our future," he said with a bright smile. "What we wanted to share with you is that Maggie is now the newest official employee at SZS, as our official media liaison!"

"Oh, that's great!" Lexi clapped excitedly, and Jake approached them, giving Maggie a hug.

"She's actually been working for us already," Jake said. "When I got back from our medical supply delivery, I shared with her a bunch of photographs and videos that I took. She's been working on some social media advertising, and if I'm not mistaken, just sold our story to a prominent Washington D.C. paper."

"I sure did," Maggie said brightly.

Alice spoke to Jake. "Maggie is the one that made that video you showed me the other day?"

"Yep."

Alice turned wide bright eyes toward Maggie. "It was fantastic! I hope he paid you extra for that because you even managed to make Jake look like a decent human being."

Everyone howled in laughter. "You're funny, Alice," Jake said to her, and the two of them stared at one another for a moment. Were they sleeping together? If they weren't, they should be because the amount of sexual tension that radiated off them was almost mind-blowing.

"No, he didn't pay me extra, Alice, but I'll keep that in mind the next time he wants me to change something out to make him look better."

"What a narcissist," Trevor joked.

"Maggie has also been working with Mike on a new website design, and on Monday, we are going to roll it out, so make sure you all take a good look at it. If things go as well as we anticipate, we are hoping to bring the rest of you PTer's on full time."

Drake put his beer in the air. "Hear! Hear! I'm ready."

"We have some other things in the works, too, and on

Monday we need to meet as a group and go over some upcoming changes," Jake continued.

"Hey, did you forget that I'm on vacation this week?" I called out.

Jake turned to me. "And if I'm not mistaken, you aren't going anywhere or doing anything. You took the time off to burn."

"Yeah, so? Coming into the office for a meeting kind of defeats the purpose."

"Well, you could not come and then find out about all of it next week when you return."

I rolled my eyes at him. "What time on Monday?"

"One, and since it is going to be all of us, let's meet at the training facility. Actually, let's make it noon, and maybe Alice can order us lunch, and we can eat while we talk about the new website and show you some of the videos that Maggie has put together."

"I'm the lunch girl now?" Alice barked, and her dark-brown eyes slit closed as she glared at him. She was almost as headstrong and volatile as our boss, and I knew she hated when he volunteered her for things that were not in her job description.

"I got it, Alice," Maggie said with a wink to Alice.

Jake shook his head and muttered something under his breath.

After that, Greg announced that they were putting the food on the grill, and we all milled around talking and snacking on finger foods while the cooking got underway with Greg and Jake.

My cellphone vibrated in the pocket of my shorts, and I pulled it out to see my sister, Holly, was calling. I stepped away from the group of people I was speaking with and answered, "Hey, Holly, what's up?"

"Harv, I need your help." She sounded close to panic, and she never sounded like that. My sister was normally calm as a cucumber.

"Are you alright?"

"Yes, I'm alright, but I need your help."

"Anything you need."

My sister was five years younger than me and one of my best friends. When I'd gone into the military, leaving her had been the hardest thing I had to do. Especially as she had been just starting high school and getting involved with boys.

When I got out of the Marines three years ago after a shoulder injury, Holly and I had clicked right back into hanging out together. Except now instead of movie night and popcorn, we had dinner dates and drinks—well, we sometimes still did movie night, too.

"Really? Anything?" she asked, and I heard the uncertainty in her voice.

"Of course, Holly. Whatever you need. I'm there for you."

"Oh, my god, Harv! You have no idea how much that means to me! Seriously, I was freaking out, but this is going to work!"

I chuckled. "Okay, what did I just volunteer for?"

"I'll explain it all on Monday. You're still off this week, right?"

"Yeah, but I need to attend a meeting Monday afternoon, why?"

"We can work around that," she said and sounded excited.

"Alright, but again, what did I volunteer for?"

"It's a surprise, but I know you will love it! It's going to be so awesome."

"You're lucky that I love you, kid."

She laughed. "Harv, I'm thirty-five years old now. I think you can stop calling me kid."

"Nope, you will always be a kid to me."

"You are hopeless. Okay, I'll text you the address of where to meet me, and wear something comfortable."

"Comfortable? What are you going to have me doing?

Moving stuff? Holy shit! You're going to make me paint, aren't you?"

She laughed. "No, nothing like that. Well, you'll be moving around a lot, but you won't be painting. Just wear comfortable clothes."

"Alright, fine."

"Love you, Harv! I appreciate this so much! I'll talk to you later."

"I'll see you on Monday," I told Holly before I hung up and returned to the group I'd been talking to.

"Problem?" Wyatt asked.

"Nah, my sister needed my help with something."

"I didn't know you had a sister," Joe said.

"Oh, yeah," Drake spoke up. "She is one fine woman."

"Hey, you watch it," I growled at him. "That is my sister you are talking about."

"Who is a grown woman and does not need you to hover over her," Drake added.

"I only hover over her because the last two men she was with did a number on her. I'm not going to let that happen again."

"You should bring her around sometime," Joe said.

I frowned at him. "Yeah, why? So you can drool and hound dog all over her? I don't think so. I just told you that I'm not going to let another guy take advantage of her, and you immediately say you want to meet her." I laughed. "You are not her type, Joe."

"Man, you have no idea how well I treat girls."

Drake busted out a laugh. "Yeah, well, maybe you'll be ready for a serious relationship with an adult woman when you stop referring to them as girls or chicks."

"I didn't call her a chick," Joe said quickly.

Wyatt laughed. "Yeah, not today, but you do use that term quite often."

"I'm talking about baby chickens." Joe grinned.

I shoved his arm. "Bullshit! Dude, there is no way I'm going to let my sister get around you. She is totally out of your league."

Drake smiled. "I have to agree with you, Melton, your sister is way above his level."

"Oh, and you think she is closer to yours?" Joe joked back.

"I didn't say that, but yeah, I'm pretty sure I'm closer to her normal standards than you are."

I held up my hand. "You all can stop right now. There is no way that Holly would date any of you meatheads. She's into artsy guys."

"Hey, I enjoy the arts," Brett said.

"Body paints are not the arts," Drake said with a laugh.

"I beg to differ," Joe tacked on, and our conversation veered off of my sister and on to other subjects.

I didn't think about my sister's request to meet her again until Sunday night when she texted me an address and reminded me to wear something comfortable.

Are you going to tell me what I'm going to be doing?

You're going to be helping me and someone else out, and you're going to have fun while you do it.

Someone else? An uneasy feeling slipped down my spine. I had a feeling I was not going to have fun with whatever my sister was roping me into.

ABOUT THE AUTHOR

Stacy Eaton is a USA Today Best Selling author and began her writing career in October of 2010. Stacy took an early retirement from law enforcement after over fifteen years of service in 2016, with her last three years in investigations and crime scene investigation to write full time.

Stacy resides in southeastern Pennsylvania with her husband, who works in law enforcement, and her teen daughter. She also has a son who is currently serving in the United States Navy and has two grandchildren.

Be sure to visit www.stacyeaton.com for updates and more information on her books.

Sign up for all the latest information on Stacy's Newsletter!

ALSO BY STACY EATON

Paranormal Romance:

My Blood Runs Blue Series

My Blood Runs Blue, Book 1 **

The Pulse of Blue Blood, Book 2 (Short Story) **

Blue Blood for Life, Book 3 **

Mixing the Blue Blood, Book 4 ***

Blue Bloods Final Destiny, Book 5 ***

The Return of Blue Blood Series:

Kristin: Blue Blood Returns, Book 1

Hugh: Blue Blood Compelled, Book 2

Zander: Blue Blood Reborn, Book 3

Lena: Blue Blood Desired, Book 4 (coming soon)

Garda ~ Welcome to the Realm

Domestic Violence – Crime - Suspense:

Whether I'll Live or Die**

Barbara's Plea

You're Not Alone**

Romantic Suspense:

Liveon ~ No Evil ***

Second Shield ***

Distorted Loyalty**

Six Days of Memories **

Second Shield II: The Return ***

Contemporary Romance:

Tempt Me Too**

Finding the Strength

Finding Love in Special Places:

Stacy's Short Story Series

Finding Love on Christmas Vacation

Finding Love on the Summer Surf

Finding Love with Dear Santa

Finding Love with a Champagne Toast

Heart of the Family Series

Mistletoe & Cocoa Kisses, Book 1 **

Roses & Champagne Kisses, Book 2 **

Orchids & Hurricane Kisses, Book 3 **

Carnations & Hot Toddy Kisses, Book 4 **

Heal Me Series

Cured, Book 1 **

Revived, Book 2

Mended, Book 3

Rescued, Book 4

The Celebration Series

Tangled in Tinsel, Book 1 **

Tears to Cheers, Book 2 **

Heathens to Hearts, Book 3 **

Rainbows Bring Riches, Book 4 ***

Sweet as Sugar, Book 5 ***

Making Mom Mad, Book 6 ***

Sparklers or Spankings, Book 7 ***

Raffles to Rattles, Book 8 ***

Flirting with Fireworks, Book 9 ***

Working under Wheels, Book 10 ***

Masquerading at Midnight, Book 11 ***

Blessings & Beans, Book 12 ***

Velvet & Vows, Book 13 ***

The Celebration Series Box Sets:

Part One: Books 1-5

Part Two: Books 6-9

Part Three: Books 10-13

The Sometimes Series:

Sometimes You Win, Book 1**

Sometimes You Lose, Book 2**

Sometimes You Play The Game, Book 3**

The Sometimes Series: Win, Lose & Play Set **

Pleasure Your Fantasies Series

Mistletoe Fantasies, Book 1 **

Whispered Fantasies, Book 2

Secret Fantasies, Book 3

The Twisted Love Series

with Amy Manemann Co-Author

Love Lorn, Book 1 (Manemann)**

Love Torn, Book 2 (Eaton)**

Love Inked, Book 3

Love Drowned, Book 4

Love Carved, Book 5

Love Trapped, Book 6

Love Crossed, Book 7

Love Twisted, Book 8

Love Lies, Book 9

Rise Again Warrior Series

Mission: Believe, Book 1 **

Mission: Accept, Book 2 **

Mission: Repair, (coming soon)

Loving a Young Series

Wesley, Book 1

Henley, Book 2

The Unexpected Series

Unexpected Packages

Unexpected Arrivals

Unexpected Trouble

Unexpected Storms

Unexpected Desires (coming soon)

Unexpected Ties (coming soon)

** These books are also available on Audio

*** These books are coming to Audio soon

List Update 10-14-20

www.ingramcontent.com/pod-product-compliance
Lightning Source LLC
Chambersburg PA
CBHW020311200626
46814CB00006BA/2189